A Dangerous Place

A Dangerous Place

The United Nations as a
Weapon in World Politics

Abraham Yeselson & Anthony Gaglione

Grossman Publishers
A Division of The Viking Press / New York / 1974

Copyright © 1974 by Abraham Yeselson and Anthony Gaglione
All rights reserved
First published in 1974 by Grossman Publishers
625 Madison Avenue, New York, N.Y. 10022
Published simultaneously in Canada by
The Macmillan Company of Canada Limited
SBN: 670-25585-8
Library of Congress Catalogue Card Number: 73-16575
Printed in U.S.A.

To Ruthie, and to Beverly, Jim-David,
Brian, and David,
for their love and loyalty

Acknowledgments

There are dozens of people to whom a word of thanks is due for the help they gave to the writing of this book: families who put up with our interminable conferences, students upon whom we inflicted our thoughts, colleagues with whom we argued them, and others. But special thanks should go to the Rutgers Research Council, whose grants contributed to the leisure that was necessary to develop the ideas in this book; to Evelyn Weil, whose patient typing and retyping of the manuscript was indispensable to getting the ideas down on paper; and to Thomas A. Stewart, whose cheerful and efficient editing helped to get the ideas into print.

Preface

A good and respected friend once explained why he avoided hospitalization. "Hospitals," he said, "are very dangerous places." The argument is irrational and frightening. Hospitals are the symbols and centers of the struggle against disease and infirmity. If hospitals *are* dangerous places, where can we turn when we are sick? Better to laugh a bit uneasily and change the topic. Even those who believe that hospitals are inefficient and sometimes grossly negligent are unprepared psychologically for such an attack. They are comfortable talking about *reforms*, but they will never accept our friend's premise that a sick man has a better chance of dying if he goes to a hospital.

Another time, in a committee considering the establishment of a school of criminal justice, a black sociologist did the same thing. There had been endless academic discussion of the deficiencies of the system of law enforcement. But no one was prepared when he said: "The most humane and beneficial thing to do for the individual and for society when a young person is caught red-handed committing a crime is to let him go." There was appreciative laughter and indulgent sophisti-

cated comments, but we were unwilling to explore the implications of what he had said. Too many unexamined but deeply
engrained beliefs were at stake. He had gone too far.

There must be somewhat the same reaction among psychi-
atrists confronted by R. D. Laing's suggestion that in an
insane world, the patients in mental institutions are sane, and
those who have adjusted to an irrational environment are
insane. The challenge is too basic both to the great majority
who have a vague but deeply held attachment to existing
values and institutions, and to the experts whose work and
reputations are undermined by any serious examination of
their original premises.

We are in the position of R. D. Laing, the black sociologist, and our friend with the fixation about hospitals. We are
no more for war than they are for madness, crime, or sickness.
We say: "The United Nations is a dangerous place." We do
not mean that it is a good institution in need of a few reforms,
or that it is usually ineffective, or that it changes nothing. It
is a weapon in international relations and should be recognized as such. As part of the armory of nations in conflict, the
United Nations contributes about as much to peace as a battle-
ship or an atomic bomb. Disputes are brought into the United
Nations in order to weaken an opponent, strengthen one's
own side, prepare for war, and support a war effort. Analyses
that project illusions are irrelevant, unrealistic, and dangerous. We do not know whether or for how long mankind will
survive in the atomic age, but its chances are poor enough
without the added burden of false hopes. It may be necessary
to strip away mythology and stand naked against the darkness,
if we are to find light.

Abraham Yeselson
Anthony Gaglione

Contents

A Dangerous Place

1 *The Arena*

The process of settling international disputes often includes difficult and delicate judgments over apparently trivial matters. Talks may founder over the shape of a table or the timing of entry into a room.[1] Similarly, the selection of a site for negotiations can have a decisive impact on their success. Jews and Arabs will not negotiate in Cairo or Jerusalem, but they did conclude armistice agreements in Cyprus. Helsinki and Vienna were satisfactorily neutral places for holding the Strategic Arms Limitation Talks between the Soviet Union and the United States. Various cities in Switzerland are often acceptable negotiating locales because of that country's policy of neutrality; selection of Geneva as host for the League of Nations was motivated by the desire to reenforce the image of the League as an impartial instrument for resolving international disputes. Among concerned experts and statesmen, there was some apprehension about the choice of New York City to house the United Nations. The issue has been raised publicly from time to time, but the consensus supports the view that the organization has been adequately insulated from its national surroundings.[2] These measures are buttressed by the theory that an organization devoted to the maintenance of international peace and security is a self-sustaining, independent center for the harmonious resolution of disputes. Thus, no matter where it happened to be located, the United Nations would provide an impartial and helpful atmosphere. According to these views, the United Nations itself is the locale.

The assertion that the United Nations is a place in and of itself raises an important question: Why do some disputing nations choose the United Nations as the site for debate or negotiations? Why Manhattan, not Cyprus or Helsinki or Paris or Geneva?

Membership in the United Nations implies a commitment to its processes and acceptance of the principles of the United Nations Charter as bases for settlement of disputes. Theoretically, then, member states acknowledge that the United Nations is the supreme spokesman for that international justice and morality to which they pledged themselves when they joined the organization. It would therefore follow that they would bring their problems to the United Nations with some confidence in the wisdom of the outcome. Presumably such actions would have the dual effect of having specific issues settled fairly and would establish desirable precedents for progress toward a peaceful world.

Obviously something has gone wrong with this vision of the role of the United Nations. There appears to be an unbridgeable gap between the general agreement and its applicability to specific disputes. Common membership in the organization has not produced common acceptance of its role. For this to be true, a minimum condition would be that the parties agree in advance that the United Nations and its processes are the suitable place and means of resolving their differences. A study of the political disputes that have preoccupied the organization reveals clearly that these vital first steps are missing. Nearly always, only one side has opted to use the United Nations. Sometimes, neither accepts the jurisdiction of the international organization when a third party initiates a complaint.* This lack of agreement is devastating to any hope that the United Nations can fulfill its primary mission to "preserve succeeding generations from the scourge of war."[3] The members, after all, are sovereign states and the United Nations is not a world government. We are, therefore, constant witnesses to a scene in which a defendant is dragged unwillingly before a judge whose jurisdiction is not acknowledged by the accused and whose verdicts cannot be enforced.

Finally, after the same drama is reenacted again and again, it becomes apparent that we, like the ancient Romans in the Coliseum, are spectators at battles between gladiators. The United Nations is an arena for combat. This startling insight transforms all of our previous perceptions and hopes for the organization. Nothing—and everything—changes. The arguments, investigations, debates, resolutions are the same as ever, but they now have nothing to do with peace and everything to do with conflict. Everything must be reinterpreted. We must never depart too far from the question, "*Who* brings *what* issues to the United Nations and *why?*" Behind this question is the need to know the relationship between the initiator and the defendant. Only if we know this can we speculate about the stakes. We must relate action or inaction by the United Nations to political objectives. But we cannot make the analysis unless we begin by examining the peculiar attributes of the United Nations for conflict purposes.

* For example, the Chilean complaint to the Security Council concerning Soviet intervention in Czechoslovakia in 1948 was opposed by both the Soviet Union and Czechoslovakia. Similar objections were raised by Hungary and the Soviet Union against consideration of the Hungarian revolt in the Security Council and General Assembly in 1956.

A Hostile Act

If settlement is not the primary objective, it is clear that states using the organization hope to *win* something at the expense of those who are forced to defend themselves in a forum chosen by their opponents. Bringing an issue to the United Nations is likely, then, to be regarded as a *hostile act*. This conclusion, so at variance with the stated objectives and general perceptions of the United Nations, is borne out by the consistency with which a variety of arguments is advanced to oppose the jurisdiction of the United Nations.

In some instances, defending states will flatly deny allegations, justify their behavior on the basis of existing treaty obligations, or contend that delicate negotiations are in progress which must not be jeopardized by United Nations meddling. Frequently a defendant will insist that the question is a matter of domestic jurisdiction, or that it is acting in either individual or collective self-defense, since the Charter prohibits interference in internal affairs and grants nations the right to defend themselves.[4] Typically charges against "colonial" powers will be met with the claim that the organization is intruding into the domestic affairs of a member state. France used this argument to dispute United Nations authority to consider complaints on Algeria, Morocco, and Tunisia.[5] By far the most repetitious employment of this defense has been made by Portugal and the Republic of South Africa, who for more than a quarter of a century have reiterated that the United Nations lacks jurisdiction to consider the problems of Angola and Mozambique, and of South West Africa (Namibia) and Apartheid. Responding to charges of aggression during and after the Six-Day War in 1967, Israel predictably insisted that it was acting in self-defense.[6] With a slight modification of this same argument, hemispheric disputes

involving the United States are invariably met with the claim
that the issues fall within the authority of the Organization of
American States,[7] while the Soviet Union defends attacks on
East European states by recourse to the Warsaw Pact.[8] In short,
no defending state ever acknowledges that it has violated the
Charter of the United Nations and is prepared to resolve a
dispute on that premise.

Inconsistencies in the success and application of such
arguments further highlight the fundamentally hostile intentions that accompany bringing issues to the United Nations.
Rarely, if ever, do outcomes turn on the substance of legal
arguments. Employing the same constitutional props on
largely similar issues, France partially succeeded in blocking
United Nations intervention with regard to North Africa,
while Portugal and the Republic of South Africa repeatedly
failed with regard to southern Africa. The crucial difference
in these as in other issues lay in the willingness of majorities
in the United Nations to endorse for political reasons one
set of arguments and, for similar reasons, to reject another.
In short, France was better able to fight back. Since fighting is
the name of the game, it is not surprising that states do not
maintain consistent positions on these arguments. India rejects
all domestic-jurisdiction claims while it is attacking the policies of colonial powers, but relied on this very defense when
attempting to privatize Indian involvement in Hyderabad
(1948), Goa (1961), and Kashmir (1962).[9] Again, the Soviet
Union dismisses Portuguese and South African protests against
interference in their domestic affairs, but relied on the same
defense in conjunction with Czechoslovakia in 1948 and Hungary in 1956.[10] Clearly, there is no agreement on the scope of
United Nations authority—nor desire to arrive at one. Regardless of what argument a nation employs, its aim is simply to
avoid a public attack at the United Nations. Legalities that

are endlessly and skillfully manipulated in defense of national prerogatives are quickly abandoned when states decide to use the organization to express hostility toward their opponents.

In a very real sense, use of the United Nations is a barometer of the level of hostility existing between nations. This becomes clear when one considers the reasoning behind nonuse of the organization in conflict situations. Nations interested in reaching agreements almost always ignore or avoid the United Nations. The overwhelming majority of quarrels among allies are settled secretly and bilaterally or within the confines of an alliance setting. The fact that Canadian-American or Soviet-Bulgarian differences do not become United Nations agenda items does not mean that these countries are always in perfect accord. It does mean that they will not or cannot risk the hostile consequences that flow from complaints to the United Nations. Even states basically at odds with one another forgo opportunities to utilize the United Nations when they are unwilling to exacerbate tensions. It is unthinkable, for example, that the Nixon administration in 1973 would jeopardize the growing détente with the Soviet Union by deliberately embarrassing the latter at the United Nations. In principle, the United States could bring the issue of the emigration of Jews from Russia to the Human Rights Commission or the General Assembly. But to do so would endanger the trend toward improved relations. Instead, Henry Kissinger quietly negotiates the issue with the Russians, and by so doing demonstrates *more* interest in constructive solutions than if the question were raised in an international forum. Most disputes, therefore, do not get to the United Nations because the countries involved are reluctant to undermine the total fabric of their relations for the short-term advantages of a possibly damaging United Nations offensive.

When "friends" use the United Nations, it indicates that their friendship is precarious. Evidence of the fragility of the North Atlantic Treaty Organization was provided when Greece and Turkey fought out the Cyprus question at the United Nations. Should the Sino-Soviet conflict now result in the exchange of charges at the United Nations, we would have further evidence of the magnitude of the breakdown of social-ist unity. If the rupture is such that the two countries abandon the possibility of finding "socialist" solutions, we can antici-pate a repetition of the crusade atmosphere that characterized Soviet-American conflicts in the organization during the Cold War.

Assaulting an enemy under any circumstances is always a calculated act. This is no less true when the attack occurs at the United Nations. We have already noted that a majority vote, not an abstract or impartial application of Charter prin-ciples, determines action or inaction at the United Nations. Calculations preceding a decision to employ the organization will estimate the reception of the member states. Recently observers have noted a decline in American "support" for the United Nations.[11] Starting from the premise that the United Nations is a vehicle for the peaceful settlement of interna-tional disputes, they view the apparent disinterest in the orga-nization as a retreat from moral principle. By implication, the United States has changed from a peace-loving state into some-thing else. Clearly, this reasoning is nonsense. The United States made maximum use of the organization (or "supported" it) during the most intense period of the Cold War. When hostile confrontation with the Soviet Union was pursued at every level and place, the United Nations was a convenient and useful weapon. During this period, the United States also commanded automatic, overwhelming majorities in the United Nations. The change in attitude toward the United Nations

results, in part, from its unsuitability for national purposes
due to the diminished intensity of the Cold War and the
membership explosion from the Third World.

For the United States, estimates of comparative utility
based on shifts in membership are made against the background of a substantial residue of influence. Other states are
in a much less enviable position. It is inconceivable, for example, that the Republic of South Africa would appeal to the
United Nations if military action were taken against her or
South West Africa by other African states. In a confrontation
at the United Nations, South Africa would be hopelessly outvoted, no matter how just its cause. It is true that Portugal,
another "minority" state, did complain ineffectively to the
Security Council when India invaded and absorbed Goa.[12]
Although Portugal made a formal record against an anticolonial tormenter, it did not risk humiliation in the General
Assembly. Israel, too, did not formally charge Egypt with violation of the Charter when President Anwar el-Sadat promised
that his country would attack Israel in 1971.[13] Should Egypt
renew the "war of attrition" in violation of the cease-fire
ordered by the Security Council, it is also unlikely that Israel
will complain to a "hostile" United Nations.* There are, then,
some states for whom the United Nations is all but completely unavailable, even when they are the victims of aggression or other hostile manifestations. This circumstance alone
shatters the illusion that the United Nations functions to
resolve international disputes on the basis of universal principles. "Justice" at the United Nations is highly selective, a
fact which imposes limitations on using the United Nations
as a means of expressing hostility.

* For an analysis of use of the United Nations during and after the
October 1973 Middle East War, see Epilogue.

Choice of Organs

We have equated bringing issues to the United Nations with the pursuit of national interest: when the organization is perceived to be compatible with the objectives of one party, it will use the United Nations. However, there are options within the organization. To the extent that the structure permits, states will choose the organ that promises maximum satisfaction of goals.[14] Furthermore, the same pragmatism underlies attitudes toward the powers and responsibilities of the different forums. These considerations help explain initial choice of organs, use of more than one body, and constitutional arguments on the functions of the Security Council and General Assembly.

The Security Council

The idea that the Great Powers could cooperate sufficiently to limit or eliminate wars has been the dominant theme of peace organizations since the nineteenth century. The Napoleonic Wars demonstrated the unpredictability and unmanageable character of modern warfare. In response to this threat, the Concert of Europe attempted to maintain a rough balance among the Great Powers. They cooperated to end or limit conflicts, suppress dangerous radical movements, and to divide the spoils so that a general war would be avoided.[15] The Concert failed with the outbreak of World War I. Framers of the Covenant of the League of Nations attempted to remedy the defects of the Concert system. The Concert, it was held, was too loosely organized and therefore could not anticipate and meet threats to international peace. World War I, it was believed, could have been avoided if the Great Powers had been organized to confer before the crisis had reached a point

of no return. The obvious answer to this failing was to institutionalize the Concert system in the League Council.[16] The
League failed. World War II was overwhelmingly more horri-
ble than the First World War. Framers of the Charter of the
United Nations employed the experience of the League and
assumptions concerning the reasons for its futility in the 1930s
to establish another peace organization.

This time, the special responsibilities of the Great Powers
for the maintenance of peace were spelled out even more
clearly than in the League Covenant. Although some concessions were made to the smaller powers, the Charter quite
explicitly places the burden for maintaining peace on the
shoulders of the five permanent members of the Security
Council.[17] The possession of the veto by the permanent members gave each the power to paralyze the Council's peace-keeping efforts.[18] The permanent members were authorized to
negotiate the establishment of military forces to implement
their authority.[19] Only the Security Council could take action
binding on the entire membership of the organization in dealing with serious threats to, or breaches of, the peace.[20]
Furthermore, the Security Council would be immediately and
always available to consider any emergency. Although small
states would be elected to the Security Council, the principle
of Great Power unanimity assured that substantive actions in
peace-keeping would depend upon the collaboration of the Big
Five.*

Cold War very quickly destroyed this expectation. Clash-
ing ideological and policy interests between the United States

---

* Substantive actions required a majority of seven of the original eleven-
member Security Council, including the concurring votes of the five
permanent members. When the Security Council was enlarged to fifteen
in 1965, substantive decisions could be taken by a majority of nine members, again including the concurrence of the permanent members.

and the Soviet Union doomed any possibility of an effective collective-security system. The two states upon which such a system depended could find virtually no areas of agreement. The conflict affected every aspect of the international organization, but its greatest impact had to be felt in the Security Council, where the decision-making process was based entirely on agreement among the permanent members.

If we keep in mind the primary responsibility of the Security Council for the maintenance of international peace, it follows that a defect of this magnitude would be fatal. Either the Security Council would not function at all when confronted by Great Power hostility, or it would consider issues and fail to take positive action. If the first alternative were adopted, it would demonstrate an acknowledgment of the relationship between Great Power harmony and the objectives and effectiveness of the Security Council. Where agreement obviously did not exist, issues would not become agenda items. Clearly the Council would have very little business, but the record would show that the Great Powers used the Council in the spirit in which it was created. Analysis of the failure of the Security Council, in these circumstances, would stress the limited number of issues considered by the Council.

In fact, however, the second alternative has been adopted. A large number of issues has been considered by the Security Council. In the greatest number of cases no positive action was taken either because of the use of the veto or because the majority voted not to act. In other instances, these divisions were reflected in the passage of innocuous resolutions. Analysts have responded by concentrating upon procedural flaws such as the debilitating effect of the veto, or upon the bad faith of the Soviet Union.[21] Some have observed that the original design based on Great Power cooperation was badly conceived.[22] They have not questioned why the Security Council has been used in spite of the expectation of failure. This consideration is crucial to our evaluation of this and other organs of the United Nations.

An understanding of the success or failure of any institution must be based upon the purposes for which the institution is used. For example, we can accept the failure of the Security Council as a peace-keeping instrument only if the Council had addressed itself to those issues wherein success was possible. The limited utility of the Security Council would then be an accurate reflection of its relevance to international peace. However, when there is a deliberate and persistent employment of the Security Council in circumstances where paralysis is inevitable, we must assume that the Security Council is being used for purposes other than the settlement of international disputes. Success or failure, therefore, is meaningful only in relation to these actual purposes.

It is our contention that these purposes are entirely related to national self-interest. Neither the language of the Charter nor the severity of a crisis is controlling. Arguments concerning the constitutionality of Security Council actions are invariably advanced and occupy a significant part of the debate. These serve only to obscure political reality. Nations will utilize the Council and endorse its actions to the degree that the Council supports national objectives. Just as bringing an issue to the United Nations in the first place is a hostile act calculated to maximize national advantage, the choice of the Security Council is a tactical decision within that context. The Council is simply part of the totality of the United Nations and may be better suited than other organs for advancing national purposes.

A state may bring an issue to the Security Council because

it is convenient. Whereas the regular sessions of the General Assembly run roughly from September to year's end, the Council is always available. The timing of a crisis may therefore influence the choice. More direct political factors will also determine selection of the Security Council. States seek advantage from the theoretically predominant role of the Security Council in peace-keeping. Having the Council take up an agenda item dramatizes the seriousness of the complaint.[23] The language of the Charter demands that certain rituals are followed. Comparatively minor border incidents or the kidnapping of a former Nazi become "serious breaches of the peace" or "situations which threaten international peace and security."[24] The structure and processes of the Security Council also encourage its use by those states that can profit thereby. It has obviously been to the advantage of the Soviet Union, as a minority state possessing the veto, to confine many issues to the Security Council rather than risk defeat in the veto-free General Assembly. In addition, minority states can control a significant portion of the debate because of the limited membership of the Council. The actual membership of the Council will also influence tactical considerations. The original eleven-member Security Council was dominated by colonial states and their allies. Four of the five permanent members and four or five of the six nonpermanent members, chosen on a geographical basis, were likely to side with the colonial powers. When membership in the Security Council was expanded to fifteen in 1965, the balance shifted sufficiently so that anticolonialists could make more effective use of that organ,[25] a trend that has been strengthened by the seating of the People's Republic of China as a permanent member.

Finally, states sometimes find the Security Council the

most useful forum for registering foreign-policy positions. Because of its small size and rather precise jurisdiction, the Council assures a minimum of diffusion for the positions being advanced. Here the passage of resolutions may be a secondary or even nonexistent goal. The advantage lies almost entirely in the clarity that a Security Council initiative lends to charges and which may be absent in the larger and more volatile General Assembly. In the long Arab-Israeli confrontation, for example, each side brought violations of cease-fires and armistices to the Security Council in order to establish formal positions in respect to raids and reprisals. A typical example was the Egyptian complaint about an Israeli armed attack in Gaza on February 28, 1955. Israel retaliated by charging that Egypt was sponsoring and supporting guerrilla and other attacks against Israel. Each sought to have the other condemned. The Israelis insisted that the Gaza attack was a response to terrorist violations of the armistice agreements from the Egyptian side. Although Israel was condemned by the Security Council, which rejected "a policy of retaliation,"[26] the Israelis nevertheless made their position a part of the record. Clarity of communication may also make the Council an especially helpful device for publicizing national policies regarding comparatively minor issues.

The General Assembly

Similar tactical considerations underline uses of the General Assembly. The "town meeting of the world" image of the United Nations achieves its clearest expression in the deliberations of the General Assembly. When the Assembly speaks, we are reminded that mankind possesses a conscience and a will which can be applied to solving the world's problems. The symbolic importance of representatives from every corner of the globe speaking their minds in their native tongues on a footing of absolute equality (as contrasted with the obviously elitist spirit prevailing in the Security Council) cannot be over-estimated. To many, this is sufficient proof of the triumph of democracy over those forces that would oppress and subjugate us all. Actually the ability of states to twist and exploit this imagery for national purposes helps to explain why they often find the General Assembly a suitable battleground.

As a forum for achieving the widest hearing for national policies, the General Assembly is a highly compatible arena for propagandistic statements. From earliest days, the Soviet bloc introduced agenda items that lent themselves to wide-ranging attacks on their Cold War enemies and assertions of socialist morality in international affairs. They forced debates on such items as "Measures to Combat the Threat of a New World War and to Strengthen Peace and Friendship" and "Peaceful Coexistence and Peaceful Relations Among States." There was no hope or real concern that their resolutions would be adopted. Western states took advantage of the same oppor-tunity, and, in more recent years, anticolonialists have used the Assembly to denounce imperialism and racism. The latter, of course, expected and won passage of resolutions.

As is true of the Security Council, the structure and processes of the General Assembly affect decisions to bring issues to that body. The one-member, one-vote pattern encour-ages those states that can anticipate majority support. For some twenty years the West enjoyed this tactical advantage on Cold War issues and more recently the Afro-Asian states have profited from control of majorities in airing and gaining support for anticolonial positions. It is amusing but probably inevitable that those who formerly controlled the General

Assembly find that the new majorities are irresponsible or immature.* In truth, of course, all that has happened is that the enlarged membership in the organization permits anti-colonialists occasionally to discomfort the West as the latter had consistently done to the Soviet bloc. States that do not expect to have their foreign policies endorsed by the Assembly may nevertheless find it expedient to propose agenda items in order to help establish their positions.

Special Representatives and Committees

An important aspect of General Assembly processes that is related to the size of the Assembly and has been politically effective is the use of special committees to deal with particular problems. In principle, these committees serve the same function as in any other legislative process. That is, they investigate issues and make reports to parent bodies. At the United Nations, this process is entirely a function of foreign policies. Majority rule decides what will be investigated and who the investigators will be, thereby fixing the results in advance. In this way a state or group of states ensures favorable reports, which become the basis for a steady stream of agenda items and resolutions. Under some circumstances, the bias may become so thoroughly institutionalized that the organization itself becomes a party to a conflict.

The tactic was first introduced and employed effectively as a Cold War weapon. Special committees established to deal

* Because of anticolonial majorities, Western powers are frequently on the receiving end of condemnatory actions by the Assembly and in its various organs. The United States called the recommendations made on one such instance as "a largely unconstructive and unfounded series of condemnations and gratuitous calls for action which at times (become) undisguised propaganda attacks on the United States. . . ." United Nations Document A/AC.109/SR.298, November 4, 1964.

with various aspects of the Korean problem consistently endorsed Western views regarding the extent of Syngman Rhee's authority and the future of the entire peninsula. The reports of one special committee, the United Nations Commission for the Unification and Rehabilitation of Korea (UNCURK), were the source of the desired Assembly resolutions until 1971, when the West decided against continuation of the tactic.[27] Special committees on the Greek and Hungarian questions produced equally satisfactory results. A United Nations Commission on the Balkans provided the basis for condemnatory resolutions against Greece's Communist neighbors until Yugoslavia's ouster from the Cominform and implementation of the Truman Doctrine eliminated any further need for the commission.[28] In 1956 the General Assembly established a Special Committee on the Problem of Hungary and also used a Special Representative to provide reports of noncooperation by Hungary as the grounds for repetitive condemnations of Hungary and the Soviet Union.[29] In none of the above examples was there any serious interest in "balance" or impartial investigation. The intention and the result were to enlist the United Nations on one side of a conflict and provide the means for automatic renewals of that verdict.

The close identification of the United Nations in recent years with anticolonialism has been largely accomplished through the successful use of the same tactic. With the creation of the Special Committee on Decolonization in 1961, the United Nations became a continuing forum for the articulation of Afro-Asian policies in the area of decolonization and racism.[30] The predominance of Afro-Asian states within the committee assures the one-sidedness of its investigations and recommendations. These become the basis for the General Assembly's unremitting attack on Apartheid, on South African and Portuguese policies in southern Africa, and on colonialism in general. Stable majorities in the Assembly guarantee passage of extreme resolutions at each session, while the debates that annually follow the committee's reports impart an almost religious flavor to the struggle for national independence.[31]

Shifting of Organs

Our assertion that the choice of organs is a function of tactical considerations is borne out by the ease with which issues are shifted between the Security Council and the General Assembly. One obvious purpose of such a move is to overcome the paralyzing effect of the veto in the Council. This incentive was clearly evident in respect to such Cold War issues as the Greek question, Korea, the Hungarian revolt, the Congo, and various "membership" issues. Although legalistic arguments are always employed, motivation in these and other issues is totally unrelated to the theoretical roles of the two organs. Neither is it linked to getting something accomplished. The same nation that shifts a dispute from the Security Council to the General Assembly in order to escape a Soviet veto on one set of issues will content itself with having achieved the desired propaganda mileage by forcing a veto on another. In short, the blurring of the respective roles of these organs and the willingness to engage in this sort of manipulation is based entirely on political expediency and the command of voting majorities.

Sometimes states will use both organs. They may consider that the Assembly will be somewhat friendlier than the Council, or they may seek wider publicity for their grievances. On occasion this will occur even when there is no chance of winning majorities in either forum. In the months before the Bay of Pigs invasion, Cuba brought its charges against the United States to the Security Council and the General Assembly. The Security Council took no action. Although the Assembly was considering the complaint when the invasion was actually launched on April 17, 1961, United States influence was so great that the Assembly could adopt only an innocuous Latin American-sponsored resolution.[32]

The flow in the early years of the United Nations was toward the General Assembly from the Security Council.[33] This development reflected Western efforts to side-step Soviet vetoes. With the membership explosion and the concentration of new members on anticolonial and other non-Cold War issues, the West began to lose confidence in the reliability of the Assembly. It was now the turn of the Afro-Asian bloc, which dominated and dictated the positions of the General Assembly on such issues as Apartheid, South West Africa, Angola, Mozambique, and Rhodesia. In 1960–1961, the Sharpesville Massacre in South Africa and rebellion in Angola were the sources of their first sorties in the Security Council. Thereafter, the use of the Security Council on these issues increased as the developing countries pressed for sanctions against the Republic of South Africa, Portugal, and Rhodesia. On the last issue, the Afro-Asians were unsuccessful in their efforts to force the United Kingdom to use military force against the rebel Rhodesian regime, but they did win passage of compulsory economic sanctions under Chapter VII of the Charter.[34] In the Security Council, the racial and colonial questions became "threats to international peace." By thus reenforcing Assembly resolutions, the Afro-Asians and the socialist bloc further isolated their enemies while elevating the seriousness of their charges.

General Strategy

A nation will appeal to the provisions of the Charter to justify a choice of organ. Loose or strict interpretations of clauses
are made to justify or camouflage tactical considerations. In
most cases, these legalisms are related to immediate concerns
and concrete issues. In addition to these ad hoc interpretations of the Charter, there are *general* preferences and dislikes.
Overall strategic considerations come into play in the form of
grand constitutional debates concerning the relative jurisdiction and powers of the General Assembly and Security Council. At stake in these confrontations is the institutionalization
of tactical advantage. The two most important of these were
the issues surrounding the Uniting for Peace Resolution and
the assessments crisis.

Uniting for Peace

At the source of the Uniting for Peace Resolution was the
most intense Cold War hostility. When the Korean War
erupted on June 25, 1950, the Soviet Union was boycotting
the Security Council in order to dramatize its demand that
representatives of the People's Republic of China replace the
Chinese Nationalist delegation in the United Nations.[35] The
boycott permitted the passage of resolutions that made the
defense of South Korea a United Nations operation under the
command of the United States. If the Soviet Union had been
present and used the veto, the United States would have
utilized the General Assembly to achieve the same end. If
proof of this was needed, it was supplied by the reaction to
the return of the Soviet delegates to the Security Council on
August 1, 1950. The United States moved to legitimize its

military operations north of the thirty-eighth parallel by having the General Assembly recommend that "all appropriate steps be taken to ensure conditions of stability throughout Korea."[36] The same resolution reaffirmed the policy of holding United Nations-supervised elections for a unified Korea and established the United Nations Commission for the Unification and Rehabilitation of Korea. Later, the General Assembly, following a Soviet veto in the Security Council, found Communist China guilty of aggression against the United Nations and recommended an arms embargo against it and North Korea. In short, it was the determination of the United States to wear the United Nations mantle for its Korean policy that underlay the initiative and adoption of the Uniting for Peace Resolution.

The Uniting for Peace Resolution was not the first effort to circumvent Soviet vetoes. In November, 1947, a similar action had been taken with establishment of the Interim Committee, or Little Assembly, which, unsuccessfully, attempted to make the Assembly permanently available for emergency actions.[37] The pressures and hostilities engendered by the Korean War provoked the more definitive attack on the veto encompassed in the Uniting for Peace Resolution of November 3, 1950.

The resolution authorized a simple majority of the Security Council to call for an emergency session of the General Assembly within twenty-four hours if the Council was paralyzed by the veto in cases involving breaches of the peace or acts of aggression. The Assembly would have "residual authority" to recommend collective action, including "the use of armed force when necessary." Other provisions created a Peace Observation Commission and a Collective Measures Committee and invited the members to hold stand-by military forces available for the use of the organization.[38] In effect the General Assembly was converted into a reserve Security Council.

Passage of the resolution was inevitable. In 1950 the United States commanded an overwhelming majority on all East-West issues, and most of the smaller states preferred the Assembly to the veto-plagued Security Council. The debate was heavily legalistic, but in truth, the constitutional arguments were irrelevant. The underlying motives emerged clearly with the extreme charges and countercharges between the giants.* The United States supported the merging of Security Council and General Assembly responsibilities on peace-keeping matters not because of an abstract commitment to collective security or peaceful settlement, but because automatic majorities in the Assembly guaranteed the endorsement of policies that squared with American interests. The Uniting for Peace Resolution reflected American faith in the persistence of Western control of General Assembly majorities and in the desire to ensure the permanent availability of the Assembly. The United States favored a stronger General Assembly because it was a pliable forum. For precisely that reason the

---

* During the debate the United States accused the Soviet Union of combining with Hitlerite Germany to bring about World War II. According to the American delegate, the United States was attempting to prevent the worldwide imposition of Soviet totalitarianism. Already, he said, many peoples had come under the "yoke represented by the USSR brand of imperialist communism." In its turn the Soviet Union asserted that American monopolies had entered into agreements with German cartels prior to World War II in order to build up the Nazi war machine. Furthermore, he alleged, the record of the United Kingdom, France, and the United States during the 1930s confirmed their support for Nazi Germany and their efforts to encourage Germany to attack the Soviet Union. The Uniting for Peace Resolution, the Soviets claimed, was a screen to renew Western aggression against the peace-loving socialist nations of the world. See *GAOR*, Plenary, Meetings 299–302, November 1–4, 1950.

Soviets opposed the move. Neither was interested in the ideals of the organization, despite their pious protestations.

Nevertheless, commentators have praised the Uniting for Peace Resolution as symptomatic of a desirable constitutional growth.[39] They have been deluded either because of their need to perceive the United Nations as a functioning, flexible, peace-keeping organization or because they equate United States policy with the principles of the Charter. Neither premise is correct. United States actions in Cuba, Guatemala, the Dominican Republic, or Vietnam are, theoretically, as subject to United Nations condemnation as are the policies of the Soviet Union or China in Korea, Hungary, Czechoslovakia, or Tibet. Majority rule is confused with the objective interpretation of Charter principles. In 1950, just about every state outside the Soviet bloc could relate national advantage to expansion of the powers of the General Assembly. The United States and its allies related the change to pursuit of the Cold War. On the other hand, a state such as India considered the General Assembly to be the better vehicle for stimulating economic development among poor nations and for attacks on colonialism. Thus despite Indian endorsement of an expansion of the Assembly's powers, she abstained on the Uniting for Peace Resolution because of its military provisions. As for the vaunted flexibility of the United Nations, it relates only to the desire of some states to choose a preferred site for the advancement of their foreign policies. Liberal interpretation of the Charter, therefore, translates into widening the choice of battlegrounds.

This, however, always occurs against the need to synchronize control of United Nations processes with the dynamics of national policy formation. States that argued so vigorously that the "primary" responsibility of the Security Council did not mean "exclusive" responsibility would reverse themselves in other circumstances. Witness the outraged protests of France and the United Kingdom, both supporters of the 1950 resolution, when they were victimized by the new procedure during the Suez crisis only six years later.[40] Nor is it conceivable that the United States would accept the enlarged powers of the 132-member General Assembly in 1973. Indeed, signs of that disenchantment could be observed in the next great constitutional debate—the assessments crisis of 1964, which was directly related to the issues raised in the Uniting for Peace Resolution.

The Assessments Crisis

The constitutional quarrel concerning the authority and jurisdiction of the two major political organs of the United Nations came to a showdown in the assessments crisis of 1964. The Soviet Union had refused to pay assessments to meet the costs of the Middle East and Congo operations. As a result, she was sufficiently in arrears so that Article 19 could apply. According to Article 19: "A Member of the United Nations which is in arrears in the payment of its financial contributions to the Organization shall have no vote in the General Assembly if the amount of its arrears equals or exceeds the amount of the contributions due from it for the preceding two full years." Arguments were familiar. The Soviet Union, joined by France, which had refused to pay for the Congo operation, confronted the United States and the United Kingdom. The former argued that the authority of the Security Council for the maintenance of international peace was exclusive and extended to methods of payment.[41] States could not be forced to pay for operations that they opposed. The Soviets charged that the Congo operation had been a coverup for colonialist designs to eliminate the Lumumba regime and impose a neo-colonialist government over the Congolese people.[42] All decisions by the General Assembly were recommendatory, including any assessments that went beyond normal administrative expenses. To insist otherwise, said the French delegate, would establish a world government which would be based on unstable majorities in the General Assembly.[43] Any economic or political operation could be recommended, and all states would be forced to bear the burden. The United States, assisted by the United Kingdom, repeated the arguments made during the Uniting for Peace debate. The organization must be sufficiently flexible to overcome paralysis in the Security Council. An overwhelming majority of the members had approved the assessments. Furthermore, an advisory opinion of the International Court of Justice agreed that the expenses for the two operations came within the compass of the General Assembly. Article 19 applied automatically. There was no discretion to vote on its application against an offender. Failure to act, insisted the United States, would constitute a breach of faith with paying members, sanction violations of the Charter, and repudiate the International Court of Justice and the rule of international law. If the only mandatory power of the General Assembly—the power to compel member states to pay their dues—were undermined because of pressure by a Great Power, other states would find it difficult to continue to support the organization.[44]

These constitutional arguments actually had little to do with the Charter, and everything to do with the demands of foreign policies. Although the Soviet Union had not been unhappy about the United Nations Emergency Force being employed to ensure the evacuation of British, French, and Israeli troops from Egypt in 1956, she nevertheless insisted that the General Assembly did not have authority to make assessments for the force.[45] She held that the "aggressors" should pay. From the minority perspective of the Soviet Union, acknowledgment of the Assembly's budgetary competence could compromise her objections to other, less satisfactory peace-keeping activities. Her fears were realized during the Congo crisis. At the outset, the Soviets supported the Congo force as a means of aiding the friendly Lumumba government to expel the Belgians. However, when they perceived the operation as an instrument for the overthrow and murder of Lumumba in order to establish a pro-Western, anti-Communist regime, the Soviets unleashed a furious attack against Dag Hammarskjöld. The Secretary-General had become a pawn of capitalist colonialism, they said, and, in a memorable shoe-thumping performance, Premier Nikita Khrushchev demanded that the office be headed by a "troika" consisting of three persons representing the capitalist, socialist, and developing countries.* The complexities of the Congo operation do not concern us here. It is enough to observe that the outcome was as profoundly satisfactory to the United States as it was displeasing to the Soviet Union.[46] In effect the United States, by forcing the issue on depriving the Soviet Union of its vote in the General Assembly, was demanding

---

* The association between the Russian effort to extend the veto to the Secretariat and American satisfaction with the Congo operation was made clear by the United States Ambassador Adlai Stevenson on June 5, 1961: "It is surely significant that it is since the United Nations frustrated the Communists' plan of rapid infiltration in the Congo that Mr. Khrushchev has been trying to extend his veto to the whole Organization and make sure that neither the Secretary-General nor any other organ of the United Nations shall be free to act or intervene. We by the same token must support and back with all our influence the only instrument by which the end of the Western system of colonialism can be prevented from opening the doors to the new imperialism of the East." "The United Nations, First Step Toward a World Under Law," *Department of State Bulletin*, July 10, 1961, p. 70.

that her enemy pay for what it regarded as a hostile United Nations action.[47]

The victory contemplated by the United States was not achieved. Membership in the General Assembly had changed. During the nonsession of 1964, there were 115 members compared with the original 51. Most of the newer members were Afro-Asians, and they were reluctant to take an action that could result in total withdrawal by the Soviet bloc. They feared that the United Nations would be crippled or destroyed, thereby depriving them of a weapon for the achievement of their economic and political objectives. It became clear that they would not back the United States.

With the General Assembly demonstrating its unreliability, the United States had to reassess its policies. The political basis for its constitutional position had apparently evaporated. The Afro-Asians were less interested in the Cold War than in their own problems of colonialism, racism, and economic development. France, especially, had brought home the implications of an outmoded Cold War posture. To insist that the General Assembly had compulsory authority in budget matters could place the United States in the same unenviable position as the Soviet Union. An obvious possibility was another try at the Special United Nations Fund for Economic Development (SUNFED), the repudiated attempt to have the developed countries establish a capital fund for the use of poor nations.[48] With the Assembly less compliant and capable of adopting unpalatable policies, the United States ended its support for the prerogatives of the General Assembly.

In effect, the United States joined the Soviet Union and France in opposing an unlimited budgetary power in the General Assembly. Although the retreat was cloaked in legalisms, the new policy was clear. If the Assembly were to vote assessments to pay for operations opposed by the United States, it too would refuse to pay its share. The reality of foreign-policy interests took precedence over any theoretical attitude toward the United Nations.*

In a very real sense the assessments crisis demonstrates the bankruptcy of constitutionalism as a stratagem to ensure perpetual advantages in the choice of organs. By 1964, the perceived advantages of the Uniting for Peace Resolution had already evaporated. Suez was a painful reminder to the West that the resolution was a sword with two edges. Access to the General Assembly no longer guaranteed desirable results. Indeed, there developed a renewed appreciation for the intimacy of the Security Council. The assessments crisis merely gave substance to this appreciation.

Thus far, we have described the United Nations as it is—an arena for combat. Many things have been clarified. The initial step in going to the United Nations is seen as a hostile act, a part of an overall pattern of conflict relationships. Selection of an organ or organs is part of the tactical struggle. Finally, constitutional approaches to the United Nations are a function of foreign policies. With these points established, we can go on to be more precise about *why* issues are brought to the United Nations.

Foreign policies of states are complex and they are pursued in many ways and places. The same general goals may be sought via normal diplomatic channels, within regional orga-

* In commenting on the failure of the General Assembly to act against the Soviet Union, United Nations Ambassador Arthur Goldberg said: "If any member can insist on making an exception to the principle of collective financial responsibility with respect to certain activities of the organization, the United States reserves the same option to make exceptions if, in our view, strong and compelling reasons exist for doing so." *New York Times*, August 17, 1965, p. 1–6.

nizations, at conference tables, on the battlefield, and at the United Nations. To cite only American policy in Vietnam, all of these instruments have been employed, and many of them simultaneously. The United Nations is only *one* of the many arenas of world politics. Like each of the others, it offers certain unique opportunities and limitations.

As a vehicle for the advancement of national interests, there is an obvious relationship between objectives and the appropriateness of the United Nations environment. Strategies are dictated by the availability of forums, parliamentary procedures, and the nature of the actual disputes. For analytical purposes we have divided the strategies of conflict in the United Nations into four broad categories—the politics of embarrassment, the politics of status, the politics of legitimization, and the politics of socialization—each of which will be discussed in a subsequent chapter.

There are hazards in categories. They may be arbitrary, overlapping, or vague. The existence of categories entices the researcher to force uncomfortably complex data into neat divisions. We recognize the dangers, but hope that the rewards of organization and clarity will compensate for any oversimplifications. The task is made more difficult because states will take advantage of several strategies in respect to a single issue. In dealing with more generalized tensions, such as the Cold War and anticolonialism, it is inevitable that *every* practicable strategy will be employed. Such difficulties do not disturb our thesis. All the categories are thematically consistent. They focus on the national interests that motivate consideration of disputes in the United Nations. The breakdown therefore will aid in perceiving the use of the United Nations for the accomplishment of specific ends relative to general foreign policies. It also clarifies the connection between particular processes in the United Nations and the goals themselves. Finally, it points up the relationship between strategic uses of the United Nations and prospects for the settlement of disputes and reduction of tensions. The last is especially important because it has been so completely ignored by other analysts. Introduction of any new weapon into a struggle changes other aspects of the dispute, including prospects for, and the nature of, a settlement. It follows that the inclusion of the United Nations in the arsenal of responses to a conflict situation adds another dimension whose impact will affect the outcome. In short, the categories will contribute to a better understanding of the objectives, tactics, and consequences of bringing political disputes to the United Nations.

2 *The Politics of Embarrassment*

Staunch defenders of the United Nations are faced with the task of accounting for what are perceived to be the organization's many failures—failures to stop aggression, to defend human rights, to act in time of crisis. Critics and defenders alike tend to blame the failures on weaknesses in the Charter or on the outlaw behavior of a few nations. They imply that a stronger Charter or changes in the attitudes of a few governments could give the United Nations enough authority to settle international disputes successfully. Ignored is the fact that many disputes are brought to the United Nations with no intention of a settlement. Very often states complain to the United Nations knowing full well that the organization will do nothing; the hope instead is to embarrass and hurt an opponent. What many have seen as United Nations failures are in fact successful instances of the use of the United Nations as a weapon in the politics of embarrassment. Indeed, the politics of embarrassment is characterized by an absence of any possibility or intention of influencing the substance of an issue. Frequently the matter has been resolved before it even reaches the United Nations. The purpose is to inflict some gratuitous hurt, to gain a symbolic victory where no other is possible, to express frustration and anger. Helpless rage is the apparent or real source of the complaint. When relations between states are characterized by unremitting hostility, every opportunity to embarrass is seized. Control of United Nations machinery is not essential. Even sure "losers" will employ the approach, although states controlling majorities may realize a more satisfactory psychic return.

Identification of the strategy can normally be made from the circumstances surrounding an issue, but sometimes precise motivation is uncertain.

The doubts arise where embarrassment is a tactic in support of another strategy. This is often the case. An excellent illustration is provided by the Arab offensive in the 1970s against Israel at the United Nations. Increasingly the United States has been maneuvered into the embarrassing position of using its veto or otherwise seen as standing alone in defense of Israel. Arab leaders make no secret of their purpose to influence the United States into withdrawing or reducing aid to Israel. By forcing the United States into an embarrassing position vis-à-vis the "world community," the Arabs hope to convince American officials that the diplomatic price of continuing identification with Israel is too high. Embarrassment is thus a means toward the achievement of more concrete ends.

Problems in defining motivation are clearly illustrated by two cases involving India which appear to be remarkably similar but were probably brought to the United Nations with different objectives in mind. Charges of Indian aggression in Hyderabad and Goa were based on related Charter provisions and outwardly reflected a desire for similar corrective action. While the Security Council debated, Indian troops destroyed Hyderabad's claim to independence in 1948 and liquidated Portuguese enclaves on the subcontinent in 1961.[1] On the surface, Hyderabad and Portugal sought the same relief against nearly identical threats and actions. Their real motives and expectations were probably quite different. It is entirely reasonable that the relatively unsophisticated Nizam of Hyderabad believed in 1948 that he could stimulate collective action by the Security Council to thwart the Indian invasion. Thirteen years later, Portugal had no such illusions. Faced with a certain Soviet veto in the Security Council and a hostile majority in the General Assembly, the most she could expect was to publicize aggression carried out by a leading anticolonial tormentor. India was somewhat embarrassed in both cases. For Hyderabad, that result was incidental. Portugal, however, *intended* to embarrass India. As is usually true in such politics, physical futility merged with deep hostility to provoke an attack at the United Nations.

Sudden Flare-up

It is exceedingly rare that states enjoying comparatively friendly relations will grasp the opportunity to embarrass. One example of such a sudden and explicit flare of anger between nonhostile states was the matter of Adolph Eichmann. Eichmann, a principal architect of the World War II murder of six million Jews by Germany, had in 1960 been kidnapped from Argentina and taken to Israel for trial and eventual execution. Argentina, embarrassed by this confirmation that the country had become an important refuge for ex-Nazis, demanded the return of Eichmann and punishment of the kidnappers, thus elevating the kidnapping of an individual into a situation "which created an atmosphere of insecurity and mistrust incompatible with the preservation of international peace." In the Security Council Argentina explained that negotiations with Israel had failed and that she had warned Israel that the complaint would be filed.[2] Actually, there was nothing that the Security Council could do about Eichmann. Israel was determined to try him and punish him. Having suffered embarrassment, the Argentinians reciprocated by embarrassing Israel. In effect, the Security Council debate and passage of an innocuous resolution compensated Argentina for the bad publicity the kidnapping had provoked. It is interesting that the last paragraph expressed the hope that "the traditionally friendly relations between Argentina and Israel will be advanced."[3] In the debate, too, Argentina and Israel avoided excessive recriminations. They recognized that to bring such an issue to the Security Council was a hostile act, and they did their best to limit the repercussions. Argentina succeeded in its objective—to return a hurt for a hurt.

The Cold War

The exceptional character of the Eichmann case serves to underscore the observation that a high level of hostility is the norm when the United Nations is utilized to embarrass. We would expect and do find that the Cold War would trigger such use. A classic example was the reaction to the Communist coup in Czechoslovakia in February, 1948.

The Czech Coup

The "loss" of Czechoslovakia to Communism was an especially bitter blow to the West, because that country had exemplified the Wilsonian ideals of democracy and self-determination. The coup itself had been prepared by the Munich Agreement of 1938, wartime Communist-led resistance, the liberation of the country largely by Soviet armies, and Czechoslovakia's geographical position. In its only free postwar election, the Communist Party won 38 percent of the vote, which, while denying the Party a victory at the polls, provided its leadership with strategic levers of power. Although the coup was swift and nearly bloodless, Chile, acting as surrogate for the United States, brought the issue before the Security Council, charging that the Soviet Union had created a situation that endangered international peace.[4]

The coup, of course, was over. Nothing could be done for Czechoslovakia. Yet the Western powers were determined to indict the Soviet Union publicly and, over Soviet objections that the issue was one of domestic jurisdiction, had it inscribed on the Council's agenda. The ensuing debate represents a high point of Cold War vituperation. It was charged that the Soviet Union had engineered the coup, that Valerian Zorin had transmitted the orders to key Czech Communists, and that maneuvers by the Soviet army on Czechoslovakia's borders were timed to facilitate the coup and intimidate its opponents. The United States insisted that Czechoslovakia had been enslaved by Soviet imperialism, and that a similar process was taking place throughout Eastern Europe.[5] Over bitter Soviet objections that a private individual had no standing in the Security Council, the former Czech chief delegate, Jan Papanek, testified in support of the Western charges. Papanek accused the Soviet Union of indirect aggression and political interference into the affairs of Czechoslovakia, charging in addition that without such assistance, the Communists could not have achieved power.[6]

The Soviet Union denounced the charges, insisted that the new government had gained power constitutionally, "proved" that Zorin's itinerary in Czechoslovakia had been perfectly innocent, and pointed out that there were no Soviet troops on Czech soil. Then the Soviet delegate fired off a propaganda volley of his own. The Chilean representative was pictured as a "puppet of Wall Street" who was doing the dirty work for those who controlled Chile's economy and foreign policy.[7] The real issue was American and not Soviet imperialism; the United States was angry because the Czechoslovakian people had declined to be drawn into the Marshall Plan, thus refusing to become enslaved to American monopolies.[8]

The Western states attempted to establish a committee of inquiry to continue the investigation. The Soviet Union responded by forcing a vote on whether or not the resolution was procedural, using its veto to have the issue declared substantive. The resolution was then vetoed. Following the Soviet vetoes, which should have ended the matter, the Western powers charged the Soviet Union with abusing its veto privileges. The United States declared that this abuse, although technically permissible under the Four Power agreement reached at San Francisco, could cause the United States to denounce the agreement.* Both France and the United Kingdom then stated their intention to continue to make available to the Security Council statements by Czechs concerning the coup.

The differences between the Eichmann case and this one are striking. In the former example, a single incident jarred the generally normal relations between the parties. The Security Council was used with restraint. The parties assiduously avoided having the confrontation go beyond an exchange of limited injuries. In contrast, the Czech coup provided a plat-

---

* At San Francisco, the four sponsoring powers (United States, United Kingdom, Soviet Union, and France) elaborated on the extent of the veto. They agreed that a decision concerning whether or not "a matter is procedural must be taken by a vote of seven members of the Security Council, including the concurring votes of the permanent members." It was this agreement that the United States threatened to abandon at this time. See *SCOR*, Meeting 303, May 24, 1948.

form for some of the most vicious accusations ever heard at the United Nations. The intention was to characterize the Soviet Union as an aggressive, totalitarian, imperialist state bent upon destroying the freedom and dignity of peace-loving, democratic peoples. The Soviets responded in kind. Whereas the Eichmann matter produced little or no lasting damage to Israeli-Argentinian relations, the debate on Czechoslovakia confirmed the most hard-line estimates of the intentions of East and West. The *purpose* was to exacerbate hostility, and this was achieved. Czechoslovakia provided a convenient excuse and the United Nations an admirable vehicle.

Essentially the same Cold War-inspired use of the United Nations was repeated on other occasions. These cases are normally considered as evidence of the weakness and futility of the United Nations, because of a failure to apply the principles of the Charter. This view ignores the uses of the organization as a weapon in world politics. When embarrassment is the motive, the inaction of the United Nations is irrelevant because there was never any desire or possibility that the United Nations could resolve the dispute. The correct basis of assessing the relationship of the United Nations to the dispute is in respect to the achievement of limited national conflict objectives.

The Hungarian Revolt

Every revolution seizes upon some act of violence to symbolize the break between those seeking to overturn the status quo and those presently in power. On the evening of October 23, 1956, this act occurred before the central headquarters of the national broadcasting corporation in Budapest. In the words of one account: "It was from here, perhaps even before blood was actually shed that the anguished cry, 'They are massacring the Hungarians,' spread like fire through the superheated atmosphere of the city."[9] But no revolution really begins with a single act of violence. The Hungarian revolt had many antecedents. Most immediate of these were the spread to Hungary of the general de-Stalinization movement that followed Khrushchev's secret address before the Twentieth Congress of the Soviet Communist Party, the demands of students and intellectuals for party reform, hurried reshuffling of top party and governmental posts immediately preceding the revolt, the intoxication that the "Polish October" had created in Hungary, especially among the young, and perhaps the hope that the West stood ready to support Hungary's fight for freedom. The initial uprising was followed by a rapid succession of events: the intervention by Soviet troops, the "massacre" of Kossuth Square, a brief period between October 30 and November 3 when it appeared that the revolt might be successful, and its abrupt suppression by Soviet arms on November 4.

While these events were unfolding, the United States, France, and the United Kingdom requested that the Security Council consider the threat to peace created by Soviet intervention in Hungary.[10] Over the objections of the Soviet and Hungarian delegates that consideration of the matter by the Security Council was a violation of the domestic-jurisdiction provisions of the Charter, a majority of the Council decided to place the matter on the agenda. In the debate that followed, the Soviet Union was accused of repressing the legitimate aspirations of the people of Hungary.[11] The United States submitted a resolution demanding the immediate withdrawal of Soviet troops from Hungary and affirming the right of the Hungarian people to a "government responsive to its national aspirations and well being. . . ." The Soviet Union denied all charges, linked the propaganda attack to Western concern with deflecting attention from French and British aggression in Suez, and vetoed the American resolution.[12] The United States then submitted a draft calling for an emergency meeting of the General Assembly under the provisions of the Uniting for Peace Resolution.[13]

By the time the General Assembly began its consideration of the Hungarian revolt, nothing could be done. The Imry Nagy government had fallen; the Soviet Union was in the process of shoring up its position in Hungary. Despite the futility, lengthy debates followed. The Soviets were accused of introducing a "reign of terror" in Hungary. A series of resolutions was passed condemning the Soviet Union's actions and rebuking her for defiance of the General Assembly's recommendations. Among the resolutions were two that provided for the distribution of food and other supplies to the people of Hungary and for the coordination of the activities of the United Nations High Commissioner for Refugees with those of other international agencies to handle the substantial refugee problem that had developed. Even these humanitarian efforts, however, carried with them condemnatory references to Soviet behavior. Efforts to delete these references by a group of "neutral" states were defeated by the Assembly.[14]

The intent in the Assembly was clearly to embarrass the Soviet Union before the onlooking world. Under the Uniting for Peace Resolution a two-thirds majority of the General Assembly may call upon its members to furnish whatever aid they individually decide upon to a victim of aggression. Thus if the United States and its allies wanted to respond by collective action against Russia, there was no "legal" barrier. That no help would be forthcoming was clear immediately after the Hungarian Writers Association appeal of November to the world for assistance went unheeded. Instead the West secured the passage of resolutions calling for the admission of United Nations observers into Hungary, empowering the Secretary-General to investigate the situation and finally creating a special committee of inquiry to develop the "facts" surrounding the uprising.[15] Clearly, after the government of Janos Kadar had come to power, implementation of these measures was an impossibility. The special committee, however, completed its task. After hearing 111 witnesses in Geneva, Rome, Vienna, and London, it termed the revolt a "spontaneous national uprising due to long standing grievances which had caused resentment among the people."[16] Soviet claims regarding the nature of the uprising were found to be patently false, while the role of the Soviet Union was depicted as "a massive armed intervention by one Power into the territory of another. . . ."[17] The report concluded with a blast at the Kadar government, which it found to be totally lacking in public support and violating the basic human freedoms of the Hungarian people. The issue was institutionalized through use of the special committee and, then, a Special Representative on Hungary whose reports became the basis for condemnatory resolutions for several years.

Hungary, perhaps more clearly than any other case, illustrates general misperceptions concerning conflict and the United Nations. It is widely agreed that the United Nations was a monumental failure in Hungary. A clear contrast is observed between inaction in Hungary and the application of collective security in Korea. Actually the two cases demonstrate successful but different strategies. In Korea, American involvement was accompanied by the strategy of legitimization.[18] If the United States and its allies had wanted to fight in Hungary, the Uniting for Peace Resolution would once again have facilitated legitimization by the United Nations. That was not a problem. But legitimization also required that the United States go to war in support of the Hungarian revolutionaries. Instead, the West decided to permit the revolt to be crushed. As part of *this* decision, the West opted for the politics of embarrassment at the United Nations. By forcing a Soviet veto in the Security Council, then by dominating debate and passing harsh resolutions by overwhelming majorities in the General Assembly, the United States and its friends *succeeded* in their objective of embarrassing the Russians and the Kadar government. Hungary was as much of a victory as Korea. Only the strategies were different.

Czechoslovakia and Hungary are not exceptions. The United Nations was used to embarrass the Communist bloc whenever the possibility arose. A typical instance was the censuring of Communist China for its annexation of Tibet in 1959.[19] There was obviously no chance that General Assembly action would influence Chinese behavior, even had the Communist government been represented at the United Nations. The issue was further clouded by the fact that *both* Chinese governments claimed that Tibet was part of China and that its concerns were therefore internal matters beyond United Nations competence. Indeed, embarrassment was so obviously the sole motive of the West that even non-Communist delegations questioned the propriety of United Nations action.

Although the West, and especially the United States, had the better ability to utilize the organization to embarrass its Cold War enemies, Communist bloc countries seized similar opportunities. Given their minority positions, they could not hope to force vetoes or win passage of condemnatory resolutions in the General Assembly. In substance, however, the same patterns were repeated. By forcing the United States to

defend in public vulnerable foreign policies, the other side
achieved its limited objectives. Again, we will cite only a few
illustrations.

The U-2 Incident

The "Spirit of Camp David" ended abruptly when an American U-2 spy plane was shot down a thousand miles inside
Russia on May 1, 1960. Following a cat-and-mouse game in
which American "cover" stories were destroyed by the Soviets
producing the pilot, Francis Gary Powers, President Eisenhower assumed full responsibility for the incident. Premier
Khrushchev then canceled a scheduled Paris summit meeting
and withdrew an invitation to have President Eisenhower
visit the Soviet Union.[20]
     The American government had been caught in a lie; the
Americans had been embarrassed before the world; the Soviets had had the chance to act with righteous indignation. But
the Russians were not finished. In order to exploit the incident
to the fullest possible extent, they brought the issue to the
United Nations. The Soviet Union demanded a meeting of the
Security Council to consider "aggressive acts by the United
States Air Force against the Soviet Union, creating a threat to
universal peace."[21] In essence, Mr. Khrushchev's rage and
frustration were transferred to the Security Council, where a
furious debate took place. The Soviets denounced militaristic
adventurism and the Western alliance system for endangering
world peace. Despite the obvious embarrassment of having
been caught violating Russian sovereignty, the United States
blamed the Soviet Union for the incident. The Russians had
forced the West to take measures to prevent surprise attacks
because of the Soviet Union's aggressive policies, its closed
society, and its refusal to accept the "open skies" proposal

made by President Eisenhower in 1955.[22] Predictably, the Soviet draft resolution received only two affirmative votes (Poland and the Soviet Union). Later, the Soviets asked the General Assembly to consider the same issue, but then withdrew the complaint in 1961, claiming that the Kennedy administration had abandoned the policy of military overflights of the Soviet Union.[23]

In this manner, the Soviet Union obtained a small measure of revenge. If, by some alchemy, the "Spirit of Camp David" had been maintained in spite of the U-2 incident, there would have been no Security Council meeting on the subject. Hostile acts for the sole purpose of embarrassment are not only a barometer of the level of hostility, but contribute to an atmosphere that reduces the likelihood of negotiating away the *causes* of the differences.

Dominican Republic

A number of Latin American issues have been raised also for the purpose of embarrassing the United States. One could cite the coup in Guatemala in 1954, the Bay of Pigs invasion seven years later, and the Cuban complaint during the missile crisis of 1962.* But as good an illustration as any of the use of the United Nations to embarrass the United States was in respect to the intervention in the Dominican Republic in 1965. Here, as in Hungary, there was no possibility of influencing policy after a Great Power had committed military force in favor of *its* regime.

On April 28, 1965, American marines landed in Santo

---

* UN Document S/5183, October 22, 1962. The Cuban government here demanded that the Council consider "the act of war unilaterally committed by the Government of the United States in ordering the naval blockade of Cuba."

Domingo for the officially announced purpose of protecting
American lives during the crisis that had overtaken the
Dominican Republic. However, no secret was made of the
fact that the attack was ordered to prevent the revolutionary
government of Juan Bosch, which according to fragmentary
reports was influenced by Communists, from reassuming
power.[24] Bosch had been elected to the presidency in 1963
following the overthrow of the Trujillo dictatorship in 1961.
Seven months later he was overthrown by a military coup
whose leadership was committed to establishing a "rightist
government." Without the full support of the military, however, the revolution could not be consolidated, and the country became engulfed in civil war. After over a year of American occupation, elections were held on June 1, 1966, in which
Joaquín Balaguer became president of the Dominican Republic and American fears of a "new Cuba" were laid to rest.

During this period of time the issue was before the
Security Council. Immediately following the invasion the
Soviet Union went before the Council and demanded an
immediate withdrawal of American troops from Santo
Domingo and condemnation of America's wanton interference
with the efforts of a defenseless people to achieve self-determination.[25] By 1965 the politics at the United Nations had
undergone a drastic change from what they had been in 1954,
when the United States succeeded in keeping the Guatemalan
issue off the Security Council's agenda. With a great increase
in the number and influence of so-called Third World nations,
Soviet efforts to embarrass the West, especially over issues of
this nature, would not be as easily silenced as they had been in
the past. The strategy, however, remained the same, and the
results were never in doubt.

The Soviet Union launched a bitter verbal attack upon
the United States. The United States was accused of providing

military support for dictatorship in Latin America. Charges were levied that the OAS had been pressured into establishing an Inter-American Peace Force in violation of Article 53 of the United Nations Charter. Repeated calls, all unsuccessful, were made for a formal condemnation of the United States by the Council. Although the United States was not directly condemned by the Council, its actions in the Dominican Republic were publicly questioned through the persistence of the Soviet Union, closely monitored by the Council. Nothing could be done, of course, to coerce the removal of American troops from the Dominican Republic. The Soviet purpose was to embarrass the United States by forcing it continually to justify its actions. In the face of the overwhelming evidence of their true nature, the United States could do so only lamely.[26]

Embarrassment and Colonialism

The employment of the United Nations for purposes of propaganda and embarrassment has not been confined to Cold War issues. Increasingly, the organization's suitability in this respect has been placed in the service of the anticolonial movement. Again, a complex and intense pattern of antagonisms and frustrations provides the impetus for the drum-fire of accusations and recriminations that has characterized much of the anticolonial debate. With equally little, if any, prospect of substantively affecting the outcomes of particular issues, proponents of anticolonial positions have utilized United Nations processes to develop favorable opinion on the positions they endorse and to attack and condemn their adversaries. Embarrassment is an obvious, even flagrant aspect of United Nations activity by Afro-Asians and socialists on this issue. The untiring use and manipulation of United Nations processes on all levels can be considered the definitive text on the malleability of the organization to embarrass opponents.

Nevertheless, a word of caution is necessary. In discussing the Arab-Israeli dispute above, we observed that by embarrassing the United States on the issue, the Arabs sought to reduce American aid to Israel. Similarly, anticolonialists use embarrassment to cause Western states to abandon colonial regimes. In short, embarrassment may be a tactic in a larger strategy. African states, especially, insist that their purpose is to achieve specific goals, namely, independence and majority rule in southern Africa. Granting that assumption, embarrassment is nevertheless their conscious and primary weapon. Given the determination of Portugal, South Africa, and Rhodesia to maintain their governmental systems and colonial rule, and the continued reluctance of key Western states to undermine these governments, embarrassment may be the principal injury inflicted. After more than a quarter of a century of futility, even some of the more optimistic anticolonialists may well have reached the point where they despair of achieving concrete results, and now embarrass purely to embarrass. Some evidence of this is to be found in the withdrawal of the United Kingdom and the United States from the Special Committee on Decolonization, presumably because they found the Afro-Asians too unreasonable. The designation of Puerto Rico as a non-self-governing territory, thereby opening the way to direct condemnations of the United States as a colonial power similar to South Africa and Portugal, also testifies to that combination of rage and impotence that is characteristic of the politics of embarrassment. By lumping the United States with the racist colonial regimes and subjecting it to potential humiliation in the General Assembly, the African states have deliberately provoked American hostility. They have thus tacitly admitted the failure of their efforts to persuade the United States to withdraw support from their enemies. At the least, therefore, we can be confident that, for some of the parties, the purpose is what it appears to be—to embarrass.

These remarks underline the inherent difficulty in assessing motivation, which is made even more complex when there are a large number of participants. Although the black Africans have tended to control the submission of anticolonial issues to United Nations bodies, they are supported by states that have different and varied motives. Latin Americans and Asians have their own reasons for attacking Portugal and South Africa. Even within Africa, there are a variety of motives. When the "consensus" extends to the socialist bloc, the search for motivation becomes even more tangled. Does the Soviet Union, for example, perceive the anticolonial issue as a means of embarrassing her Cold War enemies?

We need not disregard the professed Soviet interest in wars of national liberation to suspect, at least, that *at the United Nations*, the Russians use anticolonialism to embarrass the West. The year after passage of the Declaration on Non-Self-Governing Territories, the Soviet Union sponsored a resolution proposing that a one-year deadline be set for the granting of independence to peoples in eighty-eight territories.[27] The proposal was obviously designed to embarrass the Western states, since there was no reasonable possibility that they would comply with such an Assembly resolution. In arguing its case, the Russians charged that American military and financial power buttressed other colonialists, and that the establishment of foreign military bases by the United States was part of the drive to maintain the dependency of developing peoples. When the resolution was opposed by the Afro-Asians the Soviets prudentially withdrew it. Instead, an

Afro-Asian resolution was adopted that established the Special Committee on Decolonization, but without any terminal date for eliminating colonial rule.[28] It was apparent that the extreme Soviet approach was regarded as propagandistic, and the Afro-Asians acted to keep the issue from being embroiled in the Cold War.* Inevitably, the United States responded to Soviet charges. According to the American delegate, the most cruel and oppressive empire was that of the Soviet Union and China, whose enslaved nations had no voice in determining their destiny. Furthermore, the Sino-Soviet empire was the only one bent upon further expansion.[29] To which the Russians responded by praising the positive accomplishments of the socialists and reiterating their high-minded and disinterested support for the Third World.[30] In short, the Soviet-American exchange was an obvious consequence of the politics of embarrassment, whereas, at the same time, other states were apparently more interested in influencing the balance of forces. With these cautions we can proceed to examine the embarrassment aspects of anticolonial politics, keeping in mind that for some embarrassment is a means, and for others an end, and that shifts in motivation occur with the passage of time.

The process of embarrassing a colonial power begins in the Special Committee on Decolonization or in one of its subcommittees, such as those on Apartheid or South West Africa. In the committees, evidence is gathered as it would be in an adversary proceeding, to strengthen the case on one side. Petitioners are witnesses for the prosecution. No voices are heard for the defense. Testimony invariably buttresses alle-

---

* Despite unswerving socialist support for anticolonialism at the United Nations, sponsorship of anticolonial initiatives is usually confined to Afro-Asian members, and on those occasions where a "bloc" nation assumes leadership, it is normally taken away by one or more Afro-Asian members.

gations against colonial powers and their supporters. Committee members rarely engage in dialogue, since the atmosphere favors no dilution of the rhetoric and hyperbole that befit situations of moral extremes. With the exception of occasional defensive statements by Western states, such as the United States, Britain, or France, concerning their contribution to Portuguese, Rhodesian, and South African policies,[31]all of the charges go virtually unchallenged.

The futility of injecting any moderating point of view is illustrated by a Danish request for more information concerning a charge made by the African National Congress that West Germany was actively linked to former Nazis in South West Africa. The Indian delegate responded:

> *India*: The statements made by the petitioner appear to me to be sound, carefully prepared and without exaggeration; they deserve the Committee's most serious attention. The African National Congress is highly regarded by many of the Committee's members and my own delegation has been familiar with its work for many years.
>
> *USSR*: Has the petitioner any evidence that the flow of German war criminals to South Africa has ceased after the statement of concern made by the official representative of the Bonn government?
>
> *Petitioner*: There has been no decrease in the flow of former Nazis to South Africa. We firmly believe that there is a direct link between the Government of the Federal Republic of Germany and the South African Regime.
>
> *USSR*: The Representative of Denmark does not appear to have proven his point.[32]

Testimony of petitioners is thus accepted at face value with no real attempt to verify it. In order to be certain to extract the desired bases for future resolutions, witnesses are

asked leading questions. The varied motivations of participants are revealed by this practice. Communist States tend to
focus on elaborations of the effect of outside aid from NATO
or specific Western countries on colonial or racial policies,
whereas Africans and Asians place more emphasis on inhuman
conditions.[33] A typical example of the latter is the Indian
delegate noting that "a great deal has appeared in the press
about Bantustans," and then going on to ask a witness to
explain the "nature of the system and how it was used to keep
racial groups apart instead of building a multiracial society."[34] There is no defense lawyer leaping to his feet complaining that the question leads the witness and forces him to
draw conclusions. Instead, committee members gravely listen
to confirmations of their prejudices as they prepare to write
resolutions for the next General Assembly or Security Council
meeting. When the Tanzanian delegate asks: "What do the
people of South West Africa expect the United Nations to do
for them?"[35] all of the committee members are confident that
the response will fit in with the plans of the anticolonialists.
There can be no objection that the petitioner speaks for only
some of the people of South West Africa and that there might
be others with different expectations.

The Special Committee on Decolonization reports its
findings to the Fourth Committee of the General Assembly
or to the Security Council. In these forums, the quality of
debate had been established before the committee findings
regularized the flow of resolutions. As early as 1952, the
French delegate observed that: "It was hopeless to argue about
the semi-mystical idea of the original sin of Colonialism which
permitted a distinction to be made between the just who
could claim every right and the unjust whose rights were precarious and revocable at will."[36] He was not exaggerating.
Anticolonialists were on God's side. Commenting on passage

of the Declaration on Non-Self-Governing Territories in 1960, the Liberian representative said: "I am inclined to conclude that some supernatural force which we call God and others call Allah is responsible for it all. We the agitators were only instruments in God's hands."[37]

From this commanding height, exposure to retaliatory attacks for equally reprehensible behavior does not become a strategic consideration for either side. The accused can do no more than deny that they possess colonies, as the Portuguese allege, claim that issues have been oversimplified, or insist that they are legally immune because the organization is barred from violating their domestic jurisdiction.

These defenses are ignored or countered by sweeping generalizations. According to the Tunisian delegate:

> Whether we like it or not, whether force has to be used or persuasion, whether it is acceptable to the colonial countries or not, there will soon no longer be any enslaved peoples. The irrevocable march of history will certainly not be halted by the obstinacy of France in carrying on a futile and hopeless war in Algeria for the past six years; of Portugal in denying the evidence and clinging to absurd fictions; above all, of South Africa in isolating itself, despite universal reprobation, within an inhuman racism which it has raised to the status of national policy.[38]

The right of dark-skinned peoples to govern themselves could not be denied by legalisms. The Congolese delegate said:

> Freedom is not a favour begged by long-subjected peoples from their alleged masters but an indefeasible, legitimate right . . . birth in a cold country is not a title to everything there is, and birth in a hot country is not an atavism which debars one from everything, even from freedom.[39]

Although they dominate its tone, the anticolonialists cannot completely silence their opposition in the General Assembly. A random selection of debate in any year after 1961 demonstrates the use of this forum to embarrass. In 1963, for example, in discussions of South West Africa, fifty of fifty-eight statements were condemnatory.[40] Even the more moderate speeches expressed disapproval of Apartheid. Thus, the British delegate objected mildly to the constant comparisons between Apartheid and Nazi Germany's policies:

> Apartheid [does] not appear to be a philosophy of extermination or territorial expansion; its purpose [seems] rather to be to preserve political and social conditions in an age where change and progress [are] long overdue.[41]

Such niceties could be ignored, but any attempt by the South African to defend his country's policies provoked extreme reactions. The Guinean representative would "leave it to the [Fourth] Committee to appraise the fallacious and arrogant statement just made by the person who claimed to represent South Africa."[42] Similarly, the Malian delegate found the Assembly's duty "was to defend the rights of peoples, and the South African representative's testimony [is] of no use to it in [this] connection."[43] At another time, a speech by the South African resulted in the demand that the words be purged from the record as unworthy of civilized discourse. Even the *presence* of the South African delegate has been described as an insult.

The final step in embarrassing Colonial states is the passage of resolutions. Literally hundreds have been adopted. It might be expected that dry, legalistic language would prevail at this stage. In fact, the accusatorial character of the entire process is continued, revealing the intent to embarrass even when substantive steps are demanded. Take, for example, General Assembly Resolution 2262, adopted by a vote of ninety-eight to two, with eighteen abstentions, on November 3, 1967.

The resolution condemned Rhodesia and called on all states to apply the sanctions that had been voted in the Security Council. In the course of the resolution, the Rhodesian government is referred to as "the illegal racist minority regime" *nine* times. Its racial policies were described as "a crime against humanity." In addition to the attack on Rhodesia, the resolution lashed out at the United Kingdom for not taking "effective measures to bring down the illegal racist minority regime," and condemned "those States which . . . are still trading" with "the illegal racist minority regime." Furthermore, "foreign financial and other interests" supplying support for "the illegal racist minority regime" were condemned (seven separate clauses "condemn"), as were the governments of South Africa and Portugal.

Although only South Africa and Portugal voted against the resolution, the major Western states abstained. Clearly, the escalation in language and the identification of these states and their nationals with "crimes against humanity" contributed to the decision to abstain. Two years earlier, prior to the Unilateral Declaration of Independence, the vote on a comparatively mild Rhodesian resolution was 107 to 2, with 1 abstention (France).[44] By 1967, the deliberate attempt to embarrass the Western states, perhaps in recognition that policy changes would not be forthcoming, caused the estrangement. While there may be something approaching a "consensus" generally deploring colonialism and racism, the use of the United Nations to attack specific targets is invariably countered by indifference or hostility. Certainly the Soviet bloc, so often the victim of Cold War embarrassment, had reason to enjoy the discomfiture of the United States and its allies, but whether or not their embarrassment would contribute to the achievement of the *stated* policy objectives is, at best, questionable.

Conclusions

Understanding that the United Nations is often used for embarrassment purposes clarifies many things. For one, it destroys all estimates of the organization that are based upon a record of successes or failures. These analyses relate the adoption of agenda items and passage of resolutions to Charter principles and substantive modification of national behavior. From this perspective, it is commonplace, as we have pointed out, to conclude that the United Nations failed in Hungary, since the near-total mobilization of United Nations machinery against the Soviet Union and the Kadar government had no effect on conditions in Hungary. However, from the point of view of Western strategy, which was confined entirely to embarrassing the Soviet Union, the initiative on Hungary was a huge success. The Russians were no less successful, despite their inability to manipulate the organization as effectively as the United States, when they were able to maintain an embarrassing exposure of American policy in the Dominican Republic through thirty meetings of the Security Council. Unremitting hostility, combined with the unwillingness of either of the superpowers to risk thermonuclear war to prevent its enemy from imposing a particular regime on a country within its sphere of influence, explains the initiatives in the organization. Success and failure, therefore, on these, as on other embarrassment issues, are important considerations, but only in relationship to the motivations of major participants and the relative abilities, over time, of these participants to translate their desires into favorable responses at the United Nations. To understand the dynamics of these relationships one need consider only the impact of historical changes on the vulnerability of the United States to the strategy of embarrassment. Subjected to three similarly inspired attacks over its

Latin American policies, the United States was able to prevent extensive debate over Guatemala in 1954, was subjected to a full-scale attack twelve years later on the Dominican Republic, and by 1973 would be forced to veto a resolution on the Panama Canal Zone.[45]

Embarrassment politics also helps to explain why trivial incidents will be heard in the Security Council while serious breaches of the peace are ignored. For example, several times since 1963 insignificant border problems between Senegal and Portuguese Guinea involving little or no loss of life or property have been brought to the Security Council by Senegal. The Portuguese have protested their innocence and invited investigation. In the last instance, in 1972, Portugal acknowledged that a psychologically disturbed bodyguard had been responsible for the death of a Senegalese and stated their willingness to make reparation and punish the individual.[46] Each time, a condemnatory resolution was adopted despite the obvious absence of any serious issue, and even when Portugal agreed to a settlement of the problem. When such trivial matters are raised, we must question why more serious conflicts are ignored. Large-scale hostilities, such as in Nigeria, Burundi, or Sudan, do not become agenda items. The difference obviously must be found in that combination of hostility and national interest which impels Senegal to embarrass Portugal whenever there is an opportunity to do so, and the absence of similar motivation on other issues. To illustrate this point further, we could ask why the United States did not go to the United Nations when, during the Six-Day War, the American spy ship *Liberty* was severely damaged and suffered heavy casualties as a result of Israeli naval action. Would there have been similar inaction if the *Arab* side, which was charging then that the United States air force was actively aiding the Israelis, had attacked the *Liberty*? The answer is at least doubtful. But it is certain that there was *not* that conjunction of hostility and interest required to embarrass Israel in the United Nations.

Thus, if we focus on *motivation*, mysteries concerning use and nonuse of the United Nations are unraveled. Especially in respect to embarrassment issues, we understand better why the organization devotes so much time and energy to seemingly hopeless or inconsequential questions while ignoring similar and often more serious disputes.

The politics of embarrassment lends itself to complex calculations concerning motivation. At a particular point in a conflict, embarrassment may be a deliberate feature of another strategy, whereas in other instances it may become the strategy because of failure to achieve objectives. We have suggested that the latter possibility offers a useful basis for analysis of anticolonialism in southern Africa, at least for some of the states involved. In the Algerian issue, which is analyzed below, it is probable that an early effort to help the rebels shifted to an effort to embarrass the French at a later stage. These are difficult assessments because of the need to integrate actions at the United Nations with overall strategy, and also because of the diverse aims of participating states. Thus, whereas militant anticolonialists can conceive that using the United Nations to isolate South Africa will eventually force the abandonment of Apartheid,[47] the Soviet bloc may be more interested in embarrassing NATO members. Two different strategies are thus present simultaneously.

The structure and processes of the United Nations make such alliances inevitable. To use the organization as a weapon requires the mobilization of support, and it is impossible to exclude the interests of those who are drawn into the fight.[48] An interesting recent example illustrates the point. Panama, in deciding to use the United Nations against the United

States, understood that other states would welcome the opportunity to exploit the Canal Zone controversy for their purposes. Whether or not the strategy will be successful for Panama, one certain effect was to embarrass the United States by forcing a veto in the Security Council. The announcement that Panama would utilize the General Assembly in 1973 threatened a repetition of that effect.[49] Clearly, many states supporting Panama are less interested in who owns the canal than they are in embarrassing the United States. These would include Latin Americans with ancient grievances, the anticolonialists who resent American diffidence on issues of vital concern to them, the socialist states who have endured similar embarrassment many times, and allies, such as France, who recall American moralism during the Suez Canal crisis. In short, the opportunity to take a "cheap shot" is often seized, and is frequently an element in a conflict where the primary initiating state is pursuing a somewhat different strategy. The impact of this conflict strategy affects relations not only between the major protagonists but also between the accused and the states that have a less immediate interest in the issue itself.

3 _The Politics of Status_

Serious doubts exist regarding the influence that law exerts in ordering and restraining international behavior. Observance of international law on any given issue is closely linked to concrete assessments of national self-interest. If obeying the law undermines important political objectives, a nation will either disregard the law or interpret it in a manner consistent with the momentary demands of policy formation. In short, when vital interests are at stake, nations apply the law inconsistently and behave indifferently or even contemptuously when the law is applied to them. Despite these serious shortcomings in the application of international law, nations continually invoke legalisms in support of their policies and have incorporated the law into the arsenal of weapons they employ to pursue conflicting national purposes. Political leaders always defend the most outrageous breaches of international law with elaborate and often ingenious legal rationales for their actions.*

* Consider, for example, the United States justification for violating Soviet air space after an American U-2 plane was shot down deep in Russia. Charged with violating Soviet sovereignty, the American delegate blamed the Soviet Union for having refused to accept an American "open skies" plan which would have made such espionage unnecessary. It was, thus, Russian secrecy, and _not_ the overflight, that was the cause of the crisis. By implication, the right of self-defense was extended to include aerial surveillance of a potential enemy. See _SCOR_, Meetings 880–883, May 23–

Because of its close association with international law, the United Nations offers important tactical advantages to nations that can successfully exploit its processes. Legality has historically been associated with the kind of parliamentary procedures and majority decision-making that determine most outcomes at the United Nations. Favorable interpretations of general rules and specific provisions of the Charter through either the actions of the political organs or advisory opinions of the International Court of Justice add important constitutional and judicial dimensions to conflicts which, though largely political in origin, are won or lost because of the legal arguments that ultimately prevail. The politics of status centers on the control of United Nations forums, processes, and decisions in order to advance legal positions that have some bearing on the conflicting political purposes of member states.

Many quasi-legal issues, especially those involving the confirmation or achievement of status in international relations, may be profitably fought out at the United Nations. For some areas, the quarrel rages over whether or not they should be categorized as non-self-governing territories. Newly independent states regard admission into the United Nations as a final seal of acceptance of their sovereignty. In other instances—for example, former enemy states, divided states, and the People's Republic of China—admission or acceptance of delegate credentials is an important feature of their demands for prestige and respectability.

May 26, 1960. Writers on the subjct of international law, however, have suggested that even this kind of hyprocrisy has a salutary effect on international relations. See, for example, Lawrence Scheinman, "The Berlin Blockade," in Lawrence Scheinman and David Wilkinson, eds., *International Law and Political Crisis* (Boston: Little, Brown, 1968), p. 1. Professor Scheinman writes: ". . . In developing and promoting legal justification for their action, states (in a sense) draw the boundary lines of the game in play, thus it becomes more difficult for states to cast aside these ground rules."

Admission of New Members

Article 4 of the Charter lays out the procedures and qualifications for admission into the United Nations. Membership is "effected by a decision of the General Assembly upon the recommendation of the Security Council." The critical arena is the Security Council, where the veto or a majority can be used to prevent action by the General Assembly. Criteria for membership are that a state be "peace-loving" and "able and willing" to carry out its Charter obligations.[1]

At first glance, membership issues are not comparable to other political disputes. In fact, however, they are different only in that the organization's existence is a prerequisite for their manufacture. The distinction is a subtle one. Actually, positions taken on applicants are dictated by the same political considerations that govern attitudes on disputes that originate externally. During the first ten years of the life of the United Nations, membership remained essentially static. Western states pressed for the admission of those countries that would add to their majority, while the Soviet Union urged membership for Communist-bloc countries. Each side employed appropriate legalisms to defend its own favorites and oppose states sponsored by the other side. Given the much larger number of applicants being supported by the West, the Soviets were forced to resort to tenuous and unconvincing legal arguments.[2] But the legalities were no more than the language demanded by circumstances for the expression of hostile political policies. Soviet support for its allies and satellites is easy to comprehend as a responsibility flowing from leadership of the socialist world. Western political objectives were equally tangible. By forcing repeated Soviet vetoes of the same applicants, the West advanced a powerful argument toward convincing these states that they should join the anti-Communist alignment.[3] It was an effective and comparatively inexpensive tactic. Since admission to the United Nations was important to the prestige of applicants, support by a superpower was a potent inducement to lean in the desired direction. Consider, for example, its utility in Italy, where a powerful communist party threatened the pro-Western government. Respectability had to be important to Italians, who felt the need to restore the shattered image resulting from Mussolini's policies. Each veto could be converted into a blow to Italian national pride, a useful weapon for the Christian Democrats against the domestic Communists.

Given the West's majority and the political returns inherent in the membership issue, it is not surprising that the advantage was pressed in other organs. The General Assembly debated the "constitutional" issue for years and, predictably, criticized the "abuse" of the veto power by the Soviet Union.[4] The Soviet Union was denounced for violating the intentions and spirit of the Charter in preventing universal membership. To extricate itself from its embarrassing position, the Soviet Union offered a "package" deal which would trade off Communist states for a larger number of pro-Western or neutralist applicants. There was, of course, no constitutional basis for the Soviet proposal. But it offered a direct, if crude, political solution to the politically inspired impasse that had developed. For the West, however, it provided the opportunity, quickly seized upon, to add one more legalism to its arsenal. On November 17, 1947, the General Assembly requested an opinion from the International Court of Justice on the legality of the Soviet offer.[5] Since a majority of the Assembly determines the wording of submissions to the Court, the West was assured a favorable decision. "A member of the Organization," said the Court, "cannot . . . subject its affirmative vote to the additional condition that other States be admitted to membership in the United Nations together with that State."[6]

By 1955, the Western states had concluded that their policy offered diminishing returns. The Soviet Union had been unmoved by the necessity of using its veto power repeatedly, its isolation and embarrassment in the General Assembly, and the advisory opinion of the Court. By publicizing its package proposal, the Soviets made it apparent that the West was equally responsible for the logjam and for restricting the application of the principle of universality. The package was accepted. Sixteen states, four of which were Communist, were admitted.[7] Since then, with little more to be gained, the two sides traded off a few more states and ended by acting favorably on all new applicants. High moral and legal ground was quietly abandoned.

Both sides were hypocritical. Support and opposition toward an applicant clearly related more to its potential attitude in the United Nations than to its love of peace or ability to pay its dues. Yet these observations miss the point. Hypocrisy is the norm in an organization where delegates constantly clothe their real purposes in the principles of the Charter. A few more votes for or against nonbinding resolutions would make no appreciable difference in the power balance. The United States and the Soviet Union perceived and acted on the membership question as an aspect of their global struggle for power and influence. The membership dispute reflected conflict politics in much the same way as do economic aid, alliances, and military buildups. The effect, too, was the same, namely to deepen and intensify hostility and suspicion. Even "realistic" observers have failed to appreciate this. John G. Stoessinger, for example, expresses pleasure that the vetoes were "overcome."[8] Actually, if the United Nations were not a battleground, the vetoes would never have been cast. The superpowers would have consulted beforehand on applicants and taken action only when they were in agreement. Eventually, some such version of "corridor diplomacy" prevailed, but only after the organization's usefulness for conflict purposes had been exhausted.

The Divided States

While it was possible eventually to resolve the quarrel on the general membership issue, there was less room for compromise in respect to the divided states on the front lines of the Cold War—Germany, Korea, Vietnam, and China. In all of these areas, juridical status was central to a whole complex of antagonisms. The United Nations has been the scene of continuing and bitter confrontation on these issues.

Germany

It is not necessary here to dwell on the crucial failure of the Allies to agree on post-World War II policies toward Germany. Cold War was inevitably reflected in approaches to Germany. Zones of occupation hardened as common policies for the entire country foundered. Disagreements multiplied over reparations, currency, de-Nazification, and the German economy. Western currency reform and steps toward integration of West Germany were countered by the Berlin blockade. Proclamation of the Federal Republic of Germany on May 23, 1949, produced a response in kind in East Germany. It was clear that neither the United States nor the Soviet Union could expect to integrate a united Germany into its camp. The much greater size and industry in West Germany and the acceptance by Chancellor Konrad Adenauer of the policy of maximum military and economic cooperation with Western Europe and the United States meant that the West could not accept the unification of Germany at the price of neutralization. The Soviets, on the other hand, would permit the country to be unified only if it were neutralized and the East German Communist Party represented in its formation. Unless the superpowers were willing to fight World War III, neither side could impose its will on the other.

At the United Nations, there was no possibility that the West could bring the Federal Republic into the organization except at the unacceptable price of simultaneously admitting the East German regime. Short of this goal, the Western majority embellished the status of West Germany by having it elected to membership in United Nations-related bodies, such as the specialized agencies and the Economic Commission for Europe, while systematically excluding East Germany. In addition, the Federal Republic alone was granted observer status at the General Assembly. All of these steps were consistent with the Western policy of promoting its ally while downgrading the legitimacy of the German Democratic Republic.

Although policy positions had become rigid by 1949, the United States, Britain, and France nevertheless brought the case for a united Germany to the General Assembly in 1951. The Big Three proposed the establishment of a neutral commission to investigate conditions for the holding of free elections throughout Germany. The proposal was calculated to embarrass the Soviet Union by forcing it to oppose an investigation, thereby confirming Western charges of totalitarianism in East Germany. In the debate, both sides adopted predictable Cold War positions. The Soviet argument that Article 107*

* Article 107 reads: "Nothing in the present Charter shall invalidate or preclude action in relation to any state which during the Second World War has been an enemy of any signatory to the present Charter. . . ."

excluded United Nations actions in respect to Germany was brushed aside by the West. With no possibility that the commission could function in East Germany, it was established anyway, with Brazil, Iceland, the Netherlands, and Pakistan serving (Poland refused to participate).[9] Predictably, the commission reported to the next General Assembly that it had found conditions in West Germany conducive to holding free elections, but that it had received no answers from the East to any of its communications.[10] Having made their point, the Western powers allowed the commission to die.

Even the casual observer can appreciate that there was no serious interest in solving the German problem. The debate and the action were steps that the West took in order to consolidate its relationship with Chancellor Adenauer and provide support for his policies internally. At the same time, they succeeded in embarrassing the Soviet Union. Twenty years later, Chancellor Willy Brandt's *Ostpolitik* abandoned illusions and began the process that led to the admission of both Germanies into the United Nations. The contrast between a serious attempt to solve an international problem and the opportunistic use of the United Nations in this instance highlights the actual uses of the United Nations.

Korea

As in Germany, the Cold War was responsible for the division of Korea. During World War II, the Great Powers agreed in principle that the Japanese-held peninsula should eventually become free and independent. Pledges to this effect at Cairo in 1943 and Potsdam in July, 1945, were confirmed by the Moscow Foreign Ministers Conference in December, 1945. A temporary trusteeship would be established and a joint Soviet-American commission would consult with Korean representatives and establish a provisional Korean government. The division at the thirty-eighth parallel was decided upon for purposes of military convenience to facilitate the acceptance of Japanese surrender by the Soviets in the north and the Americans in the south. However, the Cold War destroyed any hope for the implementation of the Moscow agreement. After two years of fruitless negotiation, the United States brought the issue to the United Nations.

By bringing the Korean question to the General Assembly, the United States made clear that it had abandoned any hope of achieving the goal of a united, democratic Korea through bilateral negotiations with the Soviet Union. Yet there was no other peaceful method of achieving that objective. The United States could accept the division of Korea as a consequence of the Cold War or it could use the United Nations to vent its hostility toward the Soviet Union. The second option, a diplomatic escalation of the conflict, was chosen. In the Assembly, the Soviets insisted that the existence of machinery for solving the problem precluded United Nations jurisdiction.[11] Each side bitterly denounced the other for the failure of the negotiations. In the end, an American-sponsored resolution was adopted establishing a Temporary Commission on Korea, which was authorized to observe and expedite an election to be held before March 31, 1948, for the purpose of establishing a national government of Korea.[12]

As expected, the commission was barred from any access or communication with North Korea. Consequently, it could only report that it had observed the election of the government of Syngman Rhee.[13] The General Assembly dutifully declared that this government "is based on elections which were a valid expression of the free will of the electorate . . . and that this is the only such Government in Korea." A new commission on Korea was appointed to assist in extending the

Rhee government's authority throughout the peninsula.[14] The hostile debate in the Assembly was accompanied by increased tension in Korea, where clashes multiplied following the establishment of the People's Republic of Korea under Kim Il Sung.

On June 25, 1950, North Korean troops crossed the thirty-eighth parallel. The war had begun. Historians will dispute the origins of the war. We are concerned here only with the impact of the United Nations on the dispute. The action taken in the General Assembly exacerbated the conflict. It demonstrated the unwillingness of the United States to accept the status quo of a divided Korea. From the perspective of North Korea, the endorsement of Syngman Rhee's legitimacy and the refusal even to invite North Koreans to the Assembly debate must have constituted a threat to take further measures. Syngman Rhee's government had been placed in a position where any steps taken against the North could be justified as the suppression of an internal faction. Assembly support of Rhee could therefore be construed by North Koreans as a prelude to invasion. The extent to which such calculations contributed to the decision to launch the attack is speculative. It is certain, however, that the "victory" in the United Nations made the war somewhat more likely.

When, during the war, the Soviet Union ended its boycott, thus blocking further Security Council action, the General Assembly was utilized again to promote the status of the South Korean government. A resolution was adopted which recommended that "all appropriate steps be taken to ensure conditions of stability throughout Korea" and that United Nations-supervised elections be held "for the establishment of a unified, independent and democratic government in the sovereign State of Korea." A United Nations Commission for the Unification and Rehabilitation of Korea (UNCURK) was

appointed to assist in this process.[15] The prewar situation had
changed. When this resolution was passed, United Nations
forces had repelled the invasion and were sweeping north of
the thirty-eighth parallel. Now, following the anticipated military victory, United States policy in Korea, which had been
endorsed by the General Assembly, was on the verge of implementation. Only the intervention by Chinese Communist
troops frustrated the plan. Military stalemate and an eventual
truce restored the status quo ante bellum. Again, the United
States had to choose between accepting an unpleasant reality
or using the United Nations to express its hostility and frustration. Again, the latter course was adopted. For twenty
years, UNCURK reports provided the basis for condemnatory
resolutions against North Korea. In every debate, the two
sides exchanged polemics, although now there was little likelihood that they would resort to war. The Russians unsuccessfully demanded withdrawal of United States forces and the
dissolution of UNCURK. Although its majorities diminished,
the United States succeeded in continuing to prevent participation by North Korea in the debate and forced through
resolutions reaffirming the policy of holding elections to unify
the country.[16] In addition, South Korea was admitted to
United Nations-related organizations and was granted observer
status at the United Nations. Finally, in 1971, the United
States decided against reintroducing the unification of Korea
as an agenda item. The change in posture was related to the
unexpected advancement of negotiations between the two
Koreas in the next year, and perhaps to the policy of détente
which the Nixon administration was pursuing toward Peking
and Moscow. As was true for Germany, reality eventually
intervened. In Korea, however, it was necessary to overcome a
bitter war and a quarter century of United Nations debates
and resolutions.

By 1972, a curious reversal of roles had occurred at the United Nations. Since 1947, the Soviet Union had resisted discussion of the Korean item, claiming that it was a means of pursuing the Cold War by the United States. With adoption of its approach of having the Koreans discuss unification directly, the Russians tried now to have the Assembly consider its proposal for the dissolution of UNCURK and withdrawal of United States troops.[17] Although the troop issue could not be affected by any Assembly resolution (which would probably not be adopted, anyway), the Soviets wanted the satisfaction of having their position on unification of Korea confirmed at the United Nations. They were denied the opportunity as the United States argued successfully that any debate could jeopardize the ongoing negotiations. In this, the American position was correct. But this had been equally true for the twenty-five years before that understanding was forced by events.

Vietnam

The facts surrounding the United States involvement in Southeast Asia are by now familiar. With the Korean War and the efforts to isolate Communist China, the policy of containment had achieved global dimensions. Drawing lines on a map around the world was now extended to Southeast Asia, where the line would be drawn at the seventeenth parallel. The United States was determined that the Geneva Accords of 1954 would not be implemented if, as believed, this guaranteed the expansion of Communism to South Vietnam. The enormous expenditure in blood and treasure to achieve this end is well known. As one facet of this struggle, the United Nations was used.

At this time, we are concerned only with the question of juridical status, which has remained at the center of the

entire controversy. Persistent attempts to advance the cause of
the American-supported regime in South Vietnam were made
by proposing its admission into the United Nations.[18] Success, of course, would confirm the status of South Vietnam as
a sovereign, independent nation, which was and continues to
be a principal objective of American intervention in the area.
It would be a major step toward undermining the Geneva
Accords, which acknowledge the existence of only one Vietnam, as a basis for an eventual settlement. Any claim that a
proper solution would have to be based on the implementation of that agreement, including the unification of all Vietnam through elections, would be made to appear ludicrous in
the face of South Vietnam's presence as a voting member of
the United Nations.[19] In addition, any effort by the North to
achieve the same end by military action would clearly identify
the Communists as the aggressors and ease the burden of a
response on the part of the United States. It was, of course,
inevitable that the Russians would veto the admission of South
Vietnam, which they did four times.

The contrast between this case and those of Germany and
Korea reveals clearly the pure political motivation of both
sides. In Germany and Korea, where America's allies were in
possession of popular majorities, the United States pressed for
unification and free elections. There was then no thought of
accepting the simultaneous admissions of East Germany and
North Korea. The Soviets, on the other hand, insisted on the
juridical status of their clients, thereby championing recognition of separate and independent states in Germany and
Korea. But in Vietnam, positions were reversed. The United
States war effort, supplemented by its United Nations offensive,
was designed to achieve the permanent division of Vietnam.
This time it was the Russians who were advocates of popular
elections and unification. Acknowledgment of the existence of

an independent South Vietnamese government would have confirmed American victory in the war. Unquestionably, the United States would not have objected to the simultaneous admission of North Vietnam. But the Communist side was not about to surrender at the United Nations what it was not likely to lose at the ballot box and had not lost on the battlefield. The Russians understandably insisted that the question of admission of Vietnam into the United Nations must await the elections and unification as called for in the 1954 Geneva Agreements.

Status considerations also explain what might otherwise appear to be the curious reluctance of the Communists to use the Vietnam issue to attack the United States in the United Nations. Having won their objectives at Geneva, the Soviet bloc did not want to shift the struggle into the United Nations, where the question could be defined by the Western majority as a contest between two sovereign states. They even opposed a move in 1963 by fourteen Afro-Asian states to investigate suppression of the rights of Buddhists in South Vietnam by the government of Ngo Dinh Diem.[20] Although the issue was obviously embarrassing to the United States, its consideration could strengthen the juridical status of the South Vietnamese government. The Russians suggested instead that the International Control Commission established by the Geneva Conference handle any investigation.

China

The most severe blow to America's early postwar global policy was undoubtedly the fall of China. Following the Chinese Communist victory over the Nationalists in 1949, the United States persisted in its support for the latter even after the evacuation of most of Chiang Kai-shek's troops to Taiwan.

Consistent with this policy, the United States prevented delegates representing the new Peking government from replacing those loyal to Taiwan at the United Nations. It was in protest against this policy that the Soviet Union was boycotting the Security Council when North Korea attacked South Korea on June 25, 1950. While reacting militarily in Korea, the United States simultaneously placed the Seventh Fleet between the mainland and Taiwan, although China was not initially involved. Later, when United Nations troops reached China's border at the Yalu River, massive intervention by Chinese "volunteers" forced a retreat to the thirty-eighth parallel. In the General Assembly, the United States pushed through a resolution which condemned the Chinese Communists as aggressors against the United Nations and recommended sanctions against China and North Korea.[21]

With China condemned as an aggressor, the United States now led a twenty-year campaign to prevent the Communists from taking the China seat in the United Nations. Year after year the United States argued that the People's Republic was not a "peace-loving state" and should not be permitted to "shoot its way into the United Nations." This special outlaw status was justified on the ground that the Chinese Communist regime was uniquely evil in that it was the only state to have actually aggressed against the United Nations itself. The Soviets and their Communist supporters countered that the "Chiang Kai-shek clique" represented only itself, and that China, a founder of the United Nations, was being illegally denied its permanent Security Council seat as well as its place in the other organs of the United Nations. Until the 1960s, American influence was so great that the issue never became an Assembly agenda item, although the preliminary debate was as bitter as it would have been in plenary session. In the sixties changing membership forced a modification in tactics by the United States, and the pro-American position was maintained by the parliamentary device of having the Assembly treat the seating of Communist China as an "important question," requiring a two-thirds majority, rather than a procedural item concerned only with the credentials of delegates. Substantive arguments, however, remained essentially the same. Finally, in 1972, the United States lost the battle, when the enormously enlarged General Assembly refused to endorse an American ploy in favor of a two-delegation–one-China solution, which was known to be unacceptable to the People's Republic of China.[22]

Maintaining the fiction that Chiang Kai-shek retained control over China despite the overthrow of his regime by the Communists and that the hundreds of millions of Chinese who did not make the journey to Taiwan were nonetheless ruled by the Generalissimo was, at best, an extraordinary test for American policy-makers. Its credibility rested entirely on the questionable assumption that Chiang had momentarily repaired to Taiwan in preparation for his eventual assault and recapture of the mainland. Exclusion of the Communists from the United Nations represented a minimum condition for asserting the continued legitimacy of the Nationalist government. Although the outcome of the civil war in China could not be reversed, the continued presence of Chiang's delegates as permanent members of the Security Council was a most important symbolic confirmation of American policy. This, coupled with the refusal of a majority of the world's governments to accept the credentials of the Communists, helped to bolster the opinion that there was more to this policy than stubborn attachment to a defeated and discredited ally. From a more practical standpoint, the failure to seat the Communists may have made the isolation of Communist China, an objective on which the United States was expending enormous amounts of diplomatic currency, more palatable to those friends and allies whose support was being sought. In addition, the policy in the United Nations bolstered the morale of Chiang Kai-shek's government.

We might note the reversal of attitudes on the principle of universal membership. Although the United States insisted that the Chinese people were represented by the Nationalists, it was apparent that the Soviets, who had previously been charged with obstructing the admission of new members, were now the champions of universality. In truth, neither side was concerned about principle. Downgrading the status of the People's Republic of China was a predominant American foreign-policy interest, whereas the Soviets were anxious to enhance the prestige of the largest member of the socialist bloc. The importance of the United Nations as *the* supranational arbiter of governmental legitimacy escalated the stakes and deepened bitterness between the blocs. Consistency in respect to United Nations ideals was a minor victim of this mammoth political struggle.

Dependent Peoples

The close identification of the United Nations with anticolonialism is well known. To an increasingly large number of observers, the organization's record in this area is its most noteworthy success in a history otherwise littered with failure and disappointment.[23] What is not generally appreciated is the true nature of the accomplishment. Denunciations of racism and advocacy of the principle of self-determination by the United Nations do not, as many suppose, demonstrate the triumph of moral principles over power politics or the ability of international organization through its endorsement of these principles to modify the behavior of states. Instead they are the result of the most important and in many respects most successful application of the strategy of conferring or with-holding status. The development of the anticolonial position at the United Nations rests on the assertion that colonial territories enjoy a unique place in international law and politics. This special status creates, on the one hand, certain rights for the inhabitants of these areas and, on the other, a set of obligations for the colonial powers. It also proclaims a direct responsibility for the United Nations to ensure that these rights and obligations are observed. Victory for the anti-colonialists represents the most far-reaching informal amend-ment of the Charter in the history of the United Nations. The process by which this was accomplished clearly shows the relationship between the politics of status and majority rule.

The battle over responsibility for the welfare of colonial peoples was joined during the framing of the Charter in San Francisco in 1945. Smaller nations generally shared the view that colonialism was a system of human exploitation that the United Nations should work to eradicate.[24]

Understandably the colonial powers rejected this approach. "The Colonial empires," Britain's Lord Cranborne said, "have been welded into one vast machine in defense of liberty. Could we really contemplate the destruction of this machine and its separation into component parts?"[25] Great importance was attached instead to the cultural, geographical, and developmental diversity within the empires, and the unique circumstances that would have to influence each future decision regarding each colonial territory.[26] Independence, the British delegate pointed out, "should not be con-fused with liberty." Dependent peoples might eventually travel many roads to many different destinations.[27] Under no cir-cumstances, however, could the United Nations influence these decisions. Tampering with the status of colonial territories was explicitly prohibited, according to the colonial powers, by the principle of noninterference in the domestic affairs of member states.[28]

Since British concurrence was an absolute precondition to the success of the conference, it is not surprising that the colonial powers prevailed. Little more than lip service was paid to the rights and welfare of colonial peoples. In Chapter XI of the Charter the administering authorities accepted a "sacred trust . . . to promote . . . the well being of the inhabitants."[29] The manner in which this "sacred trust" would be enforced was deliberately omitted. The Charter contains no provision for international supervision of dependent areas aside from a few trust territories. The Charter in no way coerced the colonial powers into relinquishing any measure of control over their possessions to the organization.[30] No reference was made to the morality or immorality of colonialism. There is no mention of independence, even as a desired future goal. There is a vague allusion to the encouragement of "self-government," but the Charter explicitly recognizes the existence of "particular circumstances" and "varying stages of advancement" to which progress toward even this standard is subject.

The cornerstone of the Charter's provisions on dependent peoples is voluntarism. However commendable it was to include in the Charter a pious commitment to humanitarian ideals, the authority to breathe life into that commitment rested entirely with the colonial powers. Even the trusteeship system did not depart completely from this principle.[31] In short, the language of the Charter was carefully calculated to assure a minimum of interference in the administration of colonial areas.

But the victory was short-lived. The member states that

had lost in San Francisco remained committed to the destruction of colonialism. Since formal amendment required ratification by the five permanent members of the Security Council, the anticolonialists concentrated on imposing their interpretation of Chapter XI by other means. This process began at the very first session of the General Assembly. A weakness in the armor of the colonialists was Article 73e of Chapter XI, which required the regular transmission of information to the Secretary-General on social, economic, and educational conditions in colonial territories. This was apparently innocuous, since no guidance was provided to the Secretary-General beyond receipt of the information transmitted.* Furthermore, political information was deliberately excluded, and there was no implication of a supervisory role for the General Assembly.† Finally, the transmission of information was "subject to such limitation as security and constitutional considerations may require." In the absence of any guidance in the Charter itself, it had to be presumed that only the colonial powers were competent to determine the existence of such limitations.

Despite the language of the Charter, anticolonialists insisted that Article 73e had established legal obligations. For example, the Cuban delegate said that the article was "no doubt designed to indicate that the fate of non-self-governing peoples was of international importance" and that "the General Assembly has a role to fulfill. . . ."[32] Beginning with that premise, various suggestions were made as to how this might

* The exact language is: "to transmit regularly to the Secretary General *for information purposes* . . . statistical and other information of a technical nature . . ." (italics ours) .

† Although a number of members voluntarily transmitted information of a political nature, this was always with the understanding that its transmission in no way implied the acceptance of supervisory authority by the General Assembly. See *GAOR*, Fourth Committee, Meeting 984, December 3, 1959.

be accomplished.[33] After much wrangling, the General Assembly approved the creation of an ad hoc committee "to examine the Secretary General's summary and analysis of the information transmitted under Article 73e of the Charter. . . ."[34]

The creation of the committee did not appear, in itself, to be an important victory. It was established as a temporary body comprised of an equal number of administering and nonadministering members. Given its composition, the impact of the committee on the interests of the colonial powers was certain to be negligible. Its real significance was that it established a reporting relationship between the colonialists and the General Assembly.* The committee's modest terms of reference and its composition merely reflected the unhappy compromise that politics exacts from those who initiate action in the General Assembly but are unable to command majority support for everything they advocate.

Although it would be many years before a majority of the membership would endorse a definitive statement of the anticolonial thesis, every opportunity was seized to restate its principal components. Anticolonial members persistently strove to institutionalize the supervisory functions of the ad hoc committee through the creation of permanent machinery[35] and to extend the committee's jurisdiction to include the examination of political information.[36] When France, the United Kingdom, and the United States stopped sending information on a number of their dependencies,[37] without consulting the General Assembly beforehand, a lively, often

* India, the leader of the Third World at this time, later expressed this relationship in these terms: "There could be no question that the sovereignty of these territories vested in the inhabitants. For the time being that sovereignty may be latent, but it was the purpose of the United Nations . . . to activate that sovereignty and to make it a living thing." *GAOR*, Plenary, Meeting 985, December 4, 1959.

acrimonious debate developed over the legal right of the colonial powers to decide unilaterally when their obligations under the Charter had been fulfilled.[38] Following this challenge, anticolonial members called for an examination of the "factors indicative of the attainment of self-government." The purpose of the study was to crystallize opinion around the view that only through the granting of complete political independence could the duties of administering members under Chapter XI be adequately discharged.[39] The admission of Spain and Portugal to the United Nations in 1955 occasioned yet another study, this time dealing with the obligations of "new members" under Chapter XI.[40] Here, as always, the aim was to assert the competence of the General Assembly to establish the principles governing the coverage and enforceability of Chapter XI in respect to individual territories.[41]

Colonial powers understandably protested against this incremental amendment of the Charter by majority vote. They also argued that irresponsible and unenforceable resolutions foreclosed any hope of cooperation in the attainment of the goals envisioned.[42] Neither argument was persuasive. For the anticolonialists, attachment to legality or to compromise amounted to little more than a willingness to accept defeat.[43] Majority rule promised immediate returns if the votes could be made to add up. Moreover, ultimate demands for independence had to be preceded by victory in the struggle concerning the status of dependent peoples.

The admission of fifteen strongly anticolonial members to the United Nations at the fifteenth session in 1960 provided all the votes that were needed. Passage of the Declaration on Non-Self-Governing Territories at the same session crowned with victory anticolonial efforts to redefine the meaning of

Chapter XI, which had begun at the first session with the creation of the Ad Hoc Committee on Information. The declaration read in part:

> Immediate steps shall be taken in Trust and non-self-governing-territories or all other territories which have not attained independence, to transfer all powers to the peoples of those territories, without any conditions or reservations in accordance with their freely expressed will and desire . . . in order to enable them to enjoy complete independence and freedom.[44]

All that remained was to establish machinery to implement these intentions, which was promptly accomplished the following year by the creation of a special, permanent committee of seventeen members.[45]

The quarrel over the interpretation of Chapter XI had been won by the anticolonialists. The losers now found it expedient to become a part of the "consensus."[46] Actually, however, fundamental positions were not changed.*

---

* The colonial powers made this clear immediately. Upon passage of the Declaration, the American delegate said: "Like many other members of the United Nations, we regard the provisions of Chapter XI and XII of the Charter . . . as controlling so far as territories for which we are responsible are concerned." *GAOR*, Plenary, Meeting 947, December 14, 1960.

In a letter to the president of the General Assembly during the same period, the Permanent Representative of the United Kingdom and Ireland wrote: "We have made it clear throughout that we cannot accept any form of intervention in the administration of the territories for which we are responsible; and if there were any attempt to intervene in their administration, we should be bound to withdraw our cooperation. It is on this understanding that Her Majesty's Government is prepared to participate in the Committee [on Non-Self-Governing Territories]." UN Document A/5084, January 23, 1962.

Conclusions

Because the politics of status invariably is argued in legalistic and constitutional terms, it may be somewhat difficult to ascertain its importance as a conflict strategy. The language of the Charter is debated endlessly, and states adopt apparently idealistic positions based upon the spirit of the Charter and the principle of universality. In fact, the issue is fought out on the basis of conflicting national interests. That a qualification for membership in the United Nations is not really a legal issue is easily demonstrated by the obvious conjunction of interests with positions on particular applicants. No legal consideration or theoretical attachment to universality could convince the United States to sponsor admission of Outer Mongolia or the Soviet Union to lobby for Japan. There is no recorded instance in which states have actively sought to "strengthen" the United Nations by adding prestige to non-members that are also part of an "enemy" alliance.

Status politics is, then, always related to other foreign-policy goals. When the West won the credentials fight that seated a Congo delegation appointed by President Kasa-Vubu, rather than those loyal to Premier Lumumba, an important victory was won in the struggle to preserve the Congo from Soviet penetration.[47] All of the efforts to seat or in other ways enhance the prestige at the United Nations of South Korea, South Vietnam, West Germany, and the People's Republic of China were part of a Cold War that was being fought on many fronts with many weapons. Promoting the status of one side is never a substitute for fighting in other ways. The millions of lives lost in Korea and Vietnam are ample testimony to this. Status politics is a facet of struggle for which the United Nations is admirably suited.

By detailing the processes by which the anticolonialists

eventually won their argument concerning the relationship of the United Nations to non-self-governing territories, the association with ultimate goals is seen clearly. Winning the "constitutional" quarrel was a necessary precondition for using the United Nations to apply maximum pressures against colonial states. Victory had nothing to do with the language of the Charter. The attainment of an anticolonial majority, and that alone, settled the issue. When the anticolonialists lacked the votes, the guiding principles were noninterference in the domestic affairs of member states and the voluntarism written into the Charter. After the votes changed, colonialism became a violation of the Charter and a threat to international peace. Once administration of a dependent area could be defined as a crime, and the independence of all peoples became an inalienable right, the anticolonialists were freed to pursue other strategies in the United Nations.

4 *The Politics of Legitimization*

The politics of legitimization represents the most ambitious use of United Nations processes to advance national interest. There are four prerequisites: (1) the beneficiary state must be actively engaged in a conflict that it is determined to win; (2) the stakes must be high enough to warrant something approaching total mobilization of support; (3) the dispute itself should offer at least a reasonable opportunity that it can be successfully exploited at the United Nations; and (4) the initiating state or states must have the requisite influence in the international organization.

These demands severely limit the number of disputes that qualify as legitimization of policy. Colonial issues have been excluded because the enlistment of the United Nations on the side of the anticolonialists has not yet been accompanied by more than sporadic guerrilla activity. As a typical example, the General Assembly on November 14, 1972,[1] passed a resolution encouraging support for dissidents within the Portuguese African colonies. In this manner the ground has been laid for more important uses of legitimization politics should the African states employ more direct military means to end colonialism in southern Africa. A near ideal example of what may be termed preparatory legitimization tactic involved Egypt in 1971. Egyptian President Anwar el-Sadat had proclaimed that 1971 was the "year of decision," during which the definitive blow against Israel would be struck.* Simultaneously, he asserted that Egypt would launch a diplomatic offensive at the United Nations. The Egyptian president thereby publicized the close connection between a planned military action and the United Nations. But although the appropriate resolutions were won in the General Assembly,[2] the promised military offensive did not occur. When and if circumstances become more favorable for Egypt, we can anticipate a more complete use of the politics of legitimization.

States embarking on ambitious and possibly costly adventures in foreign policy will invariably insist that they have right on their side. This is perceived as necessary in order to obtain and sustain domestic and sometimes foreign support. Legitimization of policy at the United Nations may contribute importantly to these ends. Manipulation of Charter principles is a convenient and useful assist in portraying actions as morally justified. By controlling proceedings at the United Nations, the claim can be made that one's high standards of conduct are endorsed by "world opinion." The image of moral rectitude enhances internal cohesion and may also facilitate the task of foreign governments desirous of providing material or other support for the policy of the initiating state. When the politics of legitimization is used, there is no intention to permit the United Nations to substitute alternative solutions or modify ongoing operations. The objective is to add another dimension of support for actions planned or in progress.

Not surprisingly, only the Western powers, and especially the United States, have been capable of utilizing the United Nations successfully for legitimization purposes. As the world's

* See Epilogue.

most powerful state, actively involved in global confrontations and exercising unparalleled influence in the United Nations, the United States has had unique opportunities. Despite these advantages, certain American initiatives have been, by their nature or importance, unfit for legitimization by the United Nations. Clandestine operations in Guatemala in 1954 and the Bay of Pigs affair in Cuba in 1961 were poor issues, as was the 1965 intervention in the Dominican Republic. Circumstances required that the United States minimize United Nations consideration of these conflicts by stressing the competence of the Organization of American States. In the United Nations, despite some embarrassment, the United States successfully maintained this defensive posture. On other issues, however, the United States, and on one occasion its major allies, were in a better position to make full use of the United Nations in support of major foreign-policy operations. Indeed, these have been the most important and dangerous conflicts in the post-World War II era—the 1948 Berlin crisis, the Suez crisis of 1956, Korea, Vietnam, and the Cuban missile crisis.

Berlin, 1948

As World War II drew to its weary conclusion, the seeds for a new and deadlier confrontation were already implanted. Hardly out of their long and costly struggle with fascism, the United States and the Soviet Union faced each other as enemies. Total Cold War was signaled by failure to implement the wartime agreements on Germany. Nearly from one day to the next, defeated Germany was transformed from a hated, bloody destroyer of countless millions into an attractive prize to be cajoled or forced into adding her territory, resources, and population to the power and strategic calculations of West and East. Inevitably occupation zones became spheres of influence with each side establishing institutional frameworks designed to maximize benefits and control.[3] Had the divisions been made neatly, the situation would have been dangerous enough. The new status quo was made even more precarious, however, by the presence of the West in Berlin, deep inside the Russian zone. With Berlin as a Western outpost threatening Soviet designs in East Germany, a constant source of tension had been created. Any attempt on the part of the Soviets to put their house in order would have to include dislodging the West from its enclave. Given Russia's abiding concern in consolidating its holdings in the East, any resolve on the part of the West to frustrate or impede this process could easily bring about a major war. Nerves and will were dramatically tested in the Berlin crisis of 1948.

Agreements on common Allied policies regarding Germany, which had been reached at Potsdam in July, 1945, provided, among other things, for the treatment of Germany as a single economic unit.[4] By 1948 implementation of this and other agreements had completely broken down. Meetings of the foreign ministers and efforts in Berlin by members of the Allied Control Council also failed to produce a solution to the steadily deteriorating situation, prompting Secretary of State George C. Marshall to suggest that the Western allies arrive at a common plan for the future development of West Germany.[5] This was done. The Western zones were to be fused to form the basis for a federal republic. West Germany would be brought into the European Recovery Program, Allied economic policy would be immediately coordinated, and West Germany would be represented on a newly created international commission on the Ruhr Valley industries. On June 18 currency reforms applying to the Western zones were announced. From the Soviet perspective this action could only be viewed as an attempt to cement Western gains in West Germany and to prevent the spread of Soviet influence to that area. To accomplish a similar result, the Soviet Union, in addition to Sovietizing East Germany, would have to expel the West from Berlin. Charging that the West had violated the Potsdam Agreement through the announced currency reform, Marshal Vassily Sokolovsky on June 19 announced that the Soviet Union would take measures in Berlin to prevent the "disruption of economic life" in East Germany.[6] The blockade was on.

The Western allies now had to decide whether or not to risk war to maintain their position in Berlin. Militarily, the Soviets held overwhelming superiority in conventional forces, whereas the United States still monopolized atomic weapons. War, then, could mean that Europe would be overrun by Soviet forces and possibly devastated by atomic bombs. Despite the risk, President Truman decided on June 28 that the West would stay in Berlin.[7] Implementation of this decision always included a military option, with General Lucius Clay as a leading advocate of having a military convoy challenge the Russian readiness to fight.[8] Without abandoning this possibility, a British-American airlift began to supply the city. Negotiations continued on the highest governmental levels and in Berlin. Finally, in September it became clear that an impasse had been reached. The Russians published their version of the talks and the West responded by presenting their side and announcing that they were bringing the issue to the Security Council.[9]

The decision by the United States to go to the United Nations was consistent with the hard line adopted by the Truman administration. Britain and France followed American leadership reluctantly. Their misgivings were based on a proper understanding of dangers inherent in this move.* Diplomatic escalation to the United Nations foreclosed any further attempt at negotiation. As the approach of winter increased the risks of a military showdown because of inclement flying weather and the uncertain capacity of the airlift to fuel as well as feed ·the two and a half million West Berliners, there was no doubt about why the step was taken. The policy decision to maintain the West's status in Berlin was to be legitimized at the United Nations in order to deepen support for whatever means were currently in use or contemplated—including war—to implement that decision.†

We have observed in Chapter 1 the basically hostile intent when one party to a dispute compels its opponent to defend itself in the United Nations forum. This was especially true in the Berlin controversy because the Soviet position was so well known. The only *places* that the Soviet Union regarded as acceptable for discussions about Germany were the institu-

---

* Walter Millis, ed., *The Forrestal Diaries* (New York: Viking Press, 1951), pp. 489–490. Forrestal states: "Marshall said that [Ernest] Bevin had sent him a personal cable over the weekend. . . . Bevin's position is that he wishes, if possible, to avoid a break in the negotiations which will send the issue to the U.N. . . . Marshall said that Bevin kept referring to the fact that 'we're in the front line.'" See also Lucius Clay, *Decision in Germany* (New York: Doubleday, 1950), p. 367.

† W. Phillips Davison states: "A press report from Paris on September 23 cited "officials in close touch with the Moscow negotiations as saying that the latest diplomatic notes to the Kremlin were chiefly for the record, so that the Western public might know that every effort had been made to bridge the gap between the Soviet Union and the democracies; if, as expected, the Berlin issue was carried to the United Nations, it would be for the same purpose." Davison, *The Berlin Blockade* (Princeton: Princeton University Press, 1958), pp. 241–242. The relationship between the use of military force and its legitimization at the United Nations was clearly understood by General Clay. In discussing the implementation of his proposal to force an armed convoy through to Berlin, he writes: "When our government turned down my suggestion, I understood its desire to avoid this risk of armed conflict until the issue had been placed before the United Nations." Clay, *Decision in Germany*, p. 374.

tions established for that purpose—the Council of Foreign Ministers and the Allied Control Council. The Russians therefore argued bitterly that adoption of the agenda item would be illegal and, when they were outvoted, refused to participate in the debates.[10] Virtual monopolization of the proceedings did not deter the West, which convened Security Council meetings five times in October.[11] Nonparticipation by the Soviet Union would have been an insuperable obstacle to a peaceful resolution of the problem, *if that had been the purpose behind bringing the issue.* Since it was not, Soviet silence simply eased the task of the Western allies. Unchallenged, they proceeded to drape their policy in the ideals of the Charter while portraying the blockade as Soviet aggression.[12] Making this record was the sole purpose. In this the West was aided by a Soviet veto of a resolution, sponsored by the nonpermanent members of the Security Council, which would have called for an end to the Soviet blockade in exchange for a renewal of negotiations among the Big Four on the currency problem in Berlin.[13] The veto was inevitable since Soviet policy denied the jurisdiction of the Security Council, and because the substance of the resolution asked the Russians to capitulate on Berlin in exchange for nothing except further negotiations. Nevertheless, with this veto, the West reinforced its aim of establishing the moral and legal supremacy of its Berlin policy. The editors of the *New York Times* could now write:

> The veto cannot nullify the moral validity of the judgment . . . there can be no further doubt as to who is responsible for the Berlin crisis. This, in turn, not only puts on Russia the onus for any further aggravation of the crisis, but also forces the hands of the Western Powers to take all measures necessary and permissible under the Charter to cope with the situation.[14]

Presumably, since for tactical reasons the Berlin issue had been brought to the Security Council under the enforcement provisions of Chapter VII of the Charter, the editors agreed that any action, including war, was now justified.* This was quite an accomplishment. Only three years after the end of World War II, the people of the United States and Western Europe were being prepared for another war, a war that could decimate the continent and add unknown millions of victims to the record of the nuclear age. It was even more remarkable to achieve this state of psychological preparedness if one considers that the dispute was over defeated Germany, that legal rights were at best blurred, and that no physical attack had been mounted against any of the Western countries or even their troops in Berlin.

The war did not take place. The airlift was unexpectedly effective, thereby obviating military options since the Soviet Union, for its part, avoided taking any additional measures against the West. In an interview on January 27, 1949, Joseph Stalin signaled the Soviet retreat to J. Kingsbury Smith, European manager of International News Service. Responding to a question on Berlin, the Soviet dictator made no reference to the currency issue, which had been the immediate theoretical cause for the blockade. Informal discussions between the American and Russian delegates to the United Nations established that the omission had been deliberate and led to the wider negotiations elsewhere which terminated the blockade on May 12, 1949.[15]

Observers have concentrated on those aspects of the Ber-

* If the peaceful settlement provisions of Chapter VI had been used, the three sponsoring members and the Soviet Union would have been unable to vote on the adoption of the agenda. With the Ukrainian S.S.R.'s vote supporting Russia, the West would not have had the necessary seven votes to continue the debate.

lin crisis that coincided with their search for positive United Nations contributions to peace-keeping. They have stressed the efforts of the nonpermanent members to find technical solutions, and they have lauded the meetings between United Nations delegates Philip Jessup and Jacob Malik as evidence of the importance of "corridor diplomacy."[16] Even if one grants the sincerity of the initiative by nonpermanent members, there was never any hope of success, since acceptance of United Nations jurisdiction was impossible for the Russians, and the Western Big Three were uninterested in any solutions except their own.[17] As for the argument concerning corridor diplomacy, the fact that diplomats at the United Nations were involved is meaningless. Once Joseph Stalin had decided that the Berlin adventure was a failure, he would have had no problem of communication through any embassy or a direct approach to the White House. Completely ignored is the overriding fact that by going to the United Nations the West *abandoned* diplomacy as a solution. The United Nations was used to buttress the means employed in Berlin, and when these were successful the Russians decided to negotiate their defeat.

From our perspective, the Big Three used the United Nations successfully to legitimize their foreign policy in Berlin. They demonstrated their determination and unity and mobilized popular support. The Russians eventually succumbed, and, in this sense, it can be said that the United Nations contributed to a peaceful resolution of the problem. But this approach to peace can be compared with cocking a gun (or atomic bomb) at an adversary. If the enemy surrenders, war is averted. If not, the gun is ready to go off. The success of the West in the United Nations was precisely that it used the organization well in order to cock the gun.

Suez, 1956

On July 26, 1956, President Gamal Abdel Nasser nationalized the Suez Canal Company. The action was taken as part of a sequence of hostile confrontations between Egypt and the principal Western powers. These had included: Egyptian purchase of Czech arms in 1954; French support for Egypt's arch-enemy, Israel; recognition of Communist China by Egypt in May, 1956; and withdrawal on July 19, 1956 of an Anglo-American offer of a loan to build the Aswan Dam.[18] Nasser's action, then, was an angry assertion of Egyptian nationalism against those he regarded as seeking to impose a humiliating neocolonialism on Egypt. France and Britain were the two countries most seriously affected. Although the canal was more important economically and politically to the British, France had the graver political grievances because of the support provided for Algerian rebels by Egypt. The two countries assumed the leadership in attempting to retaliate against Egypt. Although the United States was intimately involved in these efforts, there were obvious gaps in communications among the allies and differences on means. The Soviet Union, of course, strongly favored Egypt. The Western powers found an array of legal arguments with which to condemn Nasser's action. Egypt responded by insisting on its sovereign rights, and probably had the better legal case.

On August 12, a conference of the twenty-two principal users of the canal was convened in London. Egypt refused to attend, asserting that it would disregard any conclusions reached at the conference. Eighteen of the conferees adopted a proposal hammered out by Britain, France, and the United States. The key provision established a Suez Canal Board to be composed of Egypt and user states. The Canal Board would operate, maintain, and develop the canal. The four other conferees, led by Egypt's friends, India and the Soviet Union, opposed this solution and suggested a consultative group which would not contravene Egyptian sovereignty. After the conference closed, Prime Minister Robert Menzies of Australia went to Cairo to try to sell the Western plan to Nasser. Negotiations collapsed in early September. A second London conference on September 21 established the Suez Canal Users' Association, which, theoretically, would administer the canal, but there was no clear agreement between the United States and Britain and France on how this was to be accomplished against the determined opposition of President Nasser. Britain and France were more inclined to use force, if necessary, whereas the United States seemed unwilling to confront that option. The impasse became complete on September 17 when President Nasser denounced the Users' Association. On September 23, France and Britain demanded a meeting of the Security Council,[19] which met three days later—exactly two months after the crisis had been precipitated by the nationalization decree.

In their excellent article on this case, Wolfgang Friedmann and Lawrence A. Collins are puzzled by the move. They write:

> What Britain and France hoped to gain by recourse to the Security Council is not clear. They would press for nothing less than full acceptance of the Eighteen Power proposal for the establishment of a Suez Canal Board. This was unacceptable to Egypt, and the Soviet Union had made it clear at the London Conference that it supported Egypt in rejecting proposals for international operation of the Canal.[20]

Actually, there is no mystery. The chronology is revealing. For two months the Western powers agonized over finding a formula that would at once acknowledge Egyptian sovereignty while permitting an international administration of the canal.

They failed. It was *after* they had failed, and *because* they had failed to arrive at a peaceful solution, that they went to the United Nations. Serious efforts to arrive at an accommodation took place *outside* the United Nations. Now that Britain and France were close to the use of force, they used the Security Council to prepare the way for war. The Security Council would *legitimize* the use of force because of the apparent failure of the United Nations to permit any other solution. To go to the United Nations with a proposal that had already been rejected by Egypt and would certainly be vetoed by the Soviet Union is difficult to understand only if it is assumed that Britain and France were interested in having the United Nations contribute to a settlement. In fact, they utilized the mythology of the United Nations as a peacekeeping organization to ease the road to war. In this they succeeded. After dominating the debate, the British-French resolution to establish a Suez Canal Board was vetoed by the Soviet Union on October 13.[21] The veto had been anticipated. Commenting on the consequences of Security Council paralysis, Lord Chancellor Viscount Kilmuir continued:

> Is it not plain that in such circumstances [where a treaty regulating the status of an international waterway is violated] States which are party to the agreement, in the fulfillment of their international obligations, have not only the right but a positive duty to take such steps as may be necessary to compel the delinquent to fulfill his international obligations?[22]

Two weeks later the steps were taken. Israel's attack on Egypt was followed by a Franco-British ultimatum demanding that Egypt and Israel withdraw from the canal area.[23] Obviously Egypt, already invaded, had no choice except to reject this summons to surrender. The Western allies proceeded to bomb and occupy key bases along the canal. They claimed, of course, that they were acting on behalf of the United Nations, which had been prevented from functioning because of the Soviet veto.

The parallels with the Berlin crises are obvious. Timing was similar. *After* the breakdown of negotiations, the Western powers utilized the United Nations to establish their moral legitimacy and to strengthen the acceptability of more violent steps. Going to the United Nations served notice to the other side that options were being reduced toward an ultimate test of wills. It was a step in support of popular mobilization for war. The enemy had to choose between retreat and a military confrontation. In Berlin, the gun was not used, and the West carried the day. Obviously in Suez France and Britain did not achieve their political objectives. But the fact that the adventure became a catastrophe because of Soviet and, especially, American opposition, should not obscure the successful use of the United Nations to legitimize policy. This time the gun that the United Nations helped to cock was fired.

The Cuban Missile Crisis

The implicit threat of a third world war which characterized the Berlin blockade was an even greater reality during the Cuban missile crisis. The opening words of Robert Kennedy's *Thirteen Days* describe the situation:

> On Tuesday morning, October 16, 1962, shortly after 9:00 o'clock, President Kennedy called and asked me to come to the White House. He said only that we were facing great trouble. Shortly afterward, in his office, he told me that a U-2 had just finished a photographic mission and that the Intelligence Community had become convinced that Russia was placing missiles and atomic weapons in Cuba.

That was the beginning of the Cuban missile crisis—a confrontation between the two giant atomic nations, the U.S. and the U.S.S.R., which brought the world to the abyss of nuclear destruction and the end of mankind. From that moment in President Kennedy's office until Sunday morning, October 28, that was my whole life—and for Americans and Russians, for the whole world, it was their life as well.[24]

Life or death for much of mankind, and certainly for most Americans and Russians, hung in the balance. Presence of Russian missiles in Cuba did not, in itself, constitute a crisis, any more than did American missiles in Turkey or intercontinental ballistic missiles in Russia. The crisis arose only with President Kennedy's determination that missiles on Cuban soil were unacceptable and that, therefore, they must be removed. Installation of the missiles and the American response occurred against the background of the abortive, humiliating Bay of Pigs venture, and the enormous reservoir of fear and distrust developed over a quarter century of Cold War. Moreover, Kennedy could not afford the domestic political consequences of appearing to be "soft on Communism."

Although the option of a military test was always present during the Berlin blockade, it was a much more imminent possibility during the missile crisis, and this time both sides had nuclear weapons. Indeed, the use of force dominated the deliberations of the Executive Committee of the National Security Council, which, within five days, completed the initial planning for a strike against Cuba. It was taken for granted that should an attack be launched, there was every likelihood of countermeasures by the Soviet Union (perhaps in Berlin) which would escalate into World War III.[25]

By October 20, it was decided to impose a blockade (euphemistically termed a "quarantine" to improve its legal image) to provide at least minimal flexibility before more irrevocable steps were taken. Allies in the Organization of American States and in Europe were alerted. On October 22, President Kennedy appeared on national television to inform the American people of the magnitude of the crisis:

> The urgent transformation of Cuba into an important strategic base, by the presence of these large, long-range and clearly offensive weapons of sudden mass destruction, constitutes an explicit threat to the peace and security of all the Americas. . . . This sudden, clandestine decision to station strategic weapons for the first time outside of Soviet soil, is a deliberate, provocative, and unjustified change in the *status quo* which cannot be accepted by this country. . . . Our unswerving objective, therefore, must be to prevent the use of these missiles against this or any other country, and to secure their withdrawal or elimination from the Western Hemisphere. We will not prematurely or unnecessarily risk the costs of world wide nuclear war . . . but neither will we shrink from that risk at any time it must be faced.[26]

Outwardly at least the arena of conflict now shifted to the United Nations. All three participants—the United States, the Soviet Union, and Cuba—demanded urgent meetings of the Security Council.[27] It would be pointless to pursue the legal arguments, except perhaps to observe that Cuba and the Soviet Union were technically on the side of international law. As a sovereign state, Cuba had the right to provide for her own defense without interference from any foreign power, and the Soviet Union, in time of peace, was free to trade with any country and use the high seas for that purpose.

In fact, as intended, the United States dominated the proceedings. Having decided upon its course of action, the United States was determined to justify the policy. The highlight was Ambassador Adlai E. Stevenson's dramatic televised confrontation of the Russian ambassador with the aerial photos of the missiles—the evidence, for all the world to see, of Russian duplicity. In the course of the debates, Stevenson effectively established the moral legitimacy of American policy by references to "the world of the Charter," the "vision of San Francisco," and the United States' record of unswerving support for the ideals of the Charter. Even now, America was seeking a United Nations solution. Said Stevenson:

> The time has come for the Council to decide whether to make a serious attempt to bring peace to the world—or to let the United Nations stand idly by while the vast plan of piece-meal aggression unfolds, conducted in the hope that no single issue will seem consequential enough to mobilize the support of the free peoples. For my government, this question is not in doubt. We remain committed to the principles of the Charter of the United Nations, and we intend to defend them.[28]

Actually the future of the United Nations was irrelevant. The drama unfolding in the Security Council was being watched by tens of millions of Americans, who were being prepared psychologically for any sacrifice. At the very moment that American leaders were contemplating the possibility of destroying most of the world, they used the United Nations to transform their decisions into exercises in morality, decency, and fair play. The verbal jousts at the United Nations were orchestrated as contributions to total mobilization for total war.

War or peace would be decided by a few men seated around conference tables thousands of miles apart. For these men, the United Nations had only limited significance.[29] Their decisions were unrelated to the principles of the Charter, appeals by neutrals in the Security Council, or the frantic efforts of acting Secretary-General U Thant. Thant, on October 24, asked for an end to the blockade in exchange for a Soviet cessation of arms shipments. Premier Nikita Khrushchev agreed, but President Kennedy reasserted the demand that the missiles already in Cuba be dismantled and removed.[30] With Soviet vessels steaming toward the quarantine line, Thant appealed to both sides to avoid any contact which would lead to violence. In Theodore Sorensen's words, "Kennedy simply stated the obvious, that there would be no incidents if Soviet ships stayed away."[31]

The Soviet ships did stay away. The missiles were dismantled and returned to the Soviet Union, and the Kennedy administration agreed that it would not use force to bring down Fidel Castro's regime. Armageddon was averted by the direct communications between Khrushchev and Kennedy.

The irrelevance of the United Nations in Great Power disputes was obvious during the missile crisis. Man's fate rested on the wisdom, restraint, and calculations of two men—Kennedy and Khrushchev. They weighed the advice and arguments of close advisers and reached decisions. They had no illusions about the United Nations. It could not influence the men of power, but it could be useful as part of overall strategic calculations. By dramatically accusing the Russians of deceit and by portraying their actions in Cuba as part of a scheme to destroy the free world, Adlai Stevenson played his assigned role. With magnificent oratory, he helped prepare the American people to confront its death, if this were demanded by their government, in defense of the moral and legal principles enshrined in the Charter of the United Nations. The debate in the United Nations was not simply a reflection of the Soviet-American conflict. It was a carefully calculated *weapon* designed to facilitate the use, if necessary, of any and all other weapons.

The Korean War

In all cases of legitimization, there is an attempt to align Charter principles with national policy. American use of the United Nations during the Korean conflict demonstrates the ultimate in legitimization politics. Here, not only was the correctness of a policy affirmed through appeals to the Charter, but the policy itself became identified as the fulfillment of United Nations objectives. The merger of American political and military goals with the concept of collective security successfully converted a national military operation into an international response to aggression according to the highest ideals of the Charter.

With the invasion of South Korea on June 25, 1950, the United States was confronted with unpleasant choices. To allow North Korea to absorb the South would undermine the containment policy and strengthen domestic attacks against a government that was already accused of having "lost" China. A second choice was to provide material and logistical support for South Korea. The danger in this was that such aid would be insufficient to repel the invaders, and could lead to a deeper commitment in order to avoid defeat. Finally, the United States could join the war immediately, with all the risks attendant on fighting a land war in Asia, weakening defenses in Europe, and possible escalation into World War III. In fact, President Truman did not hesitate.[32] He never considered the abandonment of South Korea. Before two days had passed, the United States had entered the war. Mobilization of support for this executive decision was now necessary, and the United Nations served this purpose admirably.

Within hours of news of the attack, the United States brought the issue to the Security Council. An American-sponsored resolution was passed which charged North Korea with breaching the peace and called for a cease-fire and withdrawal of North Korean troops from the South. By immediately assigning blame for the war to North Korean aggression, the preliminary step for eventual legitimization of American policy was taken. A Yugoslavian suggestion to invite the North Koreans (South Korea had been seated), which would, contrary to American plans, have widened the discussions to include arguments favorable to the Communists, was easily defeated.[33] The Council would remain occupied with one matter—North Korean aggression—leaving the way open for the United States to coordinate further initiatives with its evolving policies.*

The resolution of June 25 made no mention of force. Its expressed intent was to terminate hostilities. Nevertheless, the United States, on June 26, began military operations against North Korea.[34] It was now desirable to have the Security Council endorse this action. To this end, the United States, on June 27, returned to the Council and won passage for a resolution that recommended "that the Members of the United Nations furnish such assistance to the Republic of Korea as may be necessary to repel the armed attack and to restore international peace and security in the area." During the discussion, the United States informed the Council of its naval, air, and ground operations in Korea, and claimed that these acts were consistent with the resolution of June 25. It might

* From the beginning, employment of the United Nations was part of a pattern to integrate American and United Nations policy. Acheson writes: ". . . Hickerson suggested a meeting of the UN Security Council the next morning (Sunday) to call for a cease-fire and urgent requests to our civilian and military missions in Korea for continuing information. I approved, and authorized Ernest Gross . . . to ask Trygue Lie to call the Security Council. Overnight Hickerson, Rusk, and Jessup were to work with the Pentagon . . . to get up such orders as the President might wish to issue should he decide to take further action, military or otherwise." Dean Acheson, *Present at the Creation* (New York: W. W. Norton, 1969), p. 525.

be noted that, despite the utilization of the Security Council to justify American policy, the use of force by the United States *preceded* the resolution authorizing such action. Nor did such niceties disturb Western supporters of the United States. The United Kingdom, Australia, and New Zealand placed military units at American disposal before the coalition was formalized and made into a United Nations operation on July 7, when France and the United Kingdom submitted a resolution that:

> 1) Recommended that all Members providing military forces and other assistance pursuant to the aforesaid Security Council resolutions make such forces and other assistance available to a unified command under the United States;
>
> 2) Requested the United States to designate the commander of such forces;
>
> 3) Authorized the unified command at its discretion to use the United Nations flag in the course of operations against North Korean forces concurrently with the flags of the various nations participating.*

Legitimization of this phase of the Korean War was now complete. American policy had become a United Nations exercise in collective security.

These remarkable victories at the United Nations had been made possible only because of the absence of the Soviet Union. For some six months, the Soviet Union had been boycotting the Security Council as a protest against the refusal to seat the Chinese Communists. Undoubtedly the Russians

---

* UN Document S/1587, July 7, 1950. The actual source of the initiative was, of course, American. Truman states in his memoirs: "A few days earlier I had approved a proposal prepared jointly by the Departments of State and Defense to introduce in the U.N. a resolution creating a unified command in Korea, asking us to name a commander and authorizing the use of the blue U.N. flag in Korea. This resolution was passed . . . and on the following day I named General MacArthur to the post of U.N. Commander." Harry S Truman, *Memoirs, Vol. 2: Years of Trial and Hope* (New York: Doubleday, 1956) , pp. 394–395.

considered this manifestation of solidarity with their most important ally as being more important than using their presence and veto in the Security Council at the start of the Korean War. The crucial calculation, after all, concerned the reaction of the *United States*, and not that of the United Nations. Condemnatory resolutions alone, whether vetoed or not, would not influence American policy or the outcome of the war.

Nevertheless, and due at least in part to the large-scale American military commitment to South Korea and the successful integration of the United Nations in support of the United States, the Soviets announced their return to the Security Council on August 1, the date that the Soviet delegate would assume the presidency of the Council. Both before and after August 1, the Soviet Union denounced all the United Nations resolutions as illegal. It is not our purpose to engage in an essentially pointless analysis of the legalisms. It is useful, however, to describe these objections in order to appreciate that the use made of the Charter by the United States was, at the least, opportunistic. The Soviets and their allies argued that no substantive resolutions could be passed in the absence of two permanent members, themselves and the "legal" government of China.[35] Furthermore, they insisted that since the use of force by the United States in Korea had preceded the resolution of June 27, the United States was guilty of aggression and had subsequently attempted to justify the policy by passage of a resolution. The North Korean government added that the Council's refusal to invite its participation invalidated the resolutions.[36] As for the July 7 decision to establish a United Nations command under American authority, this was a direct violation of the Charter, which provides that military enforcement actions must be planned and executed by the military staff committee that had been created for that purpose. The Western states, of course, had counterarguments.[37] They insisted that Nationalist China was the legal government; that deliberate absence from the Security Council could not be used to paralyze the Council; that the American military response on June 26 was consistent with the implications of the June 25 resolutions; that there was no need to hear North Korea; and that the United Nations command was in the spirit of the Charter. It would seem that a strict interpretation of the Charter favored the Soviet position, but the *entire* legal argument is irrelevant. The United States *had* been successful in legitimizing its policy, and the Soviet Union returned to the Security Council in order to veto any future authorizations.

It is true that the Soviet presence meant that no further American-supported resolutions could be passed. Necessarily, too, the debate changed in that the West had to respond to Soviet attacks on the decisions that had been taken and to reject the host of charges and resolutions initiated by the Soviet Union. But these tactics were a tolerable annoyance because the important resolutions had already been passed, and the ongoing United Nations military operation could not be affected by the Soviets. As matters stood, it seemed that the Soviet Union had returned too late to lock the barn door.

But a change in the military situation in Korea caused the United States to seek a new identification of the United Nations with American policy. On September 15, 1950, General Douglas MacArthur's troops outflanked the North Koreans with an amphibious landing at Inchon. Very rapidly, the United Nations forces defeated the enemy below the thirty-eighth parallel. By October 1, an attack had been launched north of the former dividing line; however, this happy turn of events had not been anticipated in the Security Council resolutions. On June 25, the Council had demanded a cease-fire and withdrawal of North Koreans above the thirty-eighth parallel. The June 27 resolution authorized military aid to the South Koreans in order to "repel aggression and to restore international peace and security to the area." If the North Koreans now sued for peace, it would seem that the United Nations had completed its mission. But military victory opened the possibility of completely crushing North Korea and establishing a pro-American government in the entire peninsula. The Truman administration seized the opportunity. The close identification of the United States with United Nations objectives made it politically desirable to expand the United Nations mandate. If the Soviets had not returned to the Security Council, this would have been done quickly and painlessly. Instead, it now became necessary to utilize the General Assembly, where the United States would have to contend with the hostility of the Soviet bloc and the reservations of certain neutralist states.

In any event, there was no particular difficulty in having resort to the General Assembly. The issue of reunification of Korea had been in the Assembly since 1947, and the report of UNCURK was certain to be on the agenda of the Assembly, which convened in regular session on September 19. Using the report of the commission as a springboard, the Western powers introduced a resolution which combined the objective of a reunified Korea with the military operations being carried out by the United Nations. After a protracted debate, the resolution was passed on October 7 by the now-traditional Cold War majority (47 votes to 5, with 7 abstentions). The operative paragraphs were:

> (a) All appropriate steps be taken to ensure stability throughout Korea;
> (b) All constituent acts be taken, including the holding of elections, under the auspices of the United Nations, for

the establishment of a unified, independent and democratic government in the sovereign State of Korea;

(c) All sections and representative bodies of the population of Korea, South and North, be invited to cooperate with the organs of the United Nations in the restoration of peace, in the holding of elections and in the establishment of a unified government;

(d) United Nations forces should not remain in any part of Korea otherwise than so far as necessary for achieving the objectives specified in sub-paragraphs (a) and (b) above.[38]

This was the final step in legitimization of American policy. All that remained was to win the war, supervise the elections, and continue a military occupation until all vestiges of Communist opposition were eliminated—all provided for by United Nations resolutions and all exactly coincidental with American aims in Korea. Massive intervention by the Chinese Communists in November, 1950, prevented the achievement of these goals, and, finally, in 1953, a truce restored something approaching the status quo ante bellum.

The Korean War stands as the most successful use of legitimization in the history of the United Nations. To clarify the positive accomplishments of legitimization, it is useful to observe what it was *not*. It never meant that United Nations policy replaced or dictated American policy. The United States set upon its course of action independently. If the Soviet Union had been present in the Security Council on June 25, the United States would not have been deterred from carrying out President Truman's decisions in Korea.* Either the same

* Acheson writes: "In response to the President's suggestions, I recommended that: . . . at the Security Council meeting called for the next morning [June 27] we should propose a new resolution calling on UN members to give Korea such help as might be needed to repel the armed attack. . . . If Malik [the Soviet Delegate] returned to the Security Council and vetoed the resolution, we would have to carry on under the existing one. If he did not return, it would pass without opposition." Acheson, *Present at the Creation*, p. 531.

vetoed resolutions would have been used to substantiate the legitimacy of American policy, or the United States would have moved immediately into the General Assembly to achieve the same result. The resolutions never interfered with complete American control of operations. Theoretically, the June 27 resolution, which recommended that members "furnish such assistance to the Republic of Korea as may be necessary to repel the armed attack," was an open invitation to *all* members to provide military support. In fact, the United States did not permit the resolution to be used except in coordination with its own policy needs. When Chiang Kai-shek, for example, attempted to ease his return to the mainland of Asia by offering to dispatch 33,000 Nationalist Chinese troops to Korea, he was rebuffed. The United States, and *not* the United Nations, decided to reject the offer because it conflicted with larger American policy considerations.[39] In fact, a coalition approach to the military operation was decided upon and implemented prior to the establishment of a United Nations command, while the countries involved and their contributions were determined by normal considerations of alliance politics. Furthermore, United Nations resolutions were ignored when they were no longer useful. If the General Assembly resolution of October 7 justified the drive to the Yalu, it was promptly forgotten when the Chinese Communist intervention made the reunification of Korea by force militarily and politically unacceptable to the Truman administration. Ironically, General MacArthur was dismissed for, in effect, insisting on fulfilling the United Nations resolution *after* that resolution conflicted with American foreign policy. When the risks outweighed perceived gains, there was no thought given to the idea that the United Nations had created any obligation for the United States.

Although the ultimate conclusion of the Korean War was

less than completely satisfactory for the United States, important advantages accrued from its legitimization in the United Nations. Before the sudden beginning of the Korean War, Korea had been for most Americans "a strange land in far off Asia."[40] Only a year before, the same administration had declined to be drawn into war on the Asian mainland to save Chiang Kai-shek's forces from complete collapse. Clearly, an executive decision to fight in Korea only five years after the end of World War II required congressional and popular support. Enthusiasm for the war was in large part created by the televised proceedings at the United Nations. The image of the United States as the champion of collective security added an extra dimension of idealism to the policy.[41] The same factors contributed to the ability of friendly governments to provide aid and military support. Contributions in defense of the Charter were politically acceptable, whereas it would have been more difficult to send troops to fight a war in a distant country with which there was not even a treaty commitment. In sum, the United Nations was a valuable instrument for maximizing domestic and foreign support for an American war.

The Vietnam War

The Korean War was both the most ambitious and most effective use of the politics of legitimization. Many factors combined to produce that fortuitous result, including the apparent certainty that North Korea had attacked the South, supported by an immediate report of a United Nations commission in South Korea; the absence of the Soviet Union from the Security Council; and the overwhelming influence of the United States in the United Nations. In contrast, American use of the

United Nations to legitimize its Vietnam policy was limited because these advantages did not exist or were, at best, less substantial.

Without attempting to detail the quarter century of American involvement in Vietnam, we can outline some of the basic developments and reasons for the war being an unsuitable complaint from an American point of view. Beginning about 1950, the United States provided substantial aid to the French in their war against the Viet Minh led by Ho Chi Minh. This decision was partially a reaction to events in Korea and to a general hardening of the containment line throughout the world. By the time France was defeated in the battle of Dien Bien Phu on May 7, 1954, the United States was bearing 80 percent of the costs of the war.[42] The Indochina question was added to the agenda of the Geneva Conference, which had been originally convened to discuss a settlement in Korea. Although no progress was made with respect to Korea, the conference did apparently solve the Indochinese problem. The Geneva Agreements provided: for a cease-fire; recognition of Ho Chi Minh's government in the North; a provisional military demarcation line drawn at the seventeenth parallel, which "should not in any way be interpreted as constituting a political or territorial boundary"; the holding of an election in 1956 to unite the country; the nonintroduction of foreign troops or bases into the country; and the creation of a three-member International Control Commission to oversee the execution of its provisions. The United States did not sign the accords, but indicated that it would not subvert them. Nevertheless, the agreement was considered a disaster by the Eisenhower administration, which took immediate steps to prevent its implementation.[43] With American approval, the regime in the South headed by Ngo Dinh Diem (1955–1963) prevented the promised elections. With each passing year, the United

States became more and more deeply involved in maintaining an anti-Communist government in the South.[44] Discontent with Diem's rule provoked protest and insurgency, which in turn produced greater emphasis on military support by the United States. This process was significantly intensified during President John F. Kennedy's brief tenure. By October, 1963, the United States had nearly 17,000 men in Vietnam and still the civil war was going badly. The American-sanctioned coup[45] which overthrew Diem caused even more instability, and President Johnson faced the problem of either increasing the American investment or accepting the probability that an unsatisfactory government would emerge in South Vietnam. The decision was made to continue and augment support for a pro-American, anti-Communist South Vietnam. As part of this effort, the United States supported clandestine attacks and sabotage missions in North Vietnam. Although such operations had begun as early as 1954,[46] they assumed a new significance a decade later because they were now associated with plans to bomb the North on the assumption that the bombing would affect the insurgency in the South. In fact, the scenario called for "retaliatory action against North Vietnam on 72 hours notice."[47] Elaborate preparations, including lists of targets, were made. A draft resolution to be presented to the Congress was drawn up on May 25, 1964,[48] to back the anticipated escalation.

It was against this background that the Tonkin Gulf incident occurred. According to the White House version, the destroyer *Maddox*, on routine patrol in international waters off the North Vietnamese coast, was attacked on August 2 by three North Vietnamese torpedo boats. To "protect" the *Maddox*, the destroyer *C. Turner Joy* was ordered to the same waters. On the night of August 4, the North Vietnamese repeated the attack, this time against both destroyers. Within twelve hours of the second attack, American bombers were carrying out the reprisal raids. The plan called for a supportive congressional resolution.[49] Naturally, the elaborate preparation for this purpose was not revealed to the Senate, nor the fact that sabotage operations were being carried out in the vicinity of the clash, and that the North Vietnamese could easily have confused the American vessels with those supporting the clandestine attacks.

On August 4, the United States demanded that the Security Council meet "to consider the serious situation created by deliberate attacks of the Hanoi regime on United States vessels in international waters."[50] In the Council, the United States described the attacks as unprovoked and asserted that the United States had been forced to exercise its right of self-defense and had bombed North Vietnamese naval vessels and support facilities.[51] The United States, however, had not gone to the Security Council to have the incident investigated or to have the United Nations suggest solutions. The Pentagon was using every available instrument to legitimize a policy which had been decided upon months before and which was being implemented during and before the meeting of the Security Council. Legal arguments need not detain us. Self-defense was the preferred legalism because the Security Council, with American support, had, in numerous condemnations of Israel, denied the right of retaliation.[52] As anticipated, the Soviet side denounced the United States bombing as aggression, and asserted that this was one of a long series of attacks against the North.[53] In a telegram to the Soviet delegation, North Vietnam insisted that the Council lacked jurisdiction and that only the co-chairmen of the Geneva Conference had competence to consider the questions arising from the Geneva

Accords. Furthermore, they charged that the bombing was part of a pattern of attacks by the United States for the purpose of expanding the war.[54]

No action was taken by the Security Council. None had been intended. For the Pentagon, the United Nations was a useful tool to help convince the American people and the United States Congress that the escalation of the war was justified. Undoubtedly, this could have been accomplished without resort to the United Nations, but it was still impressive for many ordinary Americans and congressmen that it was the United States that had initiated the complaint in the peace-keeping organization. Although it was not crucial, the use of the United Nations helped legitimize the policy, which was endorsed by votes of 88 to 2 in the Senate and 416 to 0 in the House of Representatives. As a Pentagon analyst observed triumphantly, the reprisal raids "marked the crossing of an important threshold in the war, and it was accomplished with virtually no domestic criticism, indeed with an evident increase in public support of the Administration. The precedent for strikes against the North was thus established and at very little apparent cost."[55]

Adroit use of the United Nations helped to achieve this victory, but the trend was against easy repeat performances. The organization was becoming less available for the United States, especially on this issue. The unpopularity of the American war effort among Third World countries, which dominated the politics of the General Assembly, meant that a full-scale Assembly debate would be disastrous for the United States. After 1965, the Security Council also became less reliable. The increase in the Council's membership from eleven to fifteen enhanced the influence of the Afro-Asian states, which were likely to be critical of American policy in Vietnam. With the Communist side opposed to United Nations involvement for juridical reasons, and the United States reluctant to risk political embarrassment, the issue could hardly be raised.

The Johnson administration continued to be confronted by the unattractive options of further escalation of the war or a political defeat in the South. Since the latter was deemed unacceptable, new plans were made to punish North Vietnam. Although agreement in principle to bomb North Vietnam more intensively was reached during the presidential campaign of 1964, implementation awaited the start of President Lyndon B. Johnson's second term. Another provocation was required to begin the sustained air bombardment of the North, code-named "rolling thunder." The precipitating "incident," although not nearly so satisfactory as Gulf of Tonkin, occurred with the Viet Cong raid on a United States military advisers compound at Pleiku. Nine Americans were killed and seventy-six wounded. Within hours, forty-nine American planes carried out the first raid in the North. The next day, the United States informed the Security Council by letter of the Viet Cong attack and the American response against the North.[56] No meeting was asked for, undoubtedly because of the difficulty of sustaining a case for bombing the North over an incident that was an inevitable consequence of increased United States involvement in the South.

Preparations were already under way for further expansion of the air war and, finally, the assumption of the ground combat role in the South. As the Pentagon Papers reveal, the government planners were continuously concerned with justifying every escalation and masking their actions by "peace offensives." These measures reflected the mounting concern with domestic and foreign criticism. Inevitably, further use of the United Nations was considered, if only to forestall an attack from that quarter. The State Department prepared the United Nations strategy, which was to be used in support of "rolling thunder" but was actually delayed until January, 1966.

After stating the plans for intensification of the war, the memo from the State Department to Ambassador Taylor went on:

> We will announce this policy of measured action in general terms and at the same time, we will go to the United Nations Security Council to make clear case that aggressor is Hanoi. We will also make it clear that we are ready and eager for "talks" to bring aggression to an end. . . . You are authorized to emphasize our conviction that announcement of readiness to talk is stronger diplomatic position than awaiting inevitable summons to Security Council by third parties. . . .
>
> a. We are determined to continue with military actions regardless of Security Council deliberations. . . .
>
> b. We consider the United Nations Security Council initiative, following another strike, essential if we are to avoid being faced with really damaging initiatives by the U.S.S.R. or perhaps by such powers as India, France, or even the United Nations.
>
> c. At an early point in the United Nations Security Council initiative, we would expect to see calls for the DRV [North Vietnam] to appear in the United Nations. If they failed to appear, as in August, this will make doubly clear that it is they who are refusing to desist, and our position in pursuing military actions against the DRV would be strengthened. For same reason we would now hope GVN [South Vietnam] itself would appear at United Nations and work closely with United States.
>
> d. With or without Hanoi, we have every expectation that any "talks" that may result from our Security Council initiative would in fact go on for many weeks or perhaps months and would above all focus constantly on the cessation of Hanoi's aggression as the precondition to any cessation of military action against the DRV. We further anticipate that any detailed discussions about any possible

eventual form of agreement returning to the essentials of the 1954 Accords would be postponed and would be sub-ordinated to the central issue. . . .[57]

The occasion for implementing the strategy was the resumption of large-scale bombing of North Vietnam on January 30, 1966. The pause in the bombing, which had begun on December 24, 1965, was one of a series of such maneuvers designed to impress North Vietnam with the dangers of refusing to accept American terms and to convince domestic and foreign opinion of the sincerity of the United States in searching for a negotiated solution of the problem.* In short, the American objective in going to the United Nations was to prove that war was peace. In recognition of the difficulty of this assignment, the United States' limited objective was to make its presentation and have the item adopted on the agenda. As the memo suggested, there were risks in having the Security Council actually debate the issue, although it was believed that these were tolerable. It was appreciated that North Vietnam would probably refuse to recognize the competence of the Security Council since they insisted that the settlement had been reached at Geneva in 1954.[58] The failure of North Vietnam to appear would give more credibility to the American contention that the other side stood in the way of peace. Of course, sophisticated observers were aware of the situation. Secretary-General Thant, for example, made clear

* For the rationale for using bombing pauses to increase pressure on Hanoi by having each pause followed by more intense bombing, see *Pentagon Papers* (New York: Bantam Books, 1971) , pp. 470–471. In his memo of November 30, 1965, to President Johnson, Secretary McNamara wrote: "It is my belief that there should be a three- or four-week pause in the program of bombing the North before we greatly increase our troop deployments to VN or intensify our strikes against the North." He emphasized that the ploy would "lay a foundation in the minds of the American public and in world opinion for such an enlarged phase of the war. . . ." *Ibid.*, p. 489.

that in respect to Vietnam, the Security Council could serve
no useful purpose, and he agreed with the North Vietnamese
that the Geneva Accords provided the basis for any progress
in reaching a settlement.[59] Nevertheless, many would believe
that the United States was showing good faith by bringing
the issue to the United Nations and would conclude that non-
appearance by North Vietnam was evidence of intransigence.

On January 31, the United States demanded an urgent
meeting of the Security Council in order to discuss a peace
conference to apply the Geneva Agreements and to arrange for
a supervised cease-fire.[60] From the State Department memo,
we know that this was a subterfuge because it had already
been decided that the United States "would continue with
military actions regardless of Security Council deliberations."
Furthermore, a principal objective of going to the United
Nations was the probability that "any detailed discussions
about any possible eventual form of agreement returning to
the essentials of the 1954 Accords would be postponed and
would be subordinated to the central issue"—North Vietnamese aggression.

Ambassador Arthur Goldberg spoke eloquently in the
debates on adoption of the agenda on February 1 and February 2. Once again, the United States was appealing to the
Security Council to fulfill its responsibility for the maintenance of international peace. The appeal to the Council was
still another dimension of the United States peace offensive.
Fully 115 governments had been consulted since the United
States had unilaterally stopped bombing the North on December 24. But the North Vietnamese continued to refuse to negotiate, presented the United States with unacceptable ultimata,
and escalated their aggression against South Vietnam.
Although these positions and actions gave the United States

no choice except to resume the bombing, good faith was being shown by this effort to have the Security Council deal with the problem.[61]

The risks in this maneuver were clear. Of course, the Soviet delegate led the counterattack, noting the hypocrisy of an appeal to the Security Council simultaneous with resumed bombing. Obviously, he said, the United Nations was being used to cover up further expansion of the war. The brutality of American aggression was described. As for the placing of the item on the agenda, the Geneva Agreements and not the Security Council were the only proper source of ending the war.[62]

In 1950, the Soviets would have stood virtually alone. By 1966, the Council had changed. Bulgaria, of course, parroted the Soviet arguments. But now France also objected to this use of the Security Council, asserting that United Nations intervention could only add to the existing confusion. And the African states on the Council were not cooperative. Mali and Nigeria agreed with France and noted that it was inappropriate to discuss a settlement at the very moment when the bombing had been resumed. Uganda observed that the United States would have demonstrated sincerity if it had asked for the meeting *during* the cessation of bombing rather than after the pause had ended. Argentina, China, Japan, the Netherlands, New Zealand, the United Kingdom, and Uruguay supported their ally.[63]

With nine votes necessary for the adoption of the agenda, the United States had only eight sure votes. For the first time in the history of the United Nations, the United States was faced with the possible embarrassment of not being able to have a proposal considered by the Security Council. If this were to happen, the "peace offensive" would be somewhat

tarnished. Jordan had the swing vote. Torn between her ties
to the Afro-Asians opposing American policy and her dependence on the United States for economic and military aid, Jordan asked for a one-day postponement in the vote on the
agenda.[64] The next day, Jordan announced her vote in favor
of adoption of the agenda. We can only speculate on how
much diplomatic currency was expended to persuade Jordan
to vote right.

Nothing more was done. The Japanese president of the
Security Council suggested that private talks be held in order
to determine how best to proceed. Three weeks later he
announced that because of divisions and the refusal by some
states to participate in these discussions, it would be unwise
for the Council to take up the question. Instead, he was
reporting to the Council in the form of a letter. In the letter
he noted the grave concern over the Vietnam War, the desira-
bility of reaching a peaceful solution, and that there seemed
to be a consensus that negotiations should take place "in an
appropriate forum in order to work out implementation of
the Geneva Accords."[65]

This apparently innocuous letter squared with the American propaganda position. It was immediately denounced by
the Soviet Union as an illegal transgression of the president's
authority, and the other states that had opposed adoption of
the agenda took similar positions. But another small victory
had been won by the United States.

Having won the agenda battle, the United States could
have forced a debate. But there was no reason to take the
risks. The vulnerability of the Vietnam policy to criticism was
accentuated by the Secretary-General's suggestion on February
17, 1966, of a three-step approach to the problem. These were
an immediate end to all bombing of North Vietnam, a scaling
down of military activity in the South, and a willingness of

all sides to begin discussions with those actually fighting (this would include the Viet Cong).[66] In contrast to these proposals, the United States had gone to the United Nations in order to justify *more* bombing, to prepare for a huge increase in America's combat role in the South, and to prevent or delay the discussions envisaged by U Thant. Thant's prestige as Secretary-General only added to American embarrassment. The proposals, which were rejected by the United States as entirely one-sided, were widely applauded in speeches during the next session of the General Assembly.[67] Considering this unfavorable atmosphere, there were obvious dangers in permitting a debate that could force the United States on the defensive. Clearly, the United States determined the "solution" announced by the Japanese delegate, since the other side refused to join the talks. To end the matter with the letter by the president of the Council was therefore eminently satisfactory. It was either fortunate or not entirely accidental that a compliant president would be presiding at the time.*

The Vietnam issue confirms the close relationship between strategy at the United Nations and on the battlefield. It should not be assumed that the policy was atypical because Pentagon planners were trapped in a maze of intrigue which caused them to adopt bizarre strategems. Although each case possesses unique features, the pattern is consistent. Thus in Vietnam, as on the Berlin issue, the Western powers took deliberate advantage of the knowledge that their opponents, because of fundamental policy requirements, were unable to respond effectively in the Security Council. The more limited value of the United Nations for the United States in respect to Vietnam flowed from the nature of the issue and an impaired ability to control majorities. The fact that the organization

* Presidents of the Security Council are rotated monthly by alphabetical progression.

was used at all in these circumstances is what is most interesting. If Korea represented the extreme in successful legitimization of a policy, Vietnam symbolizes another extreme—that of utilizing popular illusions about the United Nations for the purpose of distortion and deception.

Conclusions

The politics of legitimization requires preconditions that are not present for other strategies in the United Nations. Given the need to dominate the organization in combination with an ongoing policy operation, it is not surprising that the United States and its allies monopolized Cold War uses of legitimization. The United Nations was converted into an anti-Communist alliance in Korea. On the other issues, varying degrees of support were provided for planned or actual military actions.

There was no possibility that the minority superpower, the Soviet Union, could use the organization in the same manner. Its one initiative, probably for propaganda purposes, followed the Israeli-French-British invasion of Egypt in 1956. At that time Premier Khrushchev suggested that the United States and Russia, which was simultaneously suppressing the Hungarian revolt, use their combined military power against the aggressors. The proposal was indignantly rejected by President Eisenhower.[68] Instead, the General Assembly established the United Nations Emergency Force, which excluded Soviet troops.

The unavailability of this strategy for the Soviet Union reemphasizes the absolute need to control the political process in the United Nations. Clearly, although the anticolonialists meet this prerequisite, they lack the physical means to integrate large-scale military offensives with appropriate United Nations resolutions. They can, and do, use their majorities to endorse guerrilla resistance to colonialist or racist regimes. It is quite impossible for Portugal, Rhodesia, or South Africa to protest effectively at the United Nations against externally supported insurgents. The futility of their position was foreshadowed when the Indian invasion of Goa escaped censure.[69] To this extent, the anticolonialists have legitimized the limited martial aspects of their policy. Should more important military ventures become feasible, there is no doubt that fuller use of the politics of legitimization will be made by the anticolonialists. If, at such a time, the Western powers were to resort to the veto in the Security Council to block passage of resolutions, the General Assembly would be substituted. Ironically, the availability of the General Assembly was "legalized" by the Uniting for Peace Resolution, which was designed to legitimize Western policy in Korea. This time, the former victims of that strategy, the Soviet bloc and Communist China, would join the Afro-Asians as enthusiasts for a "liberal" interpretation of the Charter.

Discussion of the politics of legitimization reemphasizes the importance of understanding the conflict objectives of parties at the United Nations. The strategy bars any United Nations role other than as a support for independently made foreign-policy decisions. While the *image* of the organization as an instrument for the pacific settlement of disputes is useful, the underlying purposes of initiating states is always to buttress war or preparation for war. The analysis shatters the theory that if states are provided with a number of arenas, they will be less likely to use force.[70] States possessing the capacity and felt need to employ military power do not refrain from war because they could fight with words and resolutions at the United Nations. They do both simultaneously. Nor is

the record any more comforting for those who cling to the
dream that the United Nations is a last hope, which could
avert the horrors of World War III. The debate on the Cuban
missile crisis was very nearly the last debate in the organization. Should the superpowers revisit the brink of hell, we can
expect a replay of the theme that they must act to save the
world from those who have desecrated the ideals of the Charter.

5 *The Politics of Socialization*

In all conflicts the existing balance of forces is an element in determining the eventual outcome. Nations often possess unequal shares of those resources that spell victory and defeat. As a general rule it favors the stronger side to *privatize* disputes, while it is in the interest of the weaker party to *socialize* its position to outsiders in the hope of gaining the support required either to win or prevent defeat.[1] By socialization of disputes, therefore, we refer to the numerous issues that are brought to the United Nations by those who hope to add some legal, moral, or even material support to their cause because they do not otherwise possess sufficient means to win.

Of the strategies we are considering, the politics of socialization is the most common, and at the same time the most difficult to analyze. Virtually all complaints aired at the United Nations contain an element of socialization. Conflict is socialized, more or less meaningfully, merely by having it exposed to United Nations processes and bringing into play whatever added involvement and support results from this exposure. The act of having issues inscribed on the United Nations agenda, debate, demonstrations of support expressed in debates or resolutions, the establishment of United Nations presences—all alter the exclusive nature of the original dis-

putes. In short, all issues, including many already considered
as examples of embarrassment, status, and legitimization politics, might also fall into this category. Despite this overlapping
in categories, there is sufficient reason to differentiate conflict
socialization involving the United Nations as a specific *foreign-
policy objective.*

Like any other strategy, the politics of socialization has
its own peculiar problems and requirements. It is grounded
in weakness. This is likely to present the aggrieved party with
important and even insurmountable obstacles. Often the use
of socialization strategy represents a final but futile attempt to
stave off impending disaster. Where the stakes are less total,
the weak side must consider the advantages of complaining to
the United Nations if it calculates that the added hostility
engendered by this act further reduces prospects for immediate gains or jeopardizes more basic interests. At a minimum,
success depends on effective control of United Nations processes, although even command of United Nations machinery
is no assurance that socialization will be a success and inherent
weakness overcome. Without support by key states which
stand to benefit in some way from aligning themselves with
the claimant, defeat is probably equally assured.

It should be observed that not all helpless victims of
superior force have their causes aired at the United Nations.
For some, the organization is not available. The Biafran war
and the massacre of hundreds of thousands of Hutus in
Burundi are only the most spectacular among a number of
recent African "nonissues." The United Nations was similarly
unavailable to the victims of Yahya Khan's brutal suppression
of East Pakistanis, nor was there any opportunity to socialize
the plight of countless "Communists" killed by General Suhar-
to's government in Indonesia, or any number of other atroci-
ties from which the organization remains aloof. Arguments

concerning legal status may be raised to explain the indifference of the world organization.[2] Such legalisms are convenient and impressive. Actually, they shield political realities. Juridically there is little that distinguishes these from other matters in which the United Nations has been deeply involved: Tibet, Apartheid, the Algerian civil war, and various colonial issues. Impotence and isolation contribute to the silence.* Explanation of the different treatment may also be found in the relationship between the interests of member states and particular crises. Where national interest opposes the *dramatization* of injustices, these causes will remain ignored in the forums of the United Nations, although the victims may have access to less-publicized assistance.

Last Gasps: The Cases of Hyderabad and Hungary

Socialization to the United Nations must always be related to the basic objective, which is to obtain outside aid. The case of Hyderabad clearly demonstrates the futility of an appeal to the United Nations when one side is weak, isolated, and practically friendless. Because of its uncertain juridical status, Hyderabad's appeal to the Security Council for help to prevent India from crushing the regime was received with reservations. When the Council finally decided to hear the case, the members were careful to avoid offending India by making it clear that the action did not imply any judgment about Hyderabad's claims to statehood.[3] While the Council debated the issue, Indian troops invaded, brought down the government, and incorporated the territory into India. Having no other

---

* The plight of the American Indians who attempted to socialize to the United Nations grievances that they had dramatized at Wounded Knee, South Dakota, illustrates the futility of those whose weakness is compounded by political insularity. See *New York Times*, March 23, 1973.

choice, the unfortunate Nizam of Hyderabad instructed his delegate to withdraw the complaint.[4] But one outsider, Pakistan, had reason to press the issue. On Pakistan's demand, the matter was debated again, with the Pakistani delegate using the Council to stress the inconsistency in India's actions in Hyderabad as compared to Jammu and Kashmir.* It was obvious that the United Nations could do nothing about Hyderabad's fate, and no action was taken.

The case of Hyderabad is unusual in that the Nizam was appealing to the *United Nations* for help without the normal ulterior purpose of involving any particular state or states. Entirely surrounded by India, there was no place else for Hyderabad to go. The failure of the Security Council to vote on *any* resolution emphasized the hopelessness of an appeal which had no merit for member states beyond their theoretical attachment to the principles of the Charter.

When the level of hostility has reached the imminent or actual use of force, there is usually nothing that the victim can gain at the United Nations. Control of United Nations processes by supporters of Hungarian revolutionaries did not prevent the swift destruction of their cause.[5] When one's adversary is both strong and determined, successful socialization depends on calculations of risks and benefits by outsiders who can effectively intervene. The revolt in Hungary collapsed because of the unwillingness of the *United States* to defend Hungarian freedom with American blood. In the United Nations the West utilized the politics of embarrassment against the Soviet Union and the Kadar government. But for Premier

* In Jammu and Kashmir, a Hindu prince opted for accession to India despite the fact that the great majority of the population was Moslem— the exact reverse of the situation in Hyderabad. In Hyderabad, India stressed the concept of popular self-determination to justify the military attack, and Pakistan wanted that principle applied to Jammu and Kashmir. See *SCOR*, Meeting 384, December 15, 1948.

Imre Nagy and the revolutionaries, their agonized appeal to the United Nations was a last-gasp effort to socialize their struggle. Failure to stop the Soviet tanks in Hungary demonstrates the strategic limitations of socialization to the United Nations in such desperate circumstances. In truth, the Hungarian question differs little from similar appeals made by Cubans in 1960 and Guatemalans in 1954 over attempts by a strong enemy to crush their governments. Ultimately their fate, like that of Hungary, rested on the willingness of a strong outsider (the Soviet Union) actively to give support. Neither Cuba nor Guatemala was important enough to the Soviet Union to risk war with the United States.

Hyderabad and the three Cold War issues involve basically the same strategy: the socialization of conflict by one side to overcome weakness and forestall imminent destruction at the hands of a powerful enemy. In each instance success depended upon the willingness of other nations to intercede on behalf of the victim. Without that support the governments of the Nizam of Hyderabad, Imre Nagy, and Jacobo Arbenz were brought down, while that of Fidel Castro survived only because of American miscalculations.

Risks: Panama and Iran

In less desperate situations, the strategy of socialization will be more or less effective depending on its relationship to political goals, availability of the United Nations, and external factors. In short, the weaker side must make complex calculations. A fundamental consideration is that the use of the United Nations is *always a hostile act,* and the weaker side may not be willing to risk the consequences. A story in the *New York Times*[6] illustrates a typical dilemma. Panama had

obtained informal majority approval in the Security Council
to have that organ meet in Panama to consider the issue of
Panamanian rights in the Canal Zone. The initiative resulted
from dissatisfaction with negotiations to revise the Treaty of
1903, which had established United States jurisdiction in the
Zone "in perpetuity." According to the story, American officials suggested that the move "would set a dangerous precedent
of using the Security Council as a bargaining tool in influencing bilateral negotiations."* Furthermore, "the meeting could
become an exercise to embarrass the United States," especially
if Cuba seized the occasion to raise the issues of Guantanamo
Bay and Puerto Rico. As a result, a Panamanian appeal to the
United Nations "could wind up antagonizing Administration
and Congressional leaders—the very parties Panama hopes to
influence by calling attention to her long-standing grievances."
This carefully worded statement posed the basic problem for
Panama. She had to choose between using the United Nations
weapon or enduring the existing relationship with the United
States. The decision to hold the meeting, made wisely or not,
depended upon the perceived utility of socializing the issue
as opposed to the potential costs of increasing American hostility. Obviously, there are many other issues that are not
socialized to the United Nations because the dangers are un-
bearable for the weaker state. Panama felt that the advantages
outweighed the risks.

The politics of socialization is always risky. If force is
used, the enemy may respond with superior force. Dependence
on bilateral negotiations may fail because of the unwillingness

---

* This statement reveals the peculiar blindness resulting from perspective.
The very first issue brought to the Security Council was the Iranian
complaint, strongly supported by the United States, which was an effort
to "influence bilateral negotiations." The difference, of course, is that in
the Panama case the United States was the defendant.

of a powerful adversary to grant concessions. The search for outside assistance may be successful and may infuriate a stronger opponent. Socialization to the United Nations involves similar calculations. Nevertheless, the tactic has been employed many times, beginning with the very first case to come before the Security Council—Iran's complaint against the presence of Soviet troops on her soil. In somewhat similar circumstances, Syria, Lebanon, and Egypt used this weapon to help them expel the British and French from their territories. The extent to which use of the United Nations contributed to the achievement of desired goals in these cases is difficult to analyze. The Western powers probably planned to evacuate these countries anyway, and the hostility generated by the complaints did not materially alter their plans. Some, at least, have assumed that the embarrassment suffered by the Soviet Union at the United Nations contributed to its decision to evacuate northern Iran.[7] At best, it has been presumed that there was a causal relationship between Soviet conduct and United Nations influence that is inconsistent with the behavior of the Soviet Union on many other issues. It is probably more understandable to relate the Soviet withdrawal to the successful conclusion of a treaty with Iran for exploitation of oil resources in Iran's five northern provinces. The fact that they *did* withdraw following negotiation of the treaty indicates that Soviet objectives in Iran were limited. If that is true, the risk taken by Iran in bringing the issue to the United Nations may have had little to do with the outcome, which hinged on the oil treaty. This analysis is admittedly speculative, but more probable than the belief that a Great Power, determined to achieve important national objectives at the expense of a helpless opponent, would be deterred because of a complaint to the United Nations.

Surrogate Interests: The Case of Algeria

Consideration of the Algerian question at the United Nations began in 1955. The fight for Algerian independence began in earnest some months before with the outbreak of hostilities between Algerian rebels and French troops. Almost immediately the complex and often subtle web of circumstances started to unfold at the United Nations. Support for the Algerian cause was implicit in the effort by fourteen Afro-Asian states to have the matter inscribed on the General Assembly agenda.[8] French reaction, though predictable, went perhaps beyond what may have been expected. France refused to acknowledge United Nations authority in a matter which it considered to be completely within its domestic jurisdiction, but in addition withdrew itself from any discussion of Algeria and all other business before that session of the General Assembly.[9] Any hope, therefore, that the United Nations could be used to further Algerian objectives in cooperation with France was immediately shattered at a time when those objectives were still subject to negotiation. The recent French withdrawal from Indochina, and settlements concerning independence for Tunisia and Morocco, further complicated matters. French willingness to accede to the demands of independence movements in these areas raised the possibility of a negotiated settlement on Algeria and cautioned against any action that would antagonize France. Against this background, it is not surprising that India, one of the original sponsors of the resolution to include the Algerian item on the agenda, and the leader of the Third World, would suggest that the question be removed from the agenda without further debate. The unanimous adoption of this proposal confirms that at this stage the risks of socialization to the United Nations were considered unacceptable.[10]

The introduction of over 400,000 French troops in Algeria in 1955–1956 modified the assessments taken the previous year. Apparent French determination to suppress the rebellion with force rendered the prospects for settlement more remote than was previously hoped and made the question of publicly antagonizing France less important. In addition, the joint French, British, and Israeli attack on Suez in October, which Premier Guy Mollet hoped would relieve Egyptian pressure on the Algerian conflict, failed. President Nasser emerged with increased prestige and influence throughout the Arab world. These developments removed the inhibitions that had dominated the strategy a year earlier.

France, too, was eager for combat. Without abandoning the position that his country would tolerate no meddling in Algeria by the General Assembly, the French delegate did not oppose having the United Nations debate the issue. Instead he took the occasion to lash out at Egypt and to denounce what he called a "systematic campaign of denigration against France."[11] France blamed outside powers, and, in particular, Egypt for inciting the rebellion, training terrorists, and supplying weapons.[12] It is clear that the French merely wished to have the record reflect their position and that their participation in no way indicated a willingness to enter into a dialogue on Algeria at the United Nations; for the most part France declined thereafter to respond to any charges and confined her remarks essentially to denying United Nations jurisdiction in the matter. With Egypt leading the attack, the Afro-Asians pressed for passage of a resolution that would commit the United Nations to support self-determination for the Algerians. Lacking the requisite majority, they were denied their victory and were forced to accept an innocuous resolution expressing the hope that, "in a spirit of cooperation, a peaceful, democratic and just solution will be found."[13]

The contrast in the use of the United Nations from one year to the next is striking. When there appeared to be some possibility of a negotiated settlement, the Afro-Asians abandoned even the discussion of the issue. With full-scale civil war in progress and hostility at a peak between themselves and France, they became unconcerned about adding to French intransigence. In any case, the strategy was no longer designed to modify directly French behavior. The Afro-Asians had other goals. They were using debates and votes in the peace-keeping organization to provide moral support to the Algerian war effort. Additionally, their object was to stimulate doubts among the Western allies, especially the United Kingdom and the United States, about the wisdom of excessive support for France in Algeria. In the Cold War atmosphere of the time, socialization of this issue implied the threat of some Western loss to the Communist side in the struggle to win the allegiance of the Third World. Use of such "blackmail" did not appear unreasonable in the light of America's failure to support France and Britain at the United Nations over Suez.

The momentum of Afro-Asian attacks on French "colonialism" in Algeria increased with each passing year. Charges became more savage and unrestrained. The United Nations was exhorted to accept a more direct and wider role in securing Algerian independence. This became especially pronounced after the passage of the declaration on Non-Self-Governing Territories in 1960, which committed the organization to the liquidation of colonialism throughout the world. To further magnify the importance of the civil war, the Security Council was asked to consider the matter as a threat to the general peace.[14] In 1960 the Afro-Asians made their most extreme demand by urging that the General Assembly "decide that a referendum be conducted in Algeria, organized, controlled and supervised by the United Nations, whereby the

Algerian people would freely determine the destiny of their entire country."[15] This would have taken the matter completely out of French hands.

Throughout the period of United Nations deliberation, France was moving spasmodically toward a settlement of the war.[16] The governments of the Fourth Republic vacillated between conciliation and repression. From November 1954 to 1958 four French cabinets fell specifically because of this issue. In 1958 metropolitan France confronted an armed invasion by the Algerian colonels. To save the Fourth Republic General Charles de Gaulle was asked to assume leadership in June. The general had come to power because of the Algerian crisis and would, despite many domestic pressures, retain a fiercely personal rein on the decisions relating to its outcome. In September, 1959, de Gaulle shared his views with the French people. Settlement of the crisis would be based upon the principle of Algerian self-determination. The eventual independence of Algeria became a reality. What remained was the complicated maneuvering that would lead two and one-half years later to the final accords at Evian.

Against this background, Afro-Asian efforts at the United Nations seem unrealistic. No French government had accepted United Nations interference in Algeria. If there was any doubt about this, it was completely erased when General de Gaulle came to power. His contempt for the United Nations was well known.* His only preoccupation lay in manipulating

* In a press conference conducted on April 11, 1961, President de Gaulle described the meetings of the United Nations as "riotous and scandalous." He observed: "France does not see how she can adopt any attitude toward the United, or disunited, Nations other than that of the greatest reserve . . . she does not wish to contribute her men or her money to any present or future undertaking of this Organization—or disorganization." Quoted in J. B. Duroselle, "France and the United Nations," in Norman J. Padelford and Leland M. Goodrich, eds., The United Nations in the Balance (New York: Frederick A. Praeger, 1965), pp. 346–347.

domestic pressures. Since not even close associates were brought into his confidence, it was unthinkable that he would even consider resolutions or debates in the United Nations. He had his own plans for Algeria and he was determined to carry them out. Why then would the Afro-Asians persist, especially after de Gaulle revealed in principle his acceptance of Algeria's goals? The only possible effect would be to irritate de Gaulle, thereby injuring the Algerian cause.

The major point to be made is that the Afro-Asians were *surrogates* for the Algerian rebels. As such their own interests did not necessarily coincide with those of the revolutionaries. It is unlikely that the Algerians would have demanded a United Nations-controlled solution to their problem at a time when they were negotiating with de Gaulle. This would, indeed, have been dangerous. The Afro-Asians were willing to jeopardize the Algerian cause in order to attack France and advance the general assault on colonialism. This development should be contrasted with the tactics of Iran at a comparable point in its dispute with the Soviet Union. After negotiation of the oil treaty and agreement on a date for withdrawal of Soviet troops from their country, Iran asked the Security Council to *remove their complaint from the agenda*.[17] Thus, the Iranians, acting *directly* for their self-interest, did what they could to assure the evacuation of their country by the Soviets. It is interesting that the Western powers, led by the United States, insisted on retaining the item on the Council agenda. Like the Afro-Asians on Algeria, the West became the surrogate for Iran in order to pursue its broader political conflict with the Soviet Union. Socialization by a third party makes it necessary to differentiate the objectives of the indirect participants from those for whom they are spokesman. At times, in fact, the helper adds to the burdens of those whose cause it has adopted.

The paradox is further highlighted on anticolonial issues because it is rarely the victims who come to the United Nations for help. Instead surrogates raise the standard for the oppressed blacks of South Africa, South West Africa, the Portuguese colonies, and Rhodesia. The goals appear to be clear: majority rule, independence, elimination of discrimination. But the initiators have varied motives. Afro-Asians and socialist states have many and different reasons for agreeing about racism and colonialism.

As surrogates they cannot avoid adopting positions consistent with their own national interests. Such interests may not coincide with those of the inhabitants of Rhodesia or South Africa. Afro-Asian states do not assume the direct risks resulting from mobilizing support for the condemnation of their enemies. If whites in South Africa or Rhodesia feel threatened by their isolation in international organizations and respond by adoption of more severe racial legislation, the black inhabitants bear the consequences for a strategy they did not formulate. Indeed, racial extremism in South Africa and Rhodesia has been correlated with attacks at the United Nations. George Mudge found that racists in these countries have "capitalized on the external threat by the United Nations represented, first, in order to come to power, and secondly, in order to obtain approval of their increasingly extreme policies."[18] It is at least worthy of speculation to consider whether more appropriate measures for solution of these problems would emerge if those with a direct stake in the results were the initiators.

Outside Help: The Case of Indonesia

Not surprisingly, the crucial variable in the politics of socialization is the ability to combine the use of the United Nations
with requisite external assistance. Without the mobilization
of outside support, either related to or independent of United
Nations consideration, weakness is likely to result in defeat
despite whatever actions the United Nations becomes identified with. The overwhelming importance of this connection is
clearly demonstrated in the case of Indonesia, which may
well be the most successful application of the strategy we have
been describing.

We have already stressed the importance of asking the
question, Who brings an issue to the United Nations and why?
Since Indonesian rebels, like Algerians, lacked the standing to
complain directly to the United Nations, the issue had to be
raised by outside powers. The identity and motivation of these
powers would greatly influence the nature of United Nations
deliberations and, more importantly, the impact that these
would have upon the conflict.

The conflict itself arose out of the clash between Indonesian desires for independence and Dutch determination to
reassert sovereignty throughout its island empire, temporarily
suspended because of the war. On August 17, 1945, Indonesia
declared its independence from the Dutch. Almost immediately fighting broke out between the Indonesians and the
British and India Empire troops that were in Indonesia to
supervise the Japanese surrender. British protection of Dutch
interests now became the basis for a Ukrainian complaint to
the Security Council. The Ukraine charged Britain and India
with violating Indonesian rights to self-determination under
Article 73 of the Charter and with creating a threat to international peace and security.[19] Obviously the initiative was

prompted by more than allegiance to Charter principles. It is more likely that the Soviet bloc was seeking vengeance for Iran's complaint against the Soviet Union only weeks earlier. In addition, the issue provided an excellent opportunity for the Soviets to assume a positive image in the eyes of the Third World and to embarrass the West over its suppression of liberation movements. There was even some possibility that Russian involvement in an eventual settlement of the issue would result in added influence for the Soviet Union in Southeast Asia. Clearly the Ukrainian initiative was poorly designed to advance Indonesian goals. Soviet bloc support, short of military intervention, could do little in alleviating Dutch pressures on the Indonesians. The complaint was motivated more by Cold War considerations than from a sincere desire to bring about Indonesian independence. Indeed, Indonesian interests could be advanced only by securing Western support and more precisely that of the United States.

Against this background the effect of the Ukrainian complaint was to submerge the Indonesian cause in the greater conflict between East and West and to direct the attention of the West to the strategic requirements of that contest. Debate reflected these hostilities. The Western-dominated Security Council appeared most concerned with preventing Soviet involvement on any investigatory commission and in overcoming the adverse public relations that the initiative might create in the developing countries.[20] Under these circumstances, the Security Council could not hope to act on the substance of the complaint. No resolutions were adopted.

With United Nations intervention suspended, the conflict returned to its original configuration. The Indonesians persisted in their demands for independence and appeared willing, if poorly equipped, to fight for it. The Dutch were equally determined to prevent any change in the status of the archipelago on other than their own terms. Pressures mounted on both sides. Dissident elements within the nationalist movement demanded a more aggressive stand on the part of the republic. The British, who could ill afford a costly and protracted involvement, pressured the Dutch into negotiations with the rebels.[21] Given the extreme positions taken by both sides, it was unlikely that a lasting solution could be found. Nevertheless, a compromise agreement came on November 15, 1946, at Linggadjati, and with it differences in interpretation which guaranteed renewed hostilities.[22] On July 22, 1947, the Dutch government began what it termed a "police action" against the republic.[23]

In separate letters dated July 30, 1947, the governments of India and Australia brought the Indonesian situation to the attention of the Security Council once again.[24] Although Australia made no specific accusations, the Indians charged that "without warning," Dutch forces had undertaken "large-scale military operations" against the Indonesian population. A number of resolutions were quickly adopted. The Security Council called for a cease-fire, a Consular Commission was established to observe the cease-fire and report military operations to the Council, and a three-member Committee of Good Offices was commissioned to "assist in the pacific settlement" of the dispute.[25] The cease-fire, at least momentarily, relieved Dutch military pressure on the Indonesians, while the Consular Commission and Committee of Good Offices strengthened the republic's bargaining position.

These actions can be contrasted with the inaction of the Security Council a year and a half earlier when Communist states had been the surrogates for the Indonesians. The complaint by Australia and India diminished the direct involvement of the Soviet bloc and facilitated their exclusion from exerting any influence on an eventual settlement. Obviously this was and continued to be an important consideration to the West and helps to explain why an apparent Soviet expression of cooperation in calling for a mutual withdrawal of troops was voted down,[26] and a Russian suggestion to have all members of the Security Council comprise the cease-fire commission was vetoed by France.[27] Even with the exclusion of the Soviet bloc, the Indonesians had scored a victory. However, they felt that the machinery established by the Security Council was insufficient. Because of its procolonial bias, the Consular Commission was likely to reflect Dutch interests in its reporting of cease-fire violations. It was also clear that the Committee of Good Offices would result in protracted negotiations which, combined with the Netherlands' war of attrition, would eventually erode the republic's influence in the islands. In short, the republic now needed to achieve a quick and definitive solution to guarantee its survival. It recognized that only the United States could deliver such a solution. The republic, therefore, requested that the "United States government use its influence with the government of the Netherlands and with the Security Council" toward the "establishment of an international arbitration commission."[28]

Meanwhile, prolonged and tortuous negotiations, punctuated by recurring Dutch military and police actions, steadily weakened the republic's authority.[29] A truce and conditions for further negotiations were arranged aboard the U.S.S. *Renville* in January, 1948. With another Dutch military offensive imminent, the Indonesian leaders made further concessions.[30] The Dutch issued a twenty-four-hour ultimatum, demanding unqualified acceptance of their terms. In late December, 1948, a full-scale military offensive was launched and the nationalist leaders were imprisoned. That same day, the United States called for an emergency meeting of the Security Council.[31] The meaning of this action was not lost on the Dutch. American economic and military aid was vital to the success of its policy. The Dutch delegate tried desperately to evoke the Communist menace. "The Republic," he contended, "relied for a good deal of its support on Communist leaders, and was therefore strongly influenced by Communism." There was a "constant danger" that the Communists would "one day take over complete power." He defended Dutch policies as designed to prevent the independence movement from assuming "a revolutionary and extremist course."[32]

But the United States had reached different conclusions. On December 22, America withdrew fifteen million dollars in aid from the Netherlands East Indies. The revised attitude was undoubtedly influenced by the suppression of a Communist uprising by Indonesian nationalists in September, 1948. While the Security Council was debating, the State Department revealed the reasons for its confidence in the Indonesian leaders: "The United States was mindful of the proved nationalist character of the Republican Government of President Sukarno and Prime Minister Hatta which had taken action against and eliminated a Communist revolt against its authority."[33]

This bulletin foreshadowed the hard position adopted by the United States in the Security Council. Ambassador Jessup said:

> My government can find no adequate justification by the Netherlands in Indonesia. No excuses by the Netherlands Government can conceal the fact that it has failed to comply with the Security Council's demands. I am sure that the Security Council has no intention of approving actions consolidating military victories which themselves were gained as a result of an open defiance of an order of the Security Council.[34]

Not surprisingly, the Security Council now adopted a sweeping resolution. It called for a cease-fire, release of prisoners, negotiations to establish an independent and sovereign United States of Indonesia, and set a target date of July 1, 1950, for the transfer of sovereignty.[35]

In April, 1949, the Congress of the United States continued the pressure on the Netherlands. It passed an amendment to the Economic Cooperation Bill that tied Marshall Plan aid to compliance with the Charter of the United Nations.[36] It was clear from the debate that the action was directed against the Netherlands. The Dutch capitulated. On November 2, 1949, agreements were concluded and sovereignty was transferred to the Republic of Indonesia on December 27, 1949.

Indonesia is *the* model of successful socialization. The independence movement facing a powerful and determined colonial authority could not win unless the balance of forces was modified, and this could be done only by enlisting external support. Having the issue brought to the United Nations could not assure success. In fact, the wrong surrogates harmed the rebels' cause. Soviet bloc initiative was interpreted as a hostile act directed against the West, and the reaction was beneficial to the Dutch by placing the Indonesian conflict in the context of the East-West struggle. Later appeals by India and Australia were more effective but had no appreciable impact on the dispute itself. Despite United Nations involvement, there was a steady three-year deterioration in the republican position. The Dutch were growing stronger and the nationalists weaker. By the end of 1948, the Indonesians were on the verge of capitulation.

The Indonesian cause was saved by international developments and good fortune. Between 1946 and 1949, the Cold War took definitive shape. Western Europe was being mobilized behind United States leadership against the background of the Czech coup and the Berlin blockade. Nations devastated by World War II, including the Netherlands, looked to the United States to rebuild their shattered economies. Simultaneously, a worldwide campaign to gain favor among former colonial peoples was being waged. The United States, therefore, had to judge the value of supporting European allies or nationalist movements in terms of global strategy. There was no more important confrontation of these divergent interests than in the populous and wealthy Dutch East Indies.

Everything depended on United States policy. It is impossible to determine all of the calculations that convinced the United States that its interests were best served by supporting Indonesian independence. It took more than three years to reach that determination, and it had to be made against the certainty of Dutch resentments. But the Netherlands had a poor bargaining stance because of its size, geographical location, and dependence on American aid. On the other hand, an independent and friendly Indonesia represented an important addition to American strength in Indonesia itself and throughout the Third World. In effect, the Dutch did their best to capitalize on American anti-Communism, which had been aroused by the Ukrainian complaint in 1946. But the Indonesian nationalist leaders were not Communists, and their suppression of domestic Communists convinced the State Department of their reliability. The decision in favor of the Indonesian cause was taken. The one key outsider entered the conflict and the outcome reflected the new alignment.

On the surface, the Security Council took the action that compelled the Dutch to abandon their empire. But the voice of the Security Council was identical with that of the United States. It should be recalled that in 1949 the United States dominated the Security Council. There did not exist there, or in the General Assembly, the majorities that have later endorsed anticolonial policies. Without unequivocal support by the United States of the Indonesian side, no anti-Dutch resolutions could have been adopted. British, French, and other sympathizers with the Dutch could not afford to provoke American hostility on an issue of this magnitude. Successful socialization, then, was achieved when the United States joined forces with the Indonesians. At best, the United Nations was a convenient instrument for the expression of American policy.

Anticolonialism dramatically shows the importance of getting outside help if a strategy of socialization is to be successful. Consider such issues as Apartheid, South West Africa, Rhodesia, Angola, and Mozambique. Relations between the parties have been unremittingly hostile, and the black African states do not have the requisite material means to impose their will on their enemies. In these circumstances, socialization to the United Nations is inevitable, as is the appearance of failure by the organization. With monotonous regularity, condemnatory resolutions are passed in the General Assembly and the Security Council, sanctions are recommended, a United Nations trusteeship established over South West Africa, and so forth. Nothing changes. Actually, nothing *can* change until or unless there is a lowering in the level of hostility (which use of the United Nations helps to prevent) or a change in the balance of forces. The objective of the anticolonialists is to modify the latter by mobilizing the United Nations on their side. This they have done, but the strategy contains inherent limitations. On the one side, there is the absolute determination of Rhodesia, Portugal, and South Africa to maintain their policies and positions, and they possess the means to do so. On the other hand, no single African state or combination of such states possesses sufficient power to deal with any of these problems in the manner of India when she "solved" the Goan question. From their position of weakness, therefore, they *must* involve other states in the disputes. All of the maneuvers at the United Nations are designed to do this. They cannot succeed unless key states such as the United States and Britain modify their policies in favor of the Africans. No amount of United Nations resolutions (during the 1972 session of the General Assembly *ten* resolutions were adopted on Apartheid alone) can force the Africans' enemies to accept their guilt and act accordingly or compel Britain or the United States to cooperate. Successful socialization, then, is always dependent upon *significant* external support. Its absence has been the Achilles heel of the African strategy.

There is obviously a considerable gap between the support implied by votes cast at the United Nations and the actual or potential impact these exert upon the behavior of states. The Afro-Asians mobilize overwhelming majorities which include the most powerful countries in the world, yet their victories are not converted into the kinds of actions that would permit the realization of their goals. It is one thing to force a "consensus" against colonialism and racism and a very different thing to compel the United States *not* to buy chrome from Rhodesia even after sanctions have been recommended by the Security Council. More to the point, such inconsistencies in behavior help to demonstrate the absence of a hard relationship between control of United Nations majorities and the aims to be advanced. The political expediency underlying voting at the United Nations has its own rationale, which may have only a vague relationship to substantive policy considerations. This explains why Indonesia won without an anti-colonial majority in the United Nations, while black Africa is continually frustrated despite its overwhelming domination of the organization.

The United Nations as Surrogate: The Congo

It is clearly impossible to detail the complexities and ramifications of the Congo crisis in a few pages. Our analysis will therefore concentrate on strategic aspects, especially during the first year, which culminated in the deaths of Patrice Lumumba and United Nations Secretary-General Dag Hammarskjöld. By that time, the outlines of the "solution" were established, although the operation continued for three more years.

Superficially, the Congo represents as clear a success for the politics of socialization as does Indonesia. Circumstances surrounding the original appeal for help and the ultimate results seem to support this view. The Belgian grant of independence to the Congo on June 30, 1960, was followed nearly immediately by riots, internal insurrection, and Belgian military measures to restore "law and order" and protect European civilians. Secession in mineral-rich Katanga Province by Moise Tshombe threatened to deprive the infant state of its major source of revenue and resources. In these circumstances, Premier Lumumba appealed for help. He asked *both* superpowers, the United States and the Soviet Union, to save his regime. Neither found it expedient to respond, and the embattled leader applied directly to the United Nations. This was a classic attempt by a weak victim to socialize a dispute in order to change the odds in his favor. Lumumba wanted the United Nations—or Russia, or the United States—to expel the Belgians and crush the Katanga secession. We know, of course, that the United Nations *did* respond, and eventually the objectives of the Congolese government were achieved. However, the issue is extremely complex and the comparison with Indonesia indicates important differences.

In Indonesia, the Sukarno government's goal of independence from the Netherlands ultimately succeeded, primarily because of American willingness to stand against its European ally. After the republican government convincingly demonstrated the anti-Communist character of its nationalism, the United States concluded that Indonesian independence was compatible with America's global foreign policy. The result was profoundly satisfactory to the new government. In the Congo, however, the external assistance was not provided directly by a particular state. Instead, the *United Nations*, as its role was defined by Dag Hammarskjöld, undertook the rescue mission. In this case, the interests of the third party which inevitably accompany its intervention in a dispute were primarily those of Hammarskjöld rather than the more normal national objectives, thereby complicating analysis. However, compatibility with foreign policies was always a critical component.

At the outset, it must be observed that the motives of the Secretary-General differed substantially from those of the Lumumba government. The latter wanted military aid to be used against his domestic and foreign enemies, and he would persist in this demand. Lumumba's approach coincided with the views of the Soviet Union, which nevertheless was unwilling to risk direct intervention. Hammarskjöld, on the other hand, had a completely different conception of how a United Nations force would be used. He told the Security Council that such a force would contribute to ultimate withdrawal of the Belgians and unification of the Congo by restoring order until the Congolese government could deal with internal problems. The force would act only in self-defense and would not interfere in Congolese politics. These views were more compatible with American foreign policy, which would not have permitted the United Nations to become a substitute for Russian troops. The Soviet Union agreed because there was no other realistic alternative. Furthermore, the Secretary-General perceived the United Nations role in terms of "preventive diplomacy." According to this concept, in an area of potential collision between the superpowers United Nations peace-keeping forces would insulate and contain the conflict. With both superpowers willing to acquiesce in a United Nations role, Hammarskjöld seized the opportunity to make the Congo *the* test of preventive diplomacy.

We have observed that socialization is a strategy based on weakness, and that this fact frequently proves fatal. But when aid is obtained, the weaker party may be forced to accept the interests of its savior. In this case, the conflicting motives of Lumumba and Hammarskjöld resulted in disaster for the premier. The force did *not* move against the Belgians. Furthermore, Lumumba's demand that the United Nations force act against Tshombe was denied on the basis of a recommendation by Ralph Bunche. Instead Hammarskjöld negotiated with Tshombe for the peaceful entry of United Nations troops into Katanga. When the Secretary-General refused to permit Lumumba's government to use the United Nations as a means of imposing its authority in Elisabethville, the split between the two men became irreconcilable. From Lumumba's perspective, his demands for help were not being answered. The Belgians remained, many of them transferring to Katanga, where Tshombe used them, mercenaries, and funds from the Belgian cartel, Union Minière du Haut-Congo, to solidify his position. Hammarskjöld's negotiation with Tshombe appeared to confer status on the secessionist state.

Perceiving his "helpers" as enemies, Lumumba once again sought external assistance. The United States approved and supported the Secretary-General's approach, so that source of support for Lumumba was foreclosed. Russia, however, was sharply critical of the Secretary-General, and Lumumba asked for Soviet assistance. Direct military intervention by the Russians was still out of the question. Nevertheless, they wished to strengthen Lumumba's government. They responded by providing some one hundred trucks, about thirty transport planes, and two hundred technicians. Theoretically, this assistance would enable the Congolese government to carry out the same mission that had been entrusted to the United Nations in the Congo.

However, this development produced a direct confrontation. At stake for Hammarskjöld was the concept of preventive diplomacy. Soviet support for Lumumba threatened to cause a Western reaction which could doom the insulating role of the United Nations. Lumumba, of course, was concerned only about *his* needs, and the Russians were unwilling to concede that they were barred from aiding the Congo government in its United Nations-sanctioned objectives of eliminating the Belgian "aggressors" and unifying the country.

Lumumba's actions contributed to a new governmental crisis. On September 5, 1960, President Joseph Kasa-Vubu dismissed the premier, who responded by firing the president. Cold War lines were now sharply drawn. East and West each had its man in Leopoldville. Rival delegations came to the Security Council where neither was seated. Subsequently, the West successfully utilized the politics of status in the General Assembly, which voted to accept the credentials of President Kasa-Vubu's representatives. In the Security Council, the fragile consensus was broken as the West attempted to have a resolution passed that would enshrine the principle of preventive diplomacy by deciding that "no assistance for military purposes be sent to the Congo except as part of the United Nations actions." The Soviets used their veto and the West then took advantage of Uniting for Peace Resolution procedures to bring the issue to the General Assembly, where, as anticipated, a majority supported the West. As between Kasa-Vubu and Lumumba, the *United Nations* clearly preferred Kasa-Vubu. Lumumba, after all, had demanded the ouster of United Nations troops and had violated preventive diplomacy by obtaining Russian support. It is not surprising, therefore, that the Secretariat acted in a manner that proved fatal to Lumumba. Two decisive measures were taken. The airport, which was vital for continued Soviet supplies, was closed to all but United Nations traffic. Second, the government radio, which was being used by both sides, but most damagingly by Lumumba, who was arousing the people against the United Nations, was seized by United Nations troops and denied to both Kasa-Vubu and Lumumba. These decisions were made in the field by Andrew W. Cordier, an American aide to Hammarskjöld, who later defended his deputy. It must be noted that United Nations impartiality destroyed Lumumba, who was denied the opportunity to reach the people, whereas Kasa-Vubu used the friendly transmitters in neighboring Congo—Brazzaville while Tshombe broadcast over Radio Elisabethville. Troops loyal to Kasa-Vubu besieged Lumumba and captured him. The United Nations declined to "intervene" by liberating the premier, who was turned over to the untender mercies of his archenemy Moise Tshombe. Shortly afterward, according to a United Nations investigation, Lumumba was murdered by Tshombe-hired mercenaries.

In the period that followed, the United Nations was authorized and did use force against Tshombe and his European supporters, and Hammarskjöld himself was added to the victims of the operation when his plane crashed en route to a conference with Moise Tshombe. By this time, the ultimate results of United Nations intervention were apparent.

Although Lumumba's vice-premier, Antoine Gizenga, attempted to continue as Lumumba's heir, pro-Western regimes imposed their authority on the country, and U Thant presided over the liquidation of the United Nations force on June 30, 1964. Ironically, nine days later, Moise Tshombe, responsible directly or indirectly for the deaths of both Lumumba and Hammarskjöld, became premier. Belgium and the United States now openly provided military aid to Tshombe against the insurgents, and even launched a paratrooper rescue mission for civilians in the Stanleyville area. Russia and militant African states protested futilely in the Security Council against this "aggression."

The Congo operation has been the subject of controversial interpretations. Some have contended that because of the effect of Hammarskjöld's interpretation of his authority and the obvious American satisfaction with results the entire operation was a Western conspiracy. This view is buttressed by the Secretary-General's reliance on key American aides, especially Ralph Bunche and Andrew Cordier, who made crucial decisions in the Congo. The attack on the Secretary-General by the Soviet Union added fuel to the charges. Defenders of Hammarskjöld have made just as extreme claims. United Nations apologists insist that the Secretary-General saved the Congo from complete chaos, and that his preventive diplomacy averted a probable war between the West and the Soviets.

This controversy is not likely to be resolved in a few brief statements, but it is possible to make an assessment of the relationships between strategies and results.

For the Lumumba government, socialization to the United Nations was a complete failure. It resulted in the dispatch of a force that was outside the control of the Congolese authorities and did not function to achieve its ends. While it may be argued that the Congo eventually obtained the removal of Belgian troops and unification of the country, Lumumba, who personified the government, was overthrown and murdered, partially because of United Nations action and inaction. It cannot be argued either that Hammarskjöld succeeded in his intention to strengthen the doctrine of preventive diplomacy. To appreciate this, it is unnecessary to accept or reject Soviet charges that he was a pawn of American imperialism. The *effect* of his actions was to contribute to the loss of a Soviet toe-hold in central Africa. Thus, the trend toward strengthening the Secretary-General's use of peace-keeping forces for preventive diplomacy was abruptly reversed. In effect, the Soviet proposal for a troika to replace a single Secretary-General was a means of extending the veto to any operations administered by the Secretariat. Never again would the Soviet Union entrust the United Nations with a significant operation unless the original authorization could be counter-manded if a Great Power subsequently disapproved of policy decisions. This was the death knell of preventive diplomacy, whose funeral was confirmed by the debate on the Congo-created assessments crisis.

It is rather more difficult to contradict the exaggerated claim that the United Nations force prevented war between the United States and the Soviet Union. The war did not take place, and, for some, this is all the proof that is necessary. It is doubtful that there was ever any danger of such a war. All the advantages lay with the West. It is scarcely credible that the Russians would have risked a thermonuclear war to pre-serve their brief and tenuous position in the Congo. They could reasonably hope that the Lumumba government would emerge intact and strengthened, thereby providing an oppor-tunity for an extension of Soviet influence. When their expecta-tions were shattered by the demise of Lumumba, they made no significant effort to engage the West by all-out support to Antoine Gizenga. If they wanted to risk war over the Congo, they could have responded militarily to Belgian-American aid for Tshombe or by sending troops to support insurgents following the departure of the United Nations. They did not, obviously, because the risks of such a policy far outweighed the rewards.

To sum up, socialization was a success for the Congo, but a disaster for the government that made the original appeal. Another important casualty of the operation was the concept of preventive diplomacy, which was discredited because the *effects* of the intervention favored the West. By design or not, the principal winners in the Congo crisis were the United States and various allies and African states that opposed a Soviet presence in the Congo, and also President Kasa-Vubu and other politicians associated with him. The losers were the socialist bloc and various anti-Western Third World states, Premier Lumumba and his associates, and, finally, Dag Hammarskjöld and the concept of preventive diplomacy.

Conclusion

It becomes immediately apparent that conflict socialization is a strategy of indeterminate boundaries. Socializing disputes to the United Nations often occurs in combination with other strategies. Indonesian and Algerian rebels hoped to enhance the legal status of their movements in addition to achieving the help required to expel Dutch and French troops. Afro-Asians employ the forums of the United Nations to embarrass South Africa and Portugal while at the same time they advance the legal status of various dependencies and seek outside intervention on behalf of oppressed blacks in these areas.

Precision is further undermined when the strategy is judged against the varied motives of surrogates who bring complaints to the United Nations. It is difficult, for example, to distinguish the intentions of the Soviet Union to embarrass the West over its policies on Indonesia by having the Ukraine raise the issue before the Security Council from the socialization the action implied.

Conflict socialization to the United Nations is always a reflection of existing levels of hostility. From either perspective in a dispute, use or nonuse of the United Nations as a weapon involves risks. A weak opponent seeking to involve outsiders in this manner must calculate the improbable advantages of publicizing its grievances against the added hostility this act is likely to engender in its stronger adversary. If the stakes are not total, resort to the United Nations may very well jeopardize larger interests. Indeed the strategy of socialization requires a high level of hostility. Increasing the antagonism of France or the Netherlands became relatively unimportant when judged against the survival needs of Algerian and Indonesian revolutionaries. When Iran felt that its very existence was threatened by the presence of Russian troops on its soil, concern with further inflaming Soviet-Iranian relations was cast aside in favor of socializing the dispute. Panama, too, had to weigh the advantages of seeking help at the United Nations against the consequences of deepening the rift between herself and the United States.

At best the strategy involves uncertain calculations. There is, for example, no clear causal relationship between socializing specifically to the United Nations and aid that may later materialize. The most one can say is that United Nations exposure may stimulate interest which invites support otherwise denied under less visible circumstances. Always this will depend upon the constantly shifting pattern of external interests and the responses these produce. Similarly, no connection exists between the merits of particular grievances and the consideration they receive at the United Nations or the support this induces. Again, external interests dictate whether helplessness achieves a hearing and, more importantly, if it is overcome.

Perhaps the most salient feature of the strategy is that it is grounded in weakness. Success is therefore unlikely. Nothing in the history of international organization suggests that states will be restrained in their use of superior power because of moral or legal pressures. Such considerations are equally ineffective in creating obligations for third parties to intercede on behalf of their beleaguered neighbors. In short, the socializer's weakness remains essentially fixed in a world where variations in strength occur against the background of sovereignty. These observations hold even when, as in the Congo, national interests are somewhat obscured because states permit the United Nations to function in their behalf.

6 *A Dangerous Place*

Supporters and most critics of the United Nations begin with the same premises. Apologists for the organization magnify its "victories" or assert, with little or no real evidence, the beneficial effect that the organization has had on the resolution of disputes. Critics find explanations for "failures." They demand reforms, blame a few maverick states for defying the principles of the Charter and world opinion, or lament a more general blindness to the need for world order. Many find a vague satisfaction in the simple knowledge that the United Nations exists and may contribute somehow to international peace. Others avoid serious thinking about the effectiveness of the organization by emphasizing its peripheral activities in the social and economic areas.[1] Whether the assessment is optimistic or pessimistic, there is a basis for dialogue among experts grounded in common devotion to the ideals of the Charter. The United Nations either is already or can become the one last hope for the survival of mankind. Not surprisingly, all analysis proceeds from an unflagging acceptance and endorsement of what the organization *ought* to do and moves inexorably into how it might do it better.

Herein lies the fundamental fallacy. In order for the United Nations to function as intended, it requires a sense of community, some general consensus regarding the behavioral norms and guidelines expressed in the Charter and the processes that the organization brings into play. The United Nations, however, exists in an environment distinguished by the absence of common values and characterized by disunity. Thus, just as a domestic legislature or other instrument of conflict resolution operating without a sense of community will be used to advance the conflicting aims of warring factions, so too will the United Nations be employed for the conflict purposes of member states. In effect, what the organization ought to do becomes irrelevant. The only important questions concern the nature, effectiveness, and consequences of the various conflict strategies that are used.

Failure to see this has contributed to a proliferation of misleading assumptions and confused analogies. The United Nations is constantly wrapped in the mythology of democracy.[2] General Assembly debates are viewed as replications of the process of coalition-building and compromise which occurs in the legislatures of Western democracies.[3] The superficial resemblance of the organization's structure to the division of legislative, executive, and judicial functions invokes the separation-of-powers concept that occupies so prominent a place in democratic theory. Voting and majority rule, together with the fact that for years the Western powers were apparently willing to accept majority decisions while the Communists opposed and rejected them, reenforced the analogy. Additional reference points become available in tried and tested methods of conflict resolution and in more recent psychological models of conflict reduction. The organization is viewed as a "safety valve," or as a rug under which unpleasant and possibly dangerous contingencies may be swept.[4] The physical presence of the world's diplomats in New York is said to provide a continuing communication link between many sources of possible unrest. Even when the diplomats are calling one another names, benefits are seen to mount. According to the fashionable literature of the day, ventilating frustration and aggression is a healthy form of catharsis. Thus, name-calling at the United Nations becomes a hybrid form of encounter therapy and contributes no less to a healthy world than it does in its more familiar setting to healthy individuals.

From this perspective, it is easy to understand why scholars and casual observers alike are convinced that despite serious shortcomings the United Nations exerts a positive influence on world peace. It becomes impossible to look behind the exaggerated claims and the search for hidden benefits to see the real dangers that employment of the United Nations for conflict purposes has upon the achievement of these very ideals. Completely obscured is the fact that use of the United Nations as a battleground, like other hostile acts, contributes to the intensity of disputes and diminishes possibilities for peace.

Principles

A perverse yet simple truth is that world politics is very much like a jungle. National behavior is fundamentally grounded in self-interest and survival. Obsession with the latter imparts to the nation-state system not only the law of the jungle but its morality as well. No restrictions can exist on either the use or level of violence when a nation feels threatened. Inevitably errors in assessing real dangers will occur, raising the possibility of premature or even unnecessary violence. In addition, self-interest—often poorly perceived—is the only effective curb on the appetite of a powerful state bent on a course of conquest and destruction. Thus, although the world is not in a perpetually convulsive state and nations do not always behave voraciously, war has become a permanent feature of international relations.

Under these circumstances, there can be no more important task than the establishment of acceptable boundaries for national behavior. For centuries statesmen, jurists, and political philosophers have been preoccupied with this problem. International organization represents to many the most promising advance in the development of universally accepted norms of conduct. According to the Charter of the United Nations, the members agree to settle their disputes peacefully[5] and "to refrain in their international relations from the threat or use of force against the territorial integrity or political independence of any state. . . ."[6] Furthermore, states in dispute are obligated to employ specific peaceful procedures in order to settle their differences.[7] These and other clauses in the Charter establish theoretical moral and legal constraints. Membership in the United Nations implies that nations will modify their behavior to accord with these standards. It is argued that even deviants will be influenced because they are compelled to justify policies by reference to Charter principles.[8] In short, states functioning within "the world of the Charter" will pursue their interests according to rules and guidelines that will inhibit their ability to threaten international peace and security.

This expectation has not been fulfilled. National perceptions of self-interest produce the necessary rationalizations. What we have witnessed at the United Nations is the spectacle of *all* states defending *all* policies by reference to Charter principles. There is no single instance of any state acknowledging that it has violated the Charter. In every dispute, the parties pick and choose appropriate clauses and frequently use the same ones against one another. The only consistency is in the search for legal and moral justification for national policy.

From this maze of conflicting interpretations, majorities determine the applicability of particular principles to particular disputes. Theoretically this should make possible the construction of a hierarchy of values. Actually this has not occurred. Majorities support the right of self-determination against the principle of noninterference in the domestic affairs of member states on one set of issues and reverse this order of importance on others. The right of military reprisal is accepted in some cases, denied in others. Attacks on the territorial integrity of member states based on claims of individual or collective self-defense may be either ignored or criticized. All of these decisions are reached politically. Those who can dominate the organization can and do stress any available principle in any dispute and abandon or ignore the same principle in another case. There is no right of self-determination for Ibos in Nigeria, but that right is sacred for Bantus in South Africa. The United Nations condemns Israeli use of force in response to guerrilla incursions and implicitly sanctions the assertion of "belligerent rights" by Arab states. Soviet attacks on Hungary and Czechoslovakia are violations of the Charter, but American interventions in the Caribbean are not. Some states can never be right. No matter what arguments they use, the United Nations will always find for their opponents. Even when they are the obvious victims of an attack, such as the murdered Israeli Olympic team, resolutions are passed that implicitly condemn the dead for having provoked their murder.[9] Under these circumstances, losers are not likely to endorse the priority of values which they conclude have been hypocritically formulated and inconsistently applied. Neither can the winners abstractly support principles which remain appropriate only so long as they appear serviceable.

Ironically, therefore, time-honored principles which were

incorporated into the Charter in the belief that their institutionalization would exert greater moral restraint on international politics become debased and lose their influence. They
are no longer above the fight. Instead the principles become
part of the weaponry of nations in conflict. The ad hoc, obviously opportunistic resort to Charter principles cynically
destroys any confidence in the very real role that such ideals
could have in restraining national excesses. Man's slow progress toward universally accepted norms to which all may have
appeal is reversed. The world becomes more dangerous.

On individual disputes, the dangers are more concrete.
Every issue raised in the United Nations is clothed in the
ideological language of the Charter. Differences become matters of principle. Positions are based on moral rectitude, publicly expressed, and frequently endorsed by majority votes.
The side that has captured the high ground is trapped into
demanding nothing less than complete surrender. Monopolization of morality makes for intransigence because of the impossibility of compromising with sin. On the other hand, the
losing side defends its position by similar allusions to the ideals
of the Charter. Its self-righteousness is strengthened by the
necessity of defending national policies in moral terms.
Furthermore, defeats at the United Nations are seen as con-
spiratorial attacks upon national honor, thereby arousing
chauvinistic reactions. Both become hardened in their positions. The victorious state is emboldened by majority support,
and the loser embittered by injustice.

Talk

Conflict-resolution theory stresses the importance of talk in the
solution of problems. Disputes are defined, areas of disagree-

ment are clarified, parties advance bargaining positions, the negotiability of demands is established, mutually acceptable language for inclusion in agreements is settled upon. To some experts, all this and more is seen to flow from an initial willingness to air differences at the United Nations. Since many disputes are grounded in ignorance, communications specialists suggest that the avalanche of words in the Assembly and Council chambers reduces tension by eliminating uncertainties and baring national motives.[10]

Others believe that talk, even when it is bitter and insulting, is good because it is seen as an alternative to fighting. The least inhibited language in the annals of diplomacy is recorded at the United Nations. The resources of every tongue are plumbed to evoke its most colorful insults. Meticulous research exposes cultural sensitivities to demeaning attacks upon the precious and the sacred. Diplomacy, traditionally associated with civility and courtliness, is turned on its head. Ventilation theorists allege that even these angry orations are beneficial as a means of displacing physical violence.[11] Implicit in this belief is the idea there exists a hierarchy of methods of combat in international relations, and that states, having the opportunity to fight with words, will eschew bullets and atomic bombs. As *the* great forum for expressing national fears, frustrations, and bitterness, the United Nations dampens and detours animosities that might otherwise erupt in war. A common rationality is assumed about at least two things: all states accept discord as a normal part of the international game; all the players would rather play at a reduced cost to themselves. In addition, individual aggression is considered analogous to aggressive behavior among nations. The organization is a giant barroom in which drunks argue incessantly, but never, or rarely, go outside to fight.

Some who may or may not accept the premise that vituperation contributes to international peace, discount the importance of the public record. Extreme postures are part of the ritual of public diplomacy. National leaders must adopt heroic stands and denounce their opponents with appropriate vigor. The game is understood by all the participants. Descriptions of Jews as Nazis, Russians as godless, totalitarian oppressors, Americans as capitalist imperialists, South Africans as inhuman racists, Chinese as the "new" barbarians are presumed to be shrugged off by thick-skinned diplomats. But away from the public rostrums important discussions occur in the privacy of lounges, bars, restaurants, and the intimacy of small parties. These are the famous "corridors" in which the serious business of settling international disputes takes place.[12] The world's diplomats mingle in a way that reduces fears based on ignorance. Personal friendships develop. Isolation is broken down, especially for new states, which become socialized into the ways, manners, and values of international discourse.[13]

Whether the emphasis is on the salutary effects of debate at the United Nations or on the relative unimportance of the public record, the insistence that talk is connected in some way to the accomplishment of the organization's stated objectives does not vary. In either case, we are misled. Talk is meaningful only when the discussants are interested in settling problems. Confusion arises from the tendency to identify debate at the United Nations with the purposes of the organization rather than with the objectives of those who use it.

We have in preceding chapters demonstrated that the United Nations is an arena for combat in which the participants employ various strategies for the achievement of conflict objectives. It is not surprising, therefore, that talk at the United Nations is unrelated to peaceful settlement. Issues are not narrowly defined. An agenda item concerned with financing assistance to Palestinian refugees becomes the platform for an attack on Zionist imperialism.[14] The 1948 coup in Czechoslovakia is the pretext for a wide-ranging assault on alleged Soviet responsibility for World War II and the enslavement of all Eastern Europeans. American intervention in the Dominican Republic or the Bay of Pigs invasion is made part of a generalized attack on capitalism and neocolonialism. These and any number of other examples must be contrasted with the use of talk under other circumstances where it is used to remove extraneous factors from the center of controversy and pave the way to eventual settlement.

Since no one can be excluded from United Nations debate, extremists are likely to establish its tone. In many of the Arab-Israeli confrontations, the Saudi Arabian delegate, whose country was at best secondarily involved in the conflict, led the attack. It is likely that Saudi Arabia, in the United Nations, used the Six-Day War, at least in part, in order to advance its position in the Arab world at the expense of Egypt by forcing the debate to a peak of extremism.[15] Albania has served the same function on behalf of the Chinese Communists by pressing Cold War issues beyond where the Soviet Union might have preferred.[16] On the Algerian issue in 1957, Egyptian grievances against France governed the character of the discussion. We are never quite sure if socialist states and those of black Africa are referring to the same thing when they depict conditions in southern Africa and call for corrective measures. Neither is the actual nature of the differences that exist between indigenous populations in these areas and their white "masters" clearly defined in the arguments on self-determination and racism. In short, debate acquires an escalatory quality because of the imprecise relationship of actual conflicts to what is being said and the varied motives of those who are doing the talking.

Clearly not all delegates are constantly engaged in diatribes at the United Nations. The ideas of "neutrals" are also part of the record. Some states, in fact, may be counted on to attempt consistently to inject a spirit of moderation into the discussions. However, in the United Nations arena the impact of such statements is likely to be marginal. One must recognize the critical distinction between the contribution of compromise in a conflict setting as opposed to a negotiating situation. In the latter, third-party assistance is invited and given weight based on its utility in narrowing differences. At the United Nations, however, where the debate is part of combat, nonpartisan expressions are likely to be considered as either hostile or irrelevant. "Neutrals" are usually ignored or denounced for their failure to give unqualified support to a position.

The plight of the Secretary-General is similar to that of the neutrals. Secretary-General Dag Hammarskjöld did his best to use his office to stress quiet diplomacy. By interpreting broadly his power to bring threatening situations before the Security Council, he reasoned that he could investigate and, if possible, mediate quarrels at an early stage.* He hoped that his office would be accepted by members for its disinterested devotion to international peace. Hammarskjöld's approach enjoyed a brief, limited success, largely because it was in the tradition of acceptable third-party intervention. That is, he depended on his reputation for impartiality and the willingness of the parties to invite his help. The fatal flaw is that the Secretary-General cannot be separated entirely from the politi-

---

* Upon his reelection in 1957, Hammarskjöld said: ". . . On the other hand, I believe that it is in keeping with the philosophy of the Charter that the Secretary General should be expected to act also without . . . guidance, should this appear to him necessary in order to help in filling any vacuum that may appear in the system which the Charter and traditional diplomacy provide for the safeguarding of peace and security. See Wilder Foote, ed., *Dag Hammarskjöld: Servant of Peace* (New York: Harper and Row, 1962), p. 150.

cal organs. He must carry out the directives of the Security Council and General Assembly. Inevitably, no matter how circumspect he may be, the need to function as an executive officer for operations that have been decided upon politically will bring about a clash with states opposing a particular initiative. As a result, the indispensable reputation for nonpartisanship is tarnished, and the Secretary-General is identified with the policies of sponsoring states. Trygve Lie's usefulness was destroyed because of his role in supporting the United Nations in Korea, and Hammarskjöld himself was in a similar position once the Soviet Union decided that his direction of the Congo force coincided with Western political objectives. In short, while Hammarskjöld's concept of his role was a laudable effort to depoliticize disputes, the Secretary-General cannot escape the close connection with the other organs of the United Nations.

Words and War

Students from nearly every discipline have been fascinated and intrigued by the phenomenon of war. The search for causes embraces the thinking of psychologists and philosophers, economists and scientists, historians and sociologists, anthropologists and political scientists. Literature on the subject is at once overwhelming and contradictory. War is or is not an inevitable consequence of man's nature, of God's will, of the struggle of nation-states for power, of economic competition, of ignorance, of deprivation and degradation. Theoretical formulations are endless. We need not join the quarrel to observe that modern war is a special category of aggression and violence that is intimately linked to the character that sovereignty and nationalism impart to international society. Conflict is a normal part of international behavior. Its causes may be elusive, but we are sure of one thing—it happens. Nationalism legitimizes slaughter. Killing in defense of the nation is a high moral duty, and those who do not shoulder it are ostracized, banished, imprisoned, and shot. War-makers and fighters embody the noblest virtues of the nation and are their greatest heroes. War is universal. Size, wealth, location, religion, ideology, levels of technology do not affect it. Small nations fight as ferociously as do the superpowers. The world's richest countries kill as exuberantly as the poorest. There is no discernible difference in the martial behavior of democracies or dictatorships. Countries fight where they can—at sea, in the air, in jungles, deserts, mountains, or plains. Stable and unstable regimes go to war. International links of brotherhood, civilization, class, religion, race, or ideology are no deterrents. When national battle flags are unfurled, Moslems will kill Moslems, blacks will annihilate blacks, Communists will battle Communists, workers will destroy other workers. Man's incessant struggle to harness nature has produced technology that has been employed in the service of war. Unlocking the mysteries of the atom led to the bombing of Hiroshima and Nagasaki. There is no reason to believe that there are any limits to the level of violence that nation-states are prepared to inflict on one another.

It is ridiculous to suggest that war, which has successfully resisted every conceivable constraint, is somehow rendered less likely by verbal belligerence. If this were true, statesmen in threatened countries would have been reassured by every Hitlerian tirade or speech by Mussolini. Nasserian promises to annihilate Israel would be greeted with relief by Jews in the Middle East. Even to raise these images is to demonstrate that they are irrational. Whereas a particular diplomat may experience a certain psychological satisfaction in venting his hatred, it is obviously far-fetched to assume that the cause of international peace has been advanced. Use of the United Nations for strategic reasons guarantees that debate will be used to *support* military activity. Thus, a decision to fight may be accompanied by a diplomatic offensive at the United Nations. Debates on Korea and Vietnam were used to justify military action, and discussions of Berlin, Suez, and the Cuban missile crisis were part of the preparation for war. Can anyone seriously contend that the angry oratory of Arab or black African delegates *reduces* their willingness to use or support military approaches against Israelis or Portuguese colonialists? Do Egypt or Israel disarm because they vent their hatreds at the United Nations? Did Khrushchev order tank commanders in Budapest to hold their fire because the issue was being aired in the Security Council and General Assembly? Or, on the other side, is it really credible that the United States decision to condemn the Soviet Union verbally on Hungary was a meaningful alternative to going to war? Is there a single example of a state that preferred to go to war choosing instead to talk at the United Nations? The answer to all of these questions is "no." Why, then, are so many comforted by the thought that United Nations debate is healthy and advances the cause of peace? The fundamental and recurring error stems from confusing the objectives of the organization with those of its members. Again, if one asks, "*Who* brings issues and *why?*" the misunderstanding evaporates. Talk at the United Nations is seen within the context of conflict, and its intimate relationship to violence is apparent. It is no longer possible to associate United Nations debate with negotiations and peaceful settlement. In this arena talk is a weapon, and it is used in order to achieve national objectives by any means, including war. Furthermore, verbal belligerence intensifies hostility, thereby reducing the possibility of averting war.

If public diplomatic postures are dangerous, private "corridor diplomacy" is, at best, of dubious worth. After sixteen years of parties and civilized discourse at dinners and in other congenial surroundings, Russians and Americans nearly destroyed each other and much of the rest of the world during the Cuban missile crisis. It is doubtful, too, that delegates from black African states are less incensed by American and British trade with South Africa or Rhodesia because they are treated with elaborate courtesy at dinner parties by their Anglo-Saxon counterparts. The link between personal friendships and foreign policy is tenuous or nonexistent. Henry Kissinger made no secret of his personal admiration for North Vietnam's Le Duc Tho, but the private relationship did not influence bargaining positions or the decision to bomb Hanoi and Haiphong when it was decided that Tho was not "serious."* Similarly, no amount of drinks, dinners, and quiet laughs will offset the public positions taken on issues considered important by the diplomats. In short, there may be a certain desirable impact of having diplomats interact socially; the public functions of ambassadors throughout the world are testimony to the general recognition of this need. But it is also clear that individual charm and urbanity are comparatively superficial assets and will not offset the hostility engendered by substantive policies. At the United Nations, more so than in any of the world's capitals, the advantages of social intimacy

* At a press conference on December 16, 1972, Professor Kissinger noted that "we will not be charmed into an agreement until its conditions are right." *New York Times*, December 17, 1972. The Christmas bombings of Hanoi and Haiphong followed a week later. In a televised interview after the settlement, Dr. Kissinger said: "Le Duc Tho is an impressive man. . . . He's a man of great theoretical interests and we used to joke with each other about after the peace we'd have exchanged professorships—he at Harvard and I in Hanoi." *New York Times*, February 2, 1973.

are constantly dissipated by public postures. It is not, after all, an elaborate private club dedicated to harmony and quiet rapport among its members.

Implicit in the argument concerning corridors is that public acrimony should be discounted because serious negotiations take place in private. It is, of course, true that when diplomats negotiate seriously, they do so in secret. But there is no reason to believe that they will be *more* likely to negotiate because they have engaged in public polemics. The only reasonable basis for the assumption that the corridors are constantly busy with secret parlays among the apparent warriors is that they are provided with a *place* where they may talk. We suggest that when states are serious about settling problems, they find suitable sites. Embassies, headquarters of regional organizations, ad hoc meeting places, neutral settings are always available. And when they do utilize any negotiating environment, they do not befoul it by using it for public insult and recrimination.

To this point, we have stressed the minimal relationship between talk at the United Nations and the settlement of international disputes. Our purpose is not simply to confirm the widely held belief that the organization is ineffectual. United Nations debate *does* have an impact on conflicts. Issues raised are made more difficult to resolve peacefully, and relations among states are embittered.

Debate at the United Nations violates every precept of conflict resolution. Areas of disagreement are not narrowed; they are deliberately widened. Embarrassment politics, for example, exploits even nonissues in order to humiliate opponents. Every conceivable vulnerability is probed and publicized. The most extreme positions and spokesmen become part of the dialogue. Nations are reenforced in the view that the aggressive intentions of the attackers are limitless.

Ambassador Henry Cabot Lodge, commenting on the
Soviet intention to veto a resolution to entrust the Guatemalan complaint to the Organization of American States, said:

> Why does the representative of the Soviet Union, a country
> thousands of miles away from here, undertake to veto a
> move like that? How can this action of his possibly not
> fail to make unbiased observers throughout the world come
> to the conclusion that the Soviet Union has designs on the
> American hemisphere? . . . I say to the representative of
> the Soviet Union, stay out of this hemisphere and do not
> try to start your plans and your conspiracies over here.[17]

The same questions had to be asked by Russians concerning
American interventions on issues in Eastern Europe. The
answers were probably that they seized opportunities to embarrass one another. However, more sinister conclusions may be
reached by policy-makers. Particular leaders may be reenforced
in their views concerning the total hostility of their enemies.
They can seize upon initiatives at the United Nations to
"prove" that the other side has real objectives in areas where
they may be simply doing nothing more than taking advantage of open diplomacy. With no facet of foreign policy
immune from public attack, it becomes more difficult for hostile states to determine the issues where one side may be willing
to acknowledge that the vital interests of the other should
prevail. By thus *enlarging* differences, United Nations talk
provides ammunition to decision-makers whose interests coincide with a more extensive conflict. The paths to Peking and
Moscow are made more rocky by the verbal attacks at the
United Nations. Hostile talk not only reflects an existing level
of hostility, it serves to perpetuate it. Although eventually
some effort at conciliation may have occurred, the decades of
extremist public attack made that step far more difficult.
      Insults may not in themselves provoke wars directly, but

they contribute to an atmosphere that is conducive to war. It is presumptuous to assume that public invective has a uniformly unimportant impact on all states and peoples. To do so denies cultural differences and insists that national heritages are meaningless. The debate that followed the Six-Day War in 1967 saw Arabs and socialist spokesmen unceasingly equate Israelis with Nazis.* Does it really require elaborate proofs to conclude that the odious comparison must strengthen hardliners in Israel and arouse the people against any peaceful settlement? Are there no cultural sensibilities among Afrikaners that can be wounded by the ferocious assault launched by black Africans? Do all Chinese shrug away descriptions of themselves as uniquely barbarous and warlike? The answers to these questions are clear. Verbal arrows inflict wounds.

When the objective is to solve problems it is necessary to stress positive images. No more is required than to recall the behavior of President Nixon during his voyages to Peking and Moscow. In China, he observed Chinese social customs, visited and praised symbols of Chinese culture and civilization, made a courtesy call on Chairman Mao. In Moscow, he movingly evoked the memory of Leningrad's Tania in order to emphasize the courage and steadfastness of his hosts. Everywhere, he carefully drank to those toasts that stressed friendship and good will. In sum, talk can be used for conciliation or for hostile purposes, and it can contribute to either end. At the United Nations, talk is a weapon that reduces possibilities of negotiation and peaceful settlement.

Compromise solutions require privacy and good will. If public debate at the United Nations exacerbates feelings, it is

* Commenting on a picture of captured Egyptian soldiers, the Syrian delegate said: "If anybody wants proof that Zionism is equivalent to Nazism, he has only to look at that picture." SCOR, Meeting 1361, June 14, 1967.

nevertheless assumed by some that it does provide privacy. Unfortunately, the two cannot be so easily separated. Moving into corridors means nothing more than engaging in earnest negotiation. When a hostile atmosphere is encouraged by debate, it becomes less likely that quiet diplomacy will take place. If there were any possibility that black African leaders could quietly influence particular inhuman consequences of Apartheid, it has evaporated in the great debate on colonialism and racism. The two sides exchange insults in public which create obstacles to any private discussions. Too much prestige has been invested to permit a black African to drink with the South African devil. Arabs who constantly deny the legitimacy of Israel's existence publicly have more difficulty in recognizing their enemies *anyplace*, including the lounges of the United Nations building. It makes about as much sense to ignore these barriers because some agreements are eventually reached as it would to ignore armaments races and alliances, for the same reason. The fact that states may sometimes overcome impediments to better relations is scarcely an argument for creation of these obstacles.

Decisions

In the literature and practice of international relations, third-party intervention has had a prominent role in approaches to peaceful settlement. Over the centuries, states have relied on good offices, mediation, conciliation, inquiry, arbitration, and adjudication to assist them in resolving their quarrels. The culmination of this trend is the assumption of decision-making authority by international organizations. When the United Nations acts, its verdict is interpreted as the independent, collective voice of the world community. Resolutions are the final step in democratic processes which include debate, investigation, and compromise. Furthermore, the constitutional framework within which the system operates requires solutions based on universally accepted principles of proper international behavior. A moral force has been injected into world politics which cannot be disregarded. Sovereign states must acknowledge boundaries that are fixed by decisions of the organization. This argument is especially persuasive in respect to issues, such as colonialism, that evoke overwhelming agreement among the members. The United Nations is both a mirror of the attitudes and policies of its membership and an independent influence on their behavior.[18]

These claims for international organization are misplaced. Decisions by the United Nations are *not* in the tradition of impartial assists to peaceful settlement. All such procedures require prior agreement concerning outside intervention. At the United Nations, one side rarely, if ever, accepts the organization as a suitable arbiter. The adversary relationship dominates every aspect of United Nations involvement in disputes. Only one party, and sometimes neither, accepts the legitimacy of the decision-making process. All of the democratic procedures are converted into means for acquiring advantages on specific questions. Debate is war with words, investigations are confirmations of majority attitudes, and resolutions are worded to achieve maximum political objectives. Compromises must be understood within this context. They are not between the parties. "Soft" resolutions reflect nothing more than the need to tailor demands to the tactics of the moment, and usually indicate an absence of majority support for more extreme wording. When the political climate permits, harsher language is inserted in resolutions. The clearest example of this process is found in the escalatory politics of anticolonialism, although the swelling pro-Arab majority has produced similar results in the unending Arab-Israeli conflict. In neither instance do the resolutions respond to the policies of the states that have opposed *any* United Nations intervention.

It is fairly obvious that this analysis can be utilized to further understanding of United Nations "failures" and "successes." Since decisions by the organization are actually victories for particular strategies, opponents do not accept the verdicts. When they have the ability to resist pressures, they simply disregard resolutions. This is the norm. In a few instances, as in the example of Israeli withdrawal from Sinai in 1957, a state may decide that it cannot risk the consequences of adhering to a particular policy. In 1957, Israel's allies, Britain and France, had already evacuated their troops, the United States was strongly supporting Egypt, and the Soviet Union was rattling its rockets. These considerations, and not an abstract acceptance of the authority of the United Nations, forced the Israelis to abandon their gains. In a different political setting a decade later, the Israelis could and did stand fast despite any number of hostile resolutions in the United Nations. The same kind of analysis must be applied to "acceptance" of cease-fire resolutions. States will agree to stop fighting when they perceive that their interests will be adversely affected otherwise. In the Arab-Israeli case, the Arabs have agreed to end the fighting each time that it became clear to them that further warfare would be disastrous. Israelis calculated that political dangers offset military advantages. Thus, the Israeli decision not to capture Damascus after occupying the Golan Heights in 1967 was based on the potential consequences of Soviet humiliation and loss of American support rather than on any acceptance of the jurisdiction of the Security Council.[19] Since 1953 the Security Council had not once passed a resolution satisfactory to Israel because of a normal anti-Israeli majority and total Soviet support for the

Arab side.[20] The Israelis knew full well that the Soviets would have vetoed a cease-fire resolution if the fighting had favored their enemies. Similar reasoning explains other so-called successes. Pakistanis and Indians agreed to cease-fires when exhaustion and military realities favored an end to bloodshed, and they resumed their wars in 1965 and 1971 when one or the other perceived some advantage in the use of arms.[21] We can conclude that the adversary role of the United Nations guarantees "failure" in most instances, and the rare concordance of United Nations resolutions with state behavior is explainable in terms of national interest which would have guaranteed similar actions in the absence of United Nations intervention.

But there is more. Use of the United Nations for conflict purposes does not produce a mirror image of international differences that has no material effect upon their outcome. Just as the addition of words to the weaponry of opponents intensifies hostilities, so too are United Nations resolutions dangerous additions to national arsenals. One serious consequence of the decision-making process at the United Nations is that it implicates third parties. No matter how remote a particular state may be from any issue, it must vote. Even abstentions are likely to be regarded as hostile when passions are aroused. Thus, when India abstained on a resolution to condemn Soviet intervention in Hungary, India's acceptability to the United States as a potential mediator of Cold War disputes was severely damaged. United Nations procedures create constant pressure on members to make choices. If a particular black African state wishes to maintain a neutral and helpful position vis-à-vis the Arab-Israeli dispute, it must consider the risk of alienating other Afro-Asian states in respect to issues on which it seeks their support. Politics at the United Nations, by constantly forcing states to choose up sides, progressively destroys neutral havens, which may mean the difference between war and peace.

Tensions Deepened

In world politics there are certain problems that are characterized by a whole pattern of tensions. For these situations, much more is required to defuse suspicions and fears than in the settlement of specific incidents. Confidence must be strengthened, fears allayed, good will demonstrated. Habitually positive attitudes and practices must be developed.[22] We are here concerned with: (1) the Cold War between West and East in which the survival of mankind has been at stake; (2) the struggle against racism and colonialism in southern Africa; (3) the India-Pakistan dispute, which has fueled three wars in a quarter century; and (4) the Arab-Israeli conflict, which is a constant threat to world peace. These are the issues that have dominated the time and energies of the members of the United Nations. Yet the mere availability of the United Nations for registering easy victories has deepened these tensions and reduced possibilities of peaceful settlements. By demonstrating this relationship, we can project as well the consequences in respect to similar problems that may be fought on the United Nations battlefield.

The Cold War

It is commonplace to observe that success for the United Nations was predicated on Great Power cooperation and that the Cold War doomed the original conception. Obviously, the differences between the Soviet Union and its World War II allies not only survived the war but became more intense in the postwar era. The causes of the deadly rivalry are rooted in ideological differences, decades of hostility, armaments races, economic and political competition. This complex and pervasive struggle was fought out throughout the globe, including at the United Nations. Especially in its first two decades, the United Nations was the scene of incessant combat between the superpowers. Every opportunity was seized to score propaganda victories, embarrass, or condemn. Victories were easy for the West, which forced Soviet vetoes in the Security Council and overwhelmed the Communists in the General Assembly. The United Nations was an ideal forum for polemics and for registering Western righteousness and Communist immorality. On every issue, the "opinion of mankind" confirmed that right lay with the West.

It may be that President Nixon's trips to Peking and Moscow, the arms limitation agreement, the end of American participation in the Vietnam War, the conclusion of treaties between West Germany and Eastern Europe, and the weakening of alliances have signaled at least the beginning of the end of the Cold War in the early 1970s. This expectation may or may not be premature. If the worst dangers are past, the chilling potential of the Berlin and Cuban missile crises will not be repeated. It is nevertheless important to assess the effect of the availability of the United Nations on a quarter century of Cold War.

We suggest that it was a major contributor to the perpetuation and exacerbation of tensions. Winning votes at the United Nations was easier than negotiating with a difficult and suspicious opponent. Ammunition was endless. Machinery was established to repeat condemnations on Hungary, Greece, Korea, Tibet, Czechoslovakia, and so on. Whenever an impasse was reached, whether on Berlin, Korea, or disarmament, the West could take its case to the United Nations and win.

Of course, the problems remained. The Soviet Union did not accept the Baruch Plan for nuclear disarmament or "open skies" because they were approved by majorities in the United Nations.[23] Instead, they developed their own nuclear arsenal and shot down the U-2 when the United States opened Soviet skies unilaterally. Condemnations did not alter the fate of Czechoslovakia or Hungary.

Victories at the United Nations were cheap. They involved no cost in blood and very little in treasure, and they lent an aura of righteousness to Western foreign policy. Considerable diplomatic coin was expended in developing techniques for achieving parliamentary successes. This was the golden age of American support for the United Nations, and the United States Mission emerged as a most important diplomatic post. It is not surprising, therefore, that former Chief of Mission, Ambassador Charles Yost, looks back with nostalgia on the first nineteen years of the United Nations.[24]

But all of this activity contributed to maintenance of tensions. When every chance is taken to denounce and humiliate an opponent, there can be no other result except to perpetuate hostility. Statesmen acquire habits. The habitual use of the United Nations is analogous to reliance on arms whenever one is confronted by complex and uncomfortable political phenomena. It is direct, simple, and chances for victory are comparatively easy to calculate. It is far more difficult to explore areas of agreement amid differences, to negotiate patiently for years to achieve minimal goals, to maintain composure in spite of provocations, to attempt an understanding of the sources of foreign conduct, to acknowledge complexity and attempt to unravel those strands that are susceptible to compromise. These approaches, which are essential to the easing of deep-seated tensions, were neglected in favor of harshness, moral posturing, and simplistic definitions of issues.

Tensions were maintained, a crusade atmosphere developed, and the possibility increased that a political miscalculation or accident would trigger the war that would destroy both sides.

Anticolonialism

The same reasoning applies to the other great quarrels at the United Nations. The Afro-Asians are now in a position similar to that once enjoyed by the United States. They have complete control of the machinery. Resolutions are formulated and passed with assembly-line precision. The United Nations is identified as a participant on their side. We are not here concerned with the morality, immorality, legality, or illegality of resolutions. Majorities settle all ambiguities. South Africans, Portuguese, and Rhodesians (even if they had a voice) have about as much chance of convincing the Assembly or Security Council that they have valid legal or other arguments as the Soviet Union had of carrying the day on Hungary or Korea. They are crushed by the United Nations steamroller. But, again, the issues are not solved. South Africans devise more and more repressive Apartheid legislation, Portugal beefs up its military presence in the colonies, and Rhodesia adopts South Africa's Apartheid techniques. No effort is made to explore possibilities of solving peripheral problems, technological cooperation, or gradualist approaches. Compromise becomes unthinkable. Instead, tensions are constantly refueled. It is taken for granted that force is the ultimate answer. The world looks forward to an inevitable black-white showdown. Until that day, the Afro-Asians will score their United Nations victories and resolutely refuse to consider any means of easing tensions. In fact, the habit of dominating the United Nations battlefield excludes other solutions.

India-Pakistan

The origins of the Kashmir dispute lay in the withdrawal of Britain from the Indian subcontinent, the establishment of India and Pakistan, and the equivocal status of certain former princely states. These states had the theoretical options of acceding to either India or Pakistan, or choosing independence. As a practical matter, all but three had no real choice except to be absorbed by one or the other of the larger states. The three exceptions were Hyderabad, Junagadh, and Kashmir. By refusing to accept Indian or Pakistani sovereignty by August 15, 1947, the three princes opted for independence. In Junagadh, the Moslem ruler of a largely Hindu population later acceded to Pakistan, but India, which effectively surrounded the state, used its army to force a referendum in favor of accession to India. A similar situation prevailed in Hyderabad, where the Moslem prince sought to preserve his independence. Again, the Indian army settled the issue. The Kashmir case reversed this pattern in that a Hindu prince governed a majority of Moslems. The state lay between India and Pakistan, thereby complicating an "Indian" solution by Pakistan, although she did make the effort. As the prince temporized, an uprising was followed by an invasion by Moslem tribesmen. Seeing his throne endangered, the ruler acceded to India in order to obtain military protection.[25] India sent the desired troops but at the same time, perhaps to legitimize the action, asserted support in principle for an eventual referendum.

India brought the issue to the Security Council on January 1, 1948, charging Pakistan with complicity in the invasion of Kashmir by the tribesmen. But India's case was weakened because of its equivocal attitude concerning the status of Kashmir. By asserting that Kashmir's ultimate disposition should await a plebiscite, "if necessary under international auspices," India opened the way for extensive United Nations involvement. Given the now-indeterminate relationship of Kashmir to India, the case for treating Pakistan as an aggressor was fatally weakened. Instead of condemning Pakistan, the Security Council set up machinery to solve a complicated problem. A United Nations Commission for India and Pakistan (UNCIP) was to investigate the facts and mediate. On January 29, 1948, the commission was instructed to arrange for the plebiscite and reduce violence in Kashmir. Three months later, the Security Council detailed the solution. UNCIP would secure the peace and withdrawal of forces; it would establish an interim government in Kashmir and supervise the plebiscite. The Secretary-General would appoint a plebiscite administrator to ensure a fair referendum.[26] Although Pakistan criticized aspects of the resolution, India had major objections. It was clear that the Indian government was now aware that its high-minded concern for self-determination had been taken too seriously. If a plebiscite were held, the Moslem majority would undoubtedly favor Pakistan. Indian troops had occupied two-thirds of Kashmir, including the wealthy vale of Kashmir. Unwilling to lose this prize, India began a fourteen-year filibuster during which she insisted that she adhered to the principle of a plebiscite while finding reasons for preventing the election. The United Nations was constantly involved.

A cease-fire agreement, reached on January 1, 1949, resulted in the establishment of the United Nations Mission Observers Group for India and Pakistan (UNMOGIP) to demarcate the cease-fire line and supervise the truce. With a handful of members, UNMOGIP remained in the area for over two decades. A succession of United Nations mediators was appointed. Nothing changed. Pakistan established its own puppet regime (Azad Kashmir) and pressed continuously for the plebiscite.

After 1954, the Cold War contributed to disarray in the Security Council. Pakistan began receiving American weapons. The Soviet Union became an outright supporter of India. In 1954, too, a pro-Indian constituent assembly in Kashmir ratified the act of accession with India.[27] The Indian government backed off further and further from the idea of a plebiscite. Finally, in 1962, the pose was dropped and India abandoned any commitment to popular choice. Her position now was that all of Kashmir was Indian, and the Security Council's only responsibility was to deal with Pakistani aggression.[28] Pakistan, of course, reiterated its attack on India for deyning obligations previously assumed toward the Kashmir people. Three years later, fighting erupted. India charged that regular and irregular Pakistani troops had invaded across the Kashmir cease-fire line. The war spread beyond Kashmir. Pakistan told the Security Council that an Indian attack on West Pakistan could be compared only with the aggressions by Nazi Germany.[29] Finally, on September 22, 1965, both sides accepted a cease-fire, probably because "both belligerents had taken fright at the prospects of enlarging the conflict further."[30] Withdrawal of forces followed successful mediation by the Soviet Union in Tashkent. In 1971, the rebellion in East Pakistan touched off still another war, which ended with creation of the new independent state of Bangladesh. Talks between India and Pakistan continue, and, finally, soon the division of Kashmir may be formalized and the Kashmir issue, which has been at the root of Indo-Pakistani enmity, may be settled.

This capsule presentation of a twenty-five-year dispute is not intended to be complete, nor have we tried to present all the arguments of the contestants. They have expended hundreds of thousands of words in the Security Council doing that. We are concerned only with the impact of the United Nations on the dispute. Positions were frozen in 1948, and because a decision was made at the United Nations, the parties were trapped into nonnegotiable positions. India erred in 1948 by accepting the principle of a plebiscite, perhaps because India was then justifying its actions in Junagadh and Hyderabad on similar grounds. Furthermore, India at that time aspired to leadership of the Third World, for whom self-determination was a sacred principle. Perhaps, also, India's leaders wanted to demonstrate that their foreign policy was more enlightened than that of other countries. Whatever the reasons, India soon realized its mistake. For fourteen years, debate centered on the plebiscite issue. Pakistan would accept nothing *but* a plebiscite; India could not admit that it would rather keep its share of Kashmir than permit the people to decide. Thus, the de facto partition achieved in 1949 was never accepted as the basis for an agreement. Pakistan's demand that India fulfill its promise to permit the plebiscite meant to India that Pakistan would not be content until all of Kashmir belonged to Pakistan. This, in turn, caused India to assert that the accession of Kashmir to India meant that the entire state had become part of India. In truth, once India decided that a plebiscite was a bad idea, there was no hope for a settlement except through negotiations based on actual military positions. It is largely because of United Nations involvement that no negotiations could take place. Once the plebiscite became, apparently with the consent of both sides, *the* United Nations solution, negotiation was made impossible. If both sides in fact wanted a plebiscite, the United Nations could have provided valuable, but not essential, technical assistance. Indeed, it was the mobilization of this technical apparatus at the United Nations that contributed so much to fruitless and endless concentration on a plebiscite. Two wars and twenty-five years later, the parties have, for the first time, tried seriously to end the conflict that has embittered their relations for so long. If the Indian-Pakistan talks are successful, they will accept the military status quo and give up the claims they have been making at the United Nations. United Nations resolutions will finally be abandoned as a necessary precondition for settlement. And the settlement will be reached outside of, and *in spite of,* the United Nations.

Arabs and Israelis

An example of a "balanced" decision by the United Nations is Security Council Resolution 242 (November 22, 1967). This resolution emerged after it became clear that Arab and socialist efforts to condemn Israeli aggression during and after the Six-Day War, to force an unconditional withdrawal to prewar boundaries, were unacceptable to the United States. The resolution, introduced by Britain, was adopted unanimously. Briefly, it provided for withdrawal of armed forces, the termination of belligerent claims, the right of all in the area to enjoy peace and secure boundaries, freedom of navigation through international waterways, and a fair settlement of the refugee problem. It also requested the dispatch of a mediator to assist in obtaining a settlement on the basis of the principles of the resolution. The dangers in such a balanced solution are perhaps less visible than the more normal clear-cut victories for a particular side. They are, nevertheless, real. Since the principles were an amalgam of the major demands of both sides, the resolution permitted each to concentrate on its fundamental objectives. The Arabs singled out the clauses calling for immediate withdrawal from occupied territories, and the Israelis emphasized priority for a peace settlement and the establishment of secure boundaries. Under these circumstances, Gunnar Jarring's mission was doomed. It was possible for Arabs and Israelis alike to insist that they were abiding by the resolution while condemning each other for defying the Security Council. For years the parties engaged in this non-negotiation, finding in it added confirmation of one another's intransigence. Since total Israeli withdrawal was unacceptable to Jews and a prior peace treaty was anathema to the Arabs, there was no possibility of progress. By fixing the outline of an ultimate settlement, the Security Council simply foreclosed real bargaining on whatever questions *were* susceptible to common agreement.

Normally United Nations decisions are clearer victories for one side. In the same Arab-Israeli conflict, the weight of resolutions has favored the Arabs. After 1953, Soviet policy guaranteed that no resolution opposed by the Arabs would be adopted in the Security Council. As a result, a series of condemnations of Israel for violations of the cease-fire agreements were voted.[31] The General Assembly adopted the Arab approach to the refugee problem in 1948. The resolution granted to the refugees the right to return to their former homes, and those choosing not to return were to be compensated for loss or damage to their property.[32] From that date forward, Arab states have insisted that no other solution was acceptable. With Israel refusing to jeopardize her national security by accepting a huge, hostile population, and the Arabs refusing to integrate the refugees into their economies, the issue has served to perpetuate the basic tensions of the area. In the General Assembly, also, the Arab side has obtained passage of resolutions maintaining the international status of Jerusalem[33] and demanding the unconditional evacuation of Israeli forces from territories occupied during the Six-Day

War.[34] These victories do not alter the substantive situation. Refugees remain in United Nations camps with little prospect for achieving either the Arab political goal or normal, productive lives. Jerusalem has been unified under Israeli control, and, of course, the Israelis remain in the occupied areas. In short, total United Nations victories are countered by total rejection. Every session of the General Assembly adds to the record, with the Arabs pressing for sanctions or expulsion of Israel from the organization.

With their national honor committed to solutions endorsed by the world community, the flexibility of Arab statesmen is reduced. Even if they want to, individual leaders have less chance of surviving domestically or in the Arab world if they explore alternative solutions. There is a like effect in Israel. On the eve of another Arab attack in the Security Council in August, 1973, the *New York Times* reported that condemnations at the United Nations hardened public attitudes. As a typical reaction a Hebrew University professor was quoted: "It simply infuriates me to see the United Nations, which has never been able to bring itself to flatly denounce Arab terrorism, immediately schedule a Security Council session to skewer Israel."[35]

The Arab-Israeli issue illustrates as clearly as any other the dangers to peace resulting from United Nations decisions. Basically, the threat arises from the political circumstances that accompany use of the United Nations. Since bringing the issue is a hostile act, it normally signals the breakdown or absence of negotiations. While the original complaint may reflect the existing status of the dispute, winning a United Nations verdict tends to freeze the issue at that stage. If and when the international climate changes, the parties may have great difficulty in surmounting a decision that is one-sided and impractical. The problem is further complicated when

majorities continue to endorse a policy that is rejected abso-
lutely by the loser.*

Another excellent example is the Korean issue, in which
the United States won support for its approach to unifying
the country. More than twenty years of repetitive resolutions
did not change the situation in Korea. South Korea won all
the moral victories, but North Korea remained a fact. South
Korean governments inevitably accepted the favorable United
Nations approach to unity, thereby creating internal pressures
against any other alternative. When the two sides finally
decided to try to achieve some sort of modus vivendi, an absolute but difficult precondition for the South Korean government was the abandonment of United Nations resolutions.[36]
While there seems to be some possibility that this can be
accomplished in Korea, and, perhaps, in Kashmir, there is still
considerable doubt that the barriers to peace *created by use of
the United Nations* can be overcome in the Middle East.

China

Conventional wisdom, buttressed by American guilt for having abandoned the League of Nations at birth, has supported
the principle of universal membership in the United Nations.
No single issue has symbolized the importance of this concept
more than has the admission of Communist China. Universal-
ists noted that admission to the United Nations does not
confer diplomatic recognition or imply agreement with a
country's foreign policy. In fact, they argued that the exclusion of Communist China was ill-advised precisely because
China was involved in dangerous conflicts with its neighbors.
Chinese admission was not a "reward for aggression," but was

* See Epilogue.

made all the more necessary because of aggressive behavior. After all, the United Nations was not a social club or an alliance. It was a peace-keeping organization, and in order for it to function effectively all of the potential troublemakers must come under its aegis. The world could not afford to prevent an atomic power with 800 million people from being subjected to the pacifying influence of the world organization.[37]

From our perspective these arguments are not persuasive. While insistence on a special outlaw status for China cannot be defended as advancing the cause of peace, the positive benefits from admission are not likely to materialize. It is true that serious threats to world peace are inherent in territorial disputes between China and the Soviet Union and in the bitter conflict with the United States over Taiwan. In addition, there are potential difficulties involving China in Southeast Asia, India, and Burma. Chinese relations with Japan are encumbered by nearly a century of bitterness and war. With time, too, it can be expected that China will conflict with the United States and the Soviet Union in the struggle for influence among developing countries further from its periphery. Obviously, this is a very dangerous world and its survival may depend on how well the United States, the Soviet Union, and China accommodate themselves to one another.

But does it follow that common membership in the United Nations will improve chances of avoiding nuclear war? On the basis of the record and our analysis of the United Nations, the answer is that it will not. Instead, China will be provided with a weapon it did not have before—the United Nations—and with powerful inducements to use that weapon. We have already noted the impact that the availability and use of the United Nations has had on the maintenance of Cold War tensions. Should Soviet-Chinese differences continue, we can expect similar results. The line-ups will, of course, be dif-

ferent. China can be expected to solicit support among poor
nations and emphasize the north-south axis, with themselves as
the great champion of the colored and hungry peoples of the
world. The territorial dispute with Russia will be defined as
another example of a European colonial power having raped
a weak, although more civilized, nation. Competition for leadership of the socialist bloc will be fought out in debate,
parliamentary tactics, and votes in the United Nations. It can
be argued that this scenario could be played out as easily if
China was a member of the United Nations or not. That may
be true. But the United Nations contributes to the conflict
because of the special opportunities it makes available. There
is no comparable forum for expanding disputes, embarrassing
an enemy, endorsement of extreme positions. As was true for
the Soviet-American Cold War, Sino-Soviet tensions are deeply
grounded and have complex origins. The danger is that the
parties will be less capable of developing procedures and attitudes necessary for conflict resolution because they become
accustomed to polemics and easy victories at the United
Nations.

Some American observers might consider the anticipated
Sino-Soviet confrontation at the United Nations as an opportunity for American foreign policy to take better advantage of
the split between the two giant Communist powers. Some
such benefits may develop, but they should not be confused
with improving prospects for world peace. Indeed, of more
immediate concern is the possibility of deterioration of Sino-
American relations as a consequence of Chinese presence in
the United Nations. Nixon's voyage to China was an important initiative toward adjusting to the need of establishing a
more rational relationship between the two countries. But
quite clearly it was the barest beginning. Deep-seated fears
and antagonism remain. Decades of incredibly intense hatreds

are not swept away by a single visit. If this modest initiative is to lay the foundation for increasingly constructive interchanges, it is vital that the delicate first steps are not dissipated by public charges and countercharges. It is therefore imperative that the two countries avoid bringing their differences to the United Nations. The issue that, obviously, is most likely to surface is that of Taiwan. From the Chinese perspective, Taiwan is a province of China, and it is inadmissible that China be denied jurisdiction over her own territory. The continuing presence on Taiwan of an ancient rival possessing a large army and insisting that his is the legitimate government of China magnifies the importance of the island for the Communists. On the other hand, the United States has a vast material and diplomatic interest in the Nationalist regime. Although the juridical status of Taiwan is an embarrassment for the United States, this country cannot and will not suddenly abandon Chiang's government. The trend may be in that direction, but there is no certainty about ultimate policy decisions. Presumably, American and Chinese leaders would prefer to agree to disagree on the question and permit time and new realities to work for an eventual adjustment that cannot be anticipated now.

But what would happen to this fragile tacit understanding if the issue were raised at the United Nations by China? After all, the People's Republic is now a prestigious member of the organization and occupies a permanent seat in the Security Council. Suppose that some unforeseen incident or setback infuriates the Chinese? What of the likelihood that the Chinese in their quarrels with the Soviets will be taunted at the United Nations for lacking courage or desire to challenge the United States on this issue? Furthermore, the Chinese may be tempted to initiate the complaint, knowing that they can mobilize enough socialist and Afro-Asian support to embarrass the United States in the General Assembly. If they do, they will repeat the arguments they made in 1950.[38] They will demand condemnation of the United States for aggressing against China by intervening in a civil war. The Seventh Fleet, they will say, must be removed from the Taiwan Straits, and the United States must renounce the threat of force to prevent Chinese authorities from occupying their own territory. Support for Chiang Kai-shek must be abandoned and all treaty relations abrogated, since such contracts are illegal when made with a province of a sovereign state. The United States could be expected to defend its policy by emphasizing the legitimacy of Chiang's government and treaty relations between the two countries. China will be charged with violation of the United Nations Charter for threatening the use of force. The effect of such a debate would be to favor the retention of a rigid posture by strengthening hard-liners at the expense of those in both governments who favor a more flexible line. Probably the impact would be greater in the United States, where the issue could be exploited politically against officials charged with "being soft towards Communism." A United Nations "decision" favoring China would be disastrous. It could easily destroy the impact of burgeoning economic, cultural, and diplomatic contacts between the countries.

A somewhat more subtle consequence of Chinese participation in the United Nations is that it complicates any lingering hope of reviving Dag Hammarskjöld's idea of having United Nations forces function to isolate certain conflicts from Great Power intervention. The concept of having the "blue-helmets," drawn from small, relatively uninvolved states, separate antagonists with the consent of the government on whose soil they were stationed was premised on the agreement or at least nonopposition of the superpowers. Soviet-American division in the Congo and U Thant's swift removal of the

Middle East force on President Nasser's demand in 1967 nearly doomed any further applications of this peace-keeping technique. In any case, the difficulty of gaining the approval of the United States, the Soviet Union, *and* China for operations in preventive diplomacy is obvious.

The Two Germanys

Universality has become virtually complete with the admission of the two Germanys. Their most serious difference has been over the status of Berlin, an issue that has provoked some of the most dangerous confrontations of the Cold War. There, a succession of East-West crises, beginning with the blockade in 1948, periodically dramatized the need to stabilize and defuse the situation. The success of Willy Brandt's *Ostpolitik*, which predicates the acceptance of the post-World War II status quo as a precondition for normalization of European relations, offers the first real hope that a Berlin solution can be negotiated. East and West Germany have just entered the United Nations. If that organization, as its manifold advocates insist, is the best hope for peace, there should be rejoicing that it will now have Berlin on its plate. If they were correct, German leaders would have deferred the arduous task of negotiating conditions for a Berlin agreement until they could take advantage of pacific procedures of the United Nations. In fact, however, East and West Germans were perfectly aware that it was in their interest to try to settle *before* they became members. Thus, they took advantage of a unique opportunity to resolve crucial differences prior to admission into the United Nations, thereby reducing the danger of reescalating hostility within the organization. If good-faith negotiations continue, the Berlin issue will be kept out of the United Nations.

When Nations Desire Peace

Statesmen recognize that the United Nations is a dangerous place. They therefore do their best to keep negotiable quarrels out of the organization. Quiet, bilateral diplomacy is employed to settle differences among states enjoying generally friendly relations. Only the most serious breakdown in negotiations, as in Panama's controversy with the United States on the Canal Zone, degenerates into public acrimony and possible utilization of the United Nations. Whenever practicable, regional organizations will function to prevent similar escalations. They do so in order to preserve unity for the accomplishment of common goals. Thus, disputes among black African states are shielded from the agendas of the Security Council or General Assembly. The same is true for Arabs, Latin Americans, Eastern Europeans, and NATO allies. Indeed, the measure of interstate harmony is the absence of visible antagonism. Friendly states negotiate their differences and reserve their pronouncements for compliments and success stories.

Among friends any public disapproval or condemnation is a serious breach of mutual confidence and trust. To illustrate, we need only refer to three recent incidents flowing from the Christmas, 1972, bombing of Hanoi and Haiphong by the United States. America's close ally and neighbor, Canada, registered its disapproval in a resolution passed by Parliament. The action was an unprecedented rebuke which would not have been taken if Canadian leaders had not been so deeply offended by American policy. In two other countries, disapproval was more feelingly expressed. The Swedish premier, Olof Palme, publicly compared the bombing to Nazi death camps, and Indian Prime Minister Indira Gandhi wondered aloud if the United States would have pursued so savage a policy if the victims were white rather than Asiatics. These charges of genocide and racism provoked the United States to defer receiving the Swedish ambassador and delay sending a new American ambassador to New Delhi. Secretary of State William P. Rogers angrily told a congressional committee that Palme's statement was "vitriolic and outrageous" and added that he was considering not sending an ambassador to India at all.[39] None of the three critics are "enemy" states, and that fact may explain why they did not take the further step of complaining to the United Nations—the ultimate and most hostile display of disagreements.

The same general rule applies when unfriendly states are trying to improve relations or solve specific problems. Sometimes they may be required to free an issue from the rigidities created by the prior use of the United Nations. Direct negotiations on the future of Korea is an outstanding example. Settlements of the Kashmir and Middle East problems will certainly have to follow the same course. The beginning of détente between the United States and China through direct, high-level meetings depended on willingness to abandon arguments made on the admission of China and to ignore condemnatory resolutions. All of the agreements between the United States and the Soviet Union on atomic testing, nonproliferation of atomic weapons, and arms control were reached as the result of secret bilateral negotiations and despite arguments and resolutions at the United Nations. States, then, that have serious and compelling reasons to resolve their differences, are sometimes capable of doing so even after experiencing deep hostility that manifested itself in United Nations initiatives and in spite of the obstacles thus created.

Furthermore, other major settlements have been reached with minimal or nonexistent involvement of the United Nations. For example, direct summit talks have become a dra-

matic method of attempting to cool dangerous tensions. Since
the purpose for holding the top-level meeting is to stress common interests, the participants are careful to preserve the
secrecy of their discussions and to agree on the results. Even
when little of a substantive nature can be revealed, general
statements are formulated which stress good will and amity. If
agreements have been negotiated, the summit is used to exploit
their potential for further reduction of tensions. President
Nixon's trips to Peking and Moscow and Chairman Leonid
Brezhnev's return visit to the United States are typical illustrations. Can there be any sharper contrast between these meetings and summits at the United Nations? When Premiers
Khrushchev and Castro and other national leaders lent their
prestige to the General Assembly in 1960, they came to *fight*.
Khrushchev pounded his shoe on his desk and demanded
Hammarskjöld's head for being a pawn of the West in the
Congo, and Fidel Castro, defiant and long-winded, proclaimed
the determination of the Cuban people to fight and die to preserve their independence in the face of American imperialism.
Of course, not every chief of state uses the rostrum or his shoe
so belligerently, but each one, according to particular styles
and needs, takes the opportunity to pursue national interests.
Summitry at the United Nations is simply the continuation of
conflict politics at the highest level.

7 *A Matter of Perspective*

The analysis presented in this book began with a profound dissatisfaction with the literature in the field. Too many inconsistencies and mysteries remained unexplained and too many questions were not being asked. A piecemeal approach simply produced more frustrating problems. The key, we finally realized, was a matter of perspective. When we escaped the trap of studying actions at the United Nations in the context of the purposes written into the Charter, and instead focused on the objectives of those who used the organization, everything fell into place. Motivation and perception of relative political gains, rather than an abstract attachment to Charter ideals, became the starting point of analysis. "Who brings what issues to the United Nations and why?" became the crucial question which joins use of the United Nations to world politics. Once we saw that the United Nations was an arena for conflict, actions there became susceptible to rational analysis. As in every other form of combat, the level of hostility influenced the means employed. The impact on a dispute of particular hostile acts at the United Nations could be assessed in the same way that other weapons are evaluated in a conflict setting. A host of political phenomena were explained, a framework for predictions emerged, and, perhaps most importantly, significant questions could be asked.

Motivation and the United Nations

Identification of strategies in the United Nations permitted a clear association of them with overall foreign-policy objectives. Furthermore, the unique features and limitations of the United Nations weapon appeared. At the same time, new and difficult questions had to be raised. It was apparent, for example, that statistical analyses of voting coalitions are virtually meaningless unless one asks *why* particular states vote together. Writers stress the consensus in the organization on anticolonialism. But obviously only some of the participants are seriously interested in socializing these issues in a manner that will modify the existing balance of forces in southern Africa. Quite clearly, Latin Americans, Western Europeans, socialists, many Asiatics, and others vote for resolutions in this area with differing expectations concerning the impact of action at the United Nations than those of certain militant black African states. If there is disillusionment, therefore, based on the apparent ineffectiveness of the organization, it is unevenly distributed because of the variations in the motivations of the members. Even to attempt to determine which states are utilizing an issue to embarrass others, which are simply avoiding embarrassment, which are determined to affect the substantive problems, which are asserting, in a safe way, a certain independence from a Great Power* is to raise complex questions that have not yet even been asked.

The unexplored implications of the approach are obviously large. Are there shifts in strategy on the same issue that can become apparent by a study of the quality of debate and the wording of resolutions? How often and on what issues are

---

* Latin Americans, for example, may well vote with the anticolonial bloc less because of any burning interest in freedom for black Africans and more to support an international climate that would militate against neocolonial initiatives by the United States in their hemisphere.

the intentions of surrogates synonymous with the needs of those in whose name an issue is brought? Are there significant differences in tactics on similar issues by direct complainants as opposed to surrogates?

Since national interest is the base for analysis, explanations of apparent "successes," such as in the Middle East or the Congo, must relate United Nations initiatives to the foreign policies that made them possible. In the absence of a United Nations Emergency Force in the Middle East, is it conceivable that fighting could have continued after the British and French abandoned the struggle? Given the total isolation of Israel in 1956 and the defeat suffered by Egypt, might not a settlement have been reached which would have exchanged Israeli withdrawal for security guarantees? Very importantly, did use of the United Nations Emergency Force separate the antagonists in a manner that foreclosed negotiation of the sources of hostility, thereby contributing to war in 1967? Why was it impossible to force Israeli withdrawal by use of another United Nations Emergency Force in 1967? In the Congo, why has it been so confidently assumed that the United Nations operation prevented a clash between the superpowers? Did investigators determine that the Soviet toe-hold in the Congo represented a sufficient basis for the Russians to risk thermonuclear war? On its face, this is unlikely. While the Russians were undoubtedly unhappy at being evicted by Kasa-Vubu, and expressed their displeasure by denouncing Hammarskjöld, there is every reason to believe that East-West competition for influence in the Congo would not have become a threat to world peace. In Cyprus, the essentials of the "solution" had been agreed upon before the Western powers decided that the United Nations was a somewhat more convenient tool than a NATO force. Since there was never any possibility of allowing Communist troops to participate, the concept of isolating the dispute from superpower involvement is irrelevant. To raise these issues in this way is no more than to insist that the United Nations be viewed in the context of world politics, and that its occasional limited value as an instrument of policies determined outside the organization be recognized and not exaggerated unrealistically.

If a decision to utilize the United Nations is a calculated act, so too are decisions to avoid the organization. If one can identify thirty disputes of which only ten are brought to the United Nations, it is relevant to investigate the twenty neglected issues in order to deepen one's understanding of the role that the organization plays in world politics. Indeed, non-use of the United Nations tells us nearly as much as the reverse. What is there that distinguishes particular interstate relations and/or the United Nations which results in some conflicts being aired while others are not? When a long-standing quarrel such as the Panama Canal Zone issue suddenly surfaces as an agenda item, questions must be asked about Panamanian-American relations. Does this reveal, as we contend, an upsurge of hostility? To understand Panama's initiative in 1973, it is necessary to inquire about the years when no action was taken. And what about conflicts that are extant at a particular historical moment? Who has asked why the Soviet Union did *not* complain about the mining of Haiphong—interference with freedom of the seas offered an obvious pretext—on the eve of President Nixon's trip to Moscow? Why didn't the Chinese Communists complain immediately on entering the United Nations about American "aggression" in Taiwan? The *issue* hadn't changed, but Sino-American relations had. Why is it that even the most serious differences between friendly nations, for example, the American-Japanese dispute over Okinawa, are rarely brought into the organization? Are there instances when a state has more than one grievance against other states, but resorts to the United Nations in one case and not another? If so, what does such behavior reveal about the suitability of the use of the organization for conflict purposes?

An indication of how only this last question can and should be analyzed is provided by consideration of the events in Lebanon in the spring of 1973. Israeli commandos struck in Beirut, killing some half dozen persons, including three prominent leaders of the Palestinian resistance movement. The raiders withdrew as swiftly as they had attacked. Clearly Israel had violated Lebanese sovereignty and territorial integrity. Predictably, Lebanese and other Arab leaders insisted on an emergency meeting of the Security Council. Supported by other Third World countries and the socialists, the Israeli crime was described in livid terms. Sanctions, even expulsion from the organization, were demanded. Although they failed to achieve these ends, they did succeed in having their enemy condemned, as the Security Council reiterated that Israelis had no right of retaliation against Arab guerrillas or the states that harbored, armed, and encouraged them. Arab strategy is unmistakable. They use the United Nations to isolate Israel, and especially to convince ambivalent American policy-makers that they can no longer afford to support an "international outlaw."

Apologists for the United Nations will argue that Israel *had* violated the Charter, and condemnation, or even sanctions, are a logical and necessary United Nations reaction. Otherwise the principles of the Charter become meaningless, violence and lawlessness is encouraged, and the world becomes more dangerous.

Well and good, except that they fail to consider the violence that was triggered by the Israeli raid. In Lebanon, Palestinian dissatisfaction with government policies set off widespread clashes. In late April and early May the *New York*

Times reported that thousands of guerrillas invaded Lebanon from Syria. Lebanese tanks and jet fighters participated, and hundreds died. Yet the United Nations ignored all of this. As far as the Security Council was concerned, the *only* threat to peace in Lebanon was the comparatively bloodless, two-day Israeli attack. Why didn't Lebanon complain about the Syrian-based threat to its very existence? An obvious answer is that in 1973, the Council was a suitable weapon against Israel, but not against Syria. China, the Soviet Union, Arab and Third World states would have sided with Syria against Lebanon. More important, Lebanon would have incurred extreme hostility among other Arab states whose strategy it is to define Israel as the threat to peace in the area. By going to the Security Council, an action that would have benefited Israel, Lebanon would have reduced her own chances for survival.

If we can understand Lebanon's reluctance to raise the issue, how do we explain the silence of others? Large-scale fighting on her border was a threat to Israel's security, yet that country did not appeal to the Security Council. The obvious must be restated. Israel does not have access to United Nations processes. For twenty years, the Security Council has been a weapon available only to the Arab side. It is unlikely that a majority would have permitted the issue to become an agenda item, and any debate would have been converted into another assault against Israel.

We can dispose quickly of the reticence of other countries. Arabs and their friends were anxious to keep the Syrian-Lebanese struggle private. Theoretically, the United States could have demonstrated "even-handedness" by raising the issue, but decided not to jeopardize further its interests in the Middle East. Similarly other states, including those, such as Sweden or Canada, traditionally associated with disinterested support of Charter principles, were unwilling to risk the consequences of a hostile act against Syria and the Arab world. Finally, the Secretary-General, under Article 99 of the Charter, could have called for a Security Council meeting, but to have done so would have weakened his political base in the organization.

A number of conclusions consistent with our thesis can be drawn from this rapid survey of action and inaction at the United Nations. Strategic use of the organization by Arab states against Israel is brought into sharper focus. Not only do they seize every occasion to weaken Israel, but they also oppose any intervention in the organization that will complicate their task. The seriousness of violations has nothing to do with decisions or even consideration of issues in the Security Council. To allege that condemnation of Israel for violation of the Charter is a desirable deterrent requires that silence in respect to Syria be considered an encouragement to much more serious transgressions. Charter principles are not universal. They are available only for those who can manipulate them in their own interest. To bring an issue to the United Nations against the wishes of the parties in dispute is a hostile act. All states and the Secretary-General must, accordingly, calculate the costs of such a move, and *all* place national or personal interest above devotion to Charter principles. *All* conflicts must be analyzed, not just those that become agenda items. The United Nations does not mirror world politics. It reflects *some* disputes, frequently in distortion, but the mirror is dark to others. By perceiving the United Nations as an arena for achievement of conflict purposes, a rational basis for understanding its role is established.

Another neglected aspect of United Nations impact on conflicts is the effect on domestic reactions. It is not difficult to conclude that constant defeat and threats in the United Nations influence public opinion in Israel. "Doves," such as

Abba Eban, who favor diplomatic rather than military solutions, are weakened, and the "hawks," symbolized by Moshe Dayan, are strengthened. In Rhodesia and South Africa, racial extremists have successfully exploited attacks in the United Nations to silence and eliminate moderates. More difficult to appreciate is the extent to which governments become prisoners of their victories. In Pakistan, South Korea, and the Arab states, United Nations decisions and foreign policies coincided. All have had to contend with realities that required compromises, which were made more difficult to accept because of domestic and bloc pressures favoring the public "solutions." On another level, what has been the contribution of victories at the United Nations to the maintenance of tensions and establishment of crusade atmospheres in the West and black Africa in respect to the Cold War and anticolonialism?

From the perspective that is the source of these questions, it is apparent that, despite the many existing studies of the United Nations, only a bare beginning has been made.

Reform

Reform of the United Nations must be considered from the same perspective. Reformers wish to strengthen the United Nations because they equate a stronger United Nations with improved prospects of maintaining international peace. They ignore the question Stronger for whom? Since the organization is used to advance national causes, any "improvement" will make it a more lethal weapon. This is not speculation. The United Nations has already been "reformed" informally and formally. The Uniting for Peace Resolution was intended and was widely hailed as a fundamental extraconstitutional amendment of the Charter. It signaled a basic shift in authority from the Security Council to the General Assembly. It was the supreme assault on the veto power. In truth, the Uniting for Peace Resolution was a strategic maneuver designed to provide the anti-Communist majority with a permanent means of registering condemnations or even legitimizing military sanctions against the enemy. The tactic enjoyed a limited utility, although the opportunity to mount a United Nations military action against the Soviets in Hungary was not grasped for the simple reason that the United States was unwilling to risk a thermonuclear war. By the mid-1960s, the changing membership in the General Assembly caused the sponsors of the reform to inter it in practice. When a "stronger" General Assembly was no longer strategically desirable for the West, the erstwhile reformers opted for a return to strict construction of the Charter. The only formal amendment of the Charter increased the size of the Security Council from eleven to fifteen. Its effect was to provide better representation for the developing world, which had been largely ignored in the original composition of the Council. Theoretically, the democratized Security Council would be more competent to discharge its primary responsibility for the maintenance of international peace. In fact, the effect of the reform is precisely the same as for the Uniting for Peace Resolution. This time, the Security Council rather than the General Assembly was strengthened. The chief beneficiaries, the Afro-Asians, have used their influence in the Security Council to attack their Portuguese, South African, and Rhodesian enemies. Their most important success was the adoption of compulsory, comprehensive economic and financial sanctions against Rhodesia on December 16, 1966. It is unlikely that this "milestone" in application of the peacekeeping provisions of the Charter could have been reached prior to the reform. Anti-Communists in 1950 or anticolonialists in the 1960s and 1970s may *applaud* the political objectives that were benefited by the changes. They should not, however, allow their passions to obscure the difference between conflict and conciliation.

The same reasoning applies to suggested reforms. For example, the one-state, one-vote formula in the General Assembly stimulates proposals for weighted voting so that decisions will correspond more closely to the actual size, development, and influence of the member states. The effect of the reform would be to diminish somewhat the weight of the Afro-Asians and, perhaps, tend to restore the influence of European states. If we assume this result, the only effect would be to compel marginal tactical changes based upon altered calculations of voting patterns. In another area, the chronic financial problems of the organization inspire suggestions for new and better sources of funds. But we must ask: Money for what purposes? An enriched United Nations may make it a better weapon for reaching particular objectives, and strategies will be adjusted accordingly. In short, a strengthened, richer, more "democratic" United Nations will not convert it into an effective peace-keeping instrument. The changes will evoke appropriate national responses.

Utopianism

In contrast to our strictures concerning reform, we enthusiastically endorse "utopian" schemes. The United Nations is *not* man's last hope of avoiding a third world war. Its availability and use contribute to rigidity, hostility, and tension. War is more than ever our constant companion and potential destroyer. Any heightened appreciation of the dangers of war increases the urgency and importance of "utopian" plans. Too much is at stake to abandon the struggle. Advocates of a radi-

cally different approach to world order inspire the realist
response that states are unprepared to sacrifice sovereignty for
the common good. In the absence of significant initiatives in
that direction by powerful national leaders, we can conclude
that the realists are right, at least for this moment in history.
The depressing reality makes the theoretical schemes even more
vital. They offer alternatives, and it is impossible to predict
when the availability of such options may be grasped. While
we see little in present trends to inspire optimism, it is foolish
to be dogmatic about the future. Ecological disasters, a limited
nuclear war, or, one hopes, a less drastic unanticipated cause
may convince key statesmen that they must abandon national
prerogatives to assure their survival. When Utopia is the only
realism, the thesis presented here may help in liberating imagi-
nations from the stultifying effects of the United Nations
model.

Functionalism

This book has focused on the political use of the United
Nations. If the United Nations does not contribute to the
maintenance of international peace, all of its goals are endangered. This is not to say that the economic, social, and technical activities of the United Nations and the specialized agencies are not important. They are. But these functions are
peripheral and have little relationship to the major problem
—peace in the world. Success in these areas depends upon their
nonpolitical character and becomes more doubtful as technical
issues clash with national interests. It is relatively easy to
obtain agreement on a universal postal system, but common
approaches to pollution are made difficult, if not impossible,
by unequal levels of industrialization. Poor countries demand

their opportunity to befoul the land, sea, and air before they consider proposals by developed states to relate economic growth to a healthy environment. Even if one concedes, which we do not, that multilateral technical and aid programs can contribute eventually to an atmosphere more encouraging to political negotiation, the relationship is so vague, distant, and beset by so many unknowns that it seems impossible to rely on the "functional" approach to international peace. Certainly there is nothing in the record of the League of Nations or the United Nations to indicate a positive correlation between multinational approaches to economic and social problems and political prudence. Economic, social, and technical cooperation and progress are desirable and should be applauded for humanitarian reasons, but they have little or nothing to do with war or peace. A single shot wipes out the effects of decades of nonpolitical cooperation.

A "Return" to Idealism

It would be useless to urge, as others have, that the United States return to its former position of support for the objectives and principles of the Charter. For one thing, this government, and all others, insist that they have always done precisely that. It just "happens" that foreign policy and United Nations principles coincide. An appeal to idealism is meaningless, because one nation's idealism is another nation's selfish interest. Would it make sense or do any good to suggest that the United States accept majority decisions in the United Nations when to do so would damage American interests? The General Assembly has implied that it is contrary to the principles of the Charter to maintain foreign bases or exercise political authority on the soil of another sovereign state without the latter's consent. According to a resolution, adopted unanimously, the organization "solemnly declares" that states have no right "to intervene directly or indirectly in the internal or external affairs of any other State." Further, no form of coercion could be employed to obtain "the subordination of the exercise of sovereign rights or to secure . . . advantages of any kind." The legal basis of the resolution is derived from the Charter statement that the organization is based on "the sovereign equality of the member-States." The United States, on the basis of a recommendation that it support the principles of the Charter, could now be expected to turn over the Canal Zone to Panama and Guantanamo to Cuba, since it is obvious that the United States employs military force to maintain these bases. Perhaps one day these actions will be taken. Perhaps not. Should they occur, the decisions will, as always, relate to American interest and not to an abstract attachment to the ideals of the Charter. To take another example, Puerto Rico has been defined by the Special Committee on Decolonization as a non-self-governing territory. If past practice is any guide, this step will be followed by General Assembly resolutions demanding independence for Puerto Rico. The United States would now be expected to accede, out of respect for the majority's interpretation of Charter obligations. This is about as likely to happen as would be acceptance of the principle of self-determination by India in Kashmir, the Soviet Union in Latvia, the Portuguese in Angola, or Israel in the Gaza Strip. In short, it is nonsense to propose the impossible simply because it sounds good.

Recommendations

The basic problem, of course, is the nation-state system, which has made the United Nations a dangerous place. When, how, and if that system will change we have no idea. So long as sovereign states pursue national interests with no restraints other than those that are self-imposed, the world will be wracked by turmoil and war. Nationalism remains the most powerful and destructive force in international politics. It guarantees the use of every available weapon for the benefit of the nation. Since there is no good reason to predict the demise of nationalism, and every indication that the explosion of new states and Communist unification of China tend in the opposite direction, it must be predicted that there will be no basic change in uses made of the United Nations. Substitution of anticolonialism for the Cold War represents a shift in political goals and not a decline in utilization of the United Nations for conflict purposes. If China and the Soviet Union become major antagonists, the threat to world peace will be as great as when the United States confronted the Russians. The only difference will be in the names of the gladiators who will wield the weapons.

What ends are served by a better recognition of conflict at the United Nations? At the least, clearer vision removes impediments that obscure and distort the problem of achieving international peace. That of course does not mean that the right things will be done. But at least we will not confuse the politics of conflict with the politics of peace. In the final analysis, the fate of the millions rests in the control of a few powerful decision-makers. That lesson was never more forcibly learned than during the Cuban missile crisis.

We must presume that leaders will continue to manipulate the United Nations in the service of selfish ends. Neither this nor any other book will change that. All that it can do is heighten the awareness of implications. For example, when opportunities to embarrass emerge, more thought might be given to the effects of the policy upon long-range goals. Symbolic victories may be sacrificed in favor of other discreet and effective means of registering disapproval with another country's actions. Even when it is deemed necessary to attack an opponent in a United Nations forum, little or nothing is lost by exercising verbal restraint, and the atmosphere for eventual dialogue is somewhat improved. The same approach to the wording of resolutions could be maintained, especially when, as is usually the case, the language does not affect the substantive issue. It is even not too presumptuous to suggest that the dynamic quality of world politics be considered before using the United Nations in a manner that will contribute to rigidity and hostility. Any number of illustrations come to mind, but the point can be made by reference only to Korea. After only two years of deadlock and frustration, the United States used the United Nations to lend legitimacy to its ally, South Korea, by having the organization certify an election. A terrible war and twenty-five years later, the two Koreas have begun to move cautiously towards rapprochement. The victories at the United Nations contributed to the intractability of both sides, although the resolution gave lip service to the ideals of self-determination and democracy. History cannot be replayed. It is at least conceivable that there might have been less conflict, human suffering, and danger for world peace in Korea if the opportunity to win something at the United Nations had not been taken. It is tempting to humiliate an enemy at the moment of peak hostility, but a longer view would consider that conditions can and do change, and that the freezing of positions is self-defeating.

Finally, a word about the superpowers. The concept of

Great Power harmony as an approach to world peace has obvious merit. Unfortunately, harmony cannot be dictated. The history of the Cold War at the United Nations should be studied as an object lesson in the exacerbation of tensions. Disagreements are inevitable, but they need not always result in public acrimony, self-righteous posturing, and manipulation of parliamentary procedures. The absence of unanimity can be acknowledged without using the organization to widen distances. Issues brought to the Security Council, especially, could be explored privately to ascertain whether differences can be narrowed or common approaches agreed upon. The United States alone cannot impose quiet diplomacy on the Soviet Union and China, but it can influence them in that direction.

We do not wish to imply by these observations that the United Nations, in a period of détente, becomes a valuable force for peace. When the superpowers are in basic agreement they will find the means of resolving their problems. At such a time they do not need the United Nations, and, in fact, the potential of the organization for hostile ends remains as a constant threat to progress toward accommodation. With the best will in the world, they may be driven apart. Consider the Middle East. Here the United States has been on the "losing" side, even to the point of having to use its veto to prevent an unqualified condemnation of Israel. The pressure is generated by the Arab states, and Sino-Soviet leaders, despite any simultaneous policy of easing tensions with the United States, may be compelled to provide public support for the Arabs, thereby complicating their relations with America. Similar consequences involving the Great Powers are implicit in the colonialism issue. Again, other states are likely to provide the initiative. At the same time that China and Russia may be working toward a modus vivendi with the United States, their stake in leadership of the developing world may result in support of extreme demands, even including independence for Puerto Rico, which will endanger rapprochement with the United States. It is manifestly impossible to expect that the Arabs, black Africans, or Asians will forgo their goals because the superpowers will be somewhat discomforted. Indeed, they are *more* likely, during a period of détente, to force Great Power divisions in the United Nations in order to impress the Big Three with the costs of not acceding to their policies. Thus the *New York Times*, in reporting that South Korea might force a debate in the General Assembly in 1973 on unification of Korea, observed: "A confrontation in the United Nations between South Korea (an ally of the United States) and China might jeopardize President Nixon's efforts to improve relations between Washington and Peking."

What we are suggesting, therefore, is not that the United States adopt approaches that will make the United Nations *work*. It cannot work for peace. Its political functions should be abolished. But that will not happen, because members, and especially Third-World countries that now dominate the organization, will not allow themselves to be deprived of a powerful weapon. Since this is the reality, we can recommend only that a prudential attitude govern use of the United Nations, so that its capacity to inflict injuries is limited; that voluntary institutions and devices (for example the International Court, mediation and arbitration services, hot lines, and so on) be strengthened and made more available for states seeking peaceful solutions to problems; and that the search continue for the realization of man's brightest dreams.

Epilogue: The Yom Kippur War

On October 6, 1973, Yom Kippur, Egypt and Syria struck simultaneously at Israel. The Bar-Lev line along the Suez Canal was quickly breached, and Syrian armor advanced across the Golan Heights. There was no dispute about the basic facts. All indications were that the Arabs had successfully launched a surprise attack. United Nations truce supervisors on the scene confirmed that the Arabs had initiated hostilities, and Egyptian and Syrian leaders were so delighted with their early successes that they boasted openly of having outwitted General Dayan and the famed Israeli intelligence service.

Six years earlier it had been more difficult to assign responsibility. Although it is likely that the Israelis chose the precise moment to attack on June 5, 1967, it is also true that the war atmosphere was largely created by Arab actions and threats, including: abrupt removal of the United Nations Emergency Force from Gaza and Sharmal-Sheikh on the demand of President Nasser; mobilization of Egyptian armies along Israel's border; and the blockading of the Israeli port of Elath, which the Israelis described as an act of war. One could argue that the Arabs had initiated the war with the blockade or that Israel had opened a preventive war because of a clear threat to its survival. In any event, the Security

Council acted quickly to limit the Israeli victory by ordering a cease-fire within a week. In contrast, neither Syria nor Egypt was in imminent danger in 1973, and there was no question about their having fired the first shots.

In short, an unambiguous act of aggression had been committed by one side in a dispute that has been before the United Nations for a quarter of a century. In principle, this is the most serious international crime, akin to murder on the domestic level. It was precisely to act against aggression, symbolized by the Japanese and Nazi attacks against Pearl Harbor and Poland, that the United Nations was organized in 1945. According to one's perception of the reasons for the crime, one may or may not sympathize with the criminal. But motives are ignored in the Charter. The fact of aggression is defined as the crime, and there was no doubt about the identity of the aggressors.

Yet the victim, Israel, did not even complain to the Security Council, which is charged with primary responsibility for the maintenance of international peace. Israel did not appeal to the United Nations for exactly the same reasons that a Jew in Nazi Germany did not use the German courts to protect his rights—clearly, the United Nations is a useful weapon only for the Arabs. This explains also why the American request to have the Security Council meet to recommend a cease-fire was ignored immediately after the outbreak of hostilities. The Security Council would not act unless it could serve the Arab cause. As long as there appeared to be some prospect of an Arab victory, the Council remained mute.

It is particularly interesting that the Arabs raised the issue in the General Assembly. The choice of organ is always a tactical decision. In the General Assembly, legitimization of Arab aggression would be enhanced by the sheer volume of adherents since, as the *New York Times* reported, "they could muster almost one hundred speakers in their support." In contrast, the more intimate Security Council, although heavily pro-Arab, would have considerable difficulty in avoiding discussion of a cease-fire and in drowning out the arguments of the United States and Israel.

However, when the fortunes of war changed, the Arabs quickly reversed positions. Once it was clear that the advantages of surprise and Soviet military aid were insufficient to carry the day, the Arabs were anxious to have the war end before they suffered another humiliating defeat. Now the Security Council became the preferred organ. On October 22, the Soviet-American agreement to end the war was ratified by a compliant Security Council. Even the Chinese, who were unhappy about the Soviet-American "condominium," abstained rather than veto a cease-fire that was necessary to save the Arabs from the consequences of their actions.

Such an obviously one-sided use of a cease-fire should not be misinterpreted. It is a powerful weapon of war. It encourages maximum use of war because it is a guarantee against military defeat. If the weapon must be used, the users retain the potential to renew the war at a later date. Psychologically, also, they can avoid acknowledgement of having lost on the field of battle. Indeed, the cease-fire was barely installed before the mythology that the *Arabs* had thus been denied victory began to take root.

In commenting on the frantic negotiations that prepared the way for the Geneva meetings in December, we will note only that the Arab side made every effort to involve the United Nations while the Jews opposed use of the organization. Reluctantly, the Israelis were forced to accept a *United Nations* truce force (volunteers, acceptable to *both* sides could have been installed as easily and as quickly), and Secretary-General Waldheim chaired the opening Geneva session. Nevertheless, the ultimate responsibility of the Security Council remained unclarified, with the Arabs obviously prepared to reactivate that weapon should they become dissatisfied with progress at the conference. Indeed, the major obstacle to a successful agreement remains the prominence of United Nations resolutions in bargaining positions, especially those of the Arabs.

The enormous excitement engendered by the Geneva negotiations demonstrates that there is an unarticulated awareness of the differences between these talks and those that have preoccupied the United Nations for twenty-five years. The difference is rather fundamental. It is the difference between peace and war.

Notes

1. *The Arena*

1. See, for example, Frederick H. Hartmann, *The Relations of Nations* (New York: Macmillan, 1962), pp. 92–94. Hartmann observes that the development of rules for international conferences was basically the recognition of the importance of prestige. This was clearly at the core of the dispute concerning the shape of the table that delayed the Paris negotiations on Vietnam for two months.

2. The manner in which the headquarters of the United Nations has been insulated from intrusion by New York State and United States authority is described in Stephen S. Goodspeed, *The Nature and Function of International Organizations*, second edition (New York: Oxford University Press, 1967) , pp. 106–108.

3. *Charter of the United Nations*, Preamble.

4. Article 2, Paragraph 7, of Charter reads: "Nothing contained in the present Charter shall authorize the United Nations to intervene in matters which are essentially within the domestic jurisdiction of any state or shall require the Members to submit such matters to settlement under the present Charter. . . ."

   According to Article 51: "Nothing in the present Charter shall impair the right of individual or collective self-defense if an armed attack occurs against a Member of the United Nations, until the Security Council has taken the measures necessary to maintain international peace and security."

5. See, for example, French statements on Morocco and Tunisia in the general debate, *General Assembly Official Records (GAOR)* , Plenary, Meeting 487, October 4, 1954. See also debate in the General Committee of the Assembly, Meeting 103, September 22, 1955.

6. *Security Council Official Records (SCOR)*, Meetings 1347–1348, June 5–6, 1967.

7. See for example *SCOR*, Meetings 675 and 676, June 20 and June 25, 1954. For a more general analysis of the uses made of the Organiza-

tion of American States, see Elliott Vandervanter, Jr., "NATO and the OAS," in Francis A. Beer, ed., *Alliances: Latent War Communities in the Contemporary World* (New York: Holt, Rinehart and Winston, 1970), pp. 89–119.

8. An elaboration of the Soviet application of collective self-defense appears in the "Brezhnev Doctrine" which justified Warsaw Pact intervention in Czechoslovakia in 1968. According to this view, internal disorders within the territory of a member of the "Socialist Commonwealth" obligated the governments of other members to intervene on behalf of all socialist "peoples." The presence of Russian tanks in Czechoslovakia therefore did not constitute aggression but rather the fulfillment of a legal obligation which the Soviet government had undertaken on behalf of all the peoples in the "Commonwealth."

9. In the debate on Goa, the Indian delegate maintained that it was impossible to commit aggression against one's own frontier and people. *SCOR*, Meetings 987–988, December 18, 1961. See also *SCOR*, Meeting 357, September 16, 1948, for Hyderabad, and *Yearbook of the United Nations*, 1962, p. 129, for the Indian arguments on Kashmir.

10. *SCOR*, Meeting 268, March 17, 1948; *SCOR*, Meeting 746, October 28, 1956.

11. Richard J. Walton, "The U.N. Is the Only Game In Town," *New York Times*, May 29, 1972, p. 17.

12. UN Document S/4929, *Letter of 16 August 1961 from Permanent Representative of Portugal.*

13. The Egyptian United Nations offensive was described as "a final appeal to the world's conscience and reason," before the military solution would be attempted. *New York Times*, September 21, 1971, p. 2.

14. According to Leland Goodrich: "In most instances the choice of organ is determined by what the initiating state wants or expects to achieve by submitting the question to the United Nations. . . . The likelihood of getting a favorable result is always an important consideration." *The United Nations* (New York: Thomas Y. Crowell, 1959), p. 205.

15. See Frederick L. Schuman, *International Politics*, sixth edition (New York: McGraw-Hill, 1958) , p. 207.

16. *Ibid.*

17. *Charter of the United Nations*, Article 24, Para. 1.

18. *Ibid.*, Article 27, Para. 3.

19. *Ibid.*, Article 43, Para. 3.

20. *Ibid.*, Article 24, Para. 1.

21. Lincoln P. Bloomfield, *The United Nations and U. S. Foreign Policy*, revised edition (Boston: Little, Brown, 1967) , p. 55. Professor Bloomfield observes: "So long as the Soviet Union considered itself to be virtually at war with the non-communist world, it was quite impossible to conceive a common military action against some third party."

22. *Ibid.*, p. 54. Bloomfield refers disparagingly to Franklin D. Roosevelt's naiveté in believing that the Great Powers could "somehow see to it that the rest of the world was peaceful."

23. See below, Chapter 4.

24. For example, the Senegalese complaint that Portuguese aircraft had dropped four grenades on a village resulting in the hospitalization of one person. See *SCOR*, Meetings 1024–1033, April 17–24, 1963. In a resolution adopted concerning the kidnapping of Adolph Eichmann, the Security Council noted that the action contributed to "an atmosphere of insecurity and distrust, incompatible with the preservation of peace. . . ." United Nations Document S/4349, June 23, 1960.

25. See John G. Stoessinger, *The Might of Nations,* third edition (New York: Random House, 1969), p. 258.

26. United Nations Document S/3378, March 29, 1955.

27. Typically a General Assembly resolution would read: "Having noted the Report of the United Nations Commission for the Unification and Rehabilitation of Korea . . ." the General Assembly "reaffirms that the objectives of the United Nations are to bring about by peaceful means the establishment of a unified, independent and democratic Korea under a representative form of government . . . [and] urges that continuing efforts be made to achieve these objectives . . . [and] calls upon the United Nations Commission for the Unification and Rehabilitation of Korea to continue its work . . . and to observe and report on elections throughout Korea . . ." General Assembly Resolution 1010A (XI), January 11, 1957.

28. See, for example, General Assembly Resolution 288A (IV), December 18, 1949.

29. General Assembly Resolution 1132 (XI), January 10, 1957, established the special committee, which was instructed to report its findings to the General Assembly. During the same year, by the terms of General Assembly Resolution 1133 (XI), September 14, 1957, a special representative was appointed to "report and make recommendations as he may deem advisable to the General Assembly." These reports were the bases for resolutions until 1962, when the West decided to abandon the issue of Hungary as a means of embarrassing the Soviet Union. See General Assembly Resolution 1857 (XVII), December 20, 1962, which discontinued the services of the special representative.

30. See General Assembly Resolution 1654 (XVI), November 27, 1961.

31. See below, Chapter 2.

32. General Assembly Resolution 1616 (XVI), April 1, 1961.

33. See, for example, Goodrich, *The United Nations,* p. 122.

34. Security Council Resolution 217, November 20, 1965.

35. See below, Chapter 5.

36. General Assembly Resolution 376 (V), October 7, 1950.

37. General Assembly Resolution 111 (II), November 13, 1947.

38. General Assembly Resolution 377 (V), November 3, 1950.

39. In a not untypical comment on the Uniting for Peace Resolution, Stoessinger writes: "The Charter, like a constitution, had shown itself to be amenable to interpretation in order to keep pace with changing events." Stoessinger, *The Might of Nations*, p. 263.

40. See *SCOR*, Meeting 750, October 31, 1956.

41. United Nations Document A/5729, September 11, 1964, *Letter to the Secretary General from the Acting Permanent Representative of the USSR*, details the legal position of the Soviet Union. Expenses for any peace-keeping operation, the letter states, ". . . must bc regarded as special expenses [which] are not within the competence of the General Assembly."

42. In discussing the "illegality" of Dag Hammarskjöld's direction of the Congo force, the Soviets said that he was "acting in the interests of the colonizers and in flagrant contradiction to the Charter." *Ibid.*

43. Following the assessments crisis, the French delegate reiterated this position when he said: ". . . France ascribes supreme importance to scrupulous respect for the provisions of the Charter and has been unable to endorse . . . audacious interpretations which, had they been adopted, would have been likely to have a profound effect on the balance, and consequently the effectiveness, of our institution. . . ." The Charter was ". . . limited to relations between States. . . ." *GAOR*, Plenary, Meeting 1341, September 29, 1965.

44. The United States characterized Soviet unwillingness to pay its share of peace-keeping expenses as a conflict between the Soviet Union and the United Nations which threatened to destroy the organization. See statement of Francis T. P. Plimpton, United States Delegate to the Fifth Committee, May, 1963, quoted in Stoessinger, p. 95.

45. The Soviet delegate said: "The cost of maintaining the Force should be charged to the countries which carried out the attack against Egypt in 1956." The only just solution was for ". . . the Powers responsible for the situation to assume the financial responsibility for the United Nations operations in the Middle East." *GAOR*, Plenary, Meeting 1285, December 17, 1963.

46. See, for example, David Wilkinson, "The Article 17 Crisis: The Dispute Over Financing the United Nations," in Lawrence Sheinman and David Wilkinson, eds., *International Law and Political Crisis* (Boston: Little, Brown, 1968) pp. 212–213. "Despite continuing internal disorders and confusion, the United Nations role in the Congo was ultimately much more satisfactory to the United States than to the Soviet Union or to DeGaulle's France."

47. Wilkinson notes on page 220, *ibid.*, that in addition to being "well pleased" with the Congo operation, American policy-makers thought it would be "ironic justice if they [the Russians] had to pay toward driving their own protagonists out."

48. See Inis L. Claude, Jr., *Swords Into Plowshares*, 4th ed. (New York: Random House, 1971), p. 400.

2. *The Politics of Embarrassment*

1. On Hyderabad, see *SCOR*, Meeting 359, September 20, 1948. On Goa, see *SCOR*, Meetings 987–988, December 18, 1961.
2. UN Document S/4336, June 15, 1960.
3. UN Document S/4349, June 23, 1960.
4. UN Document S/694, March 12, 1948.
5. See *SCOR*, Meeting 273, March 23, 1948.
6. See *SCOR*, Meeting 268, March 17, 1948.
7. See *SCOR*, Meeting 273, March 23, 1948.
8. *Ibid.*
9. Paul E. Zinner, *Revolution in Hungary* (New York: Columbia University Press, 1962), pp. 239–240.
10. UN Document S/3690, October 27, 1956.
11. *SCOR*, Meetings 752–754, October 28–November 4, 1956.
12. *SCOR*, Meeting 754, November 4, 1956.
13. UN Document S/3733, November 4, 1956.
14. See the amendment proposed by Ceylon, India, and Indonesia in UN Document A/3325, November 9, 1956.
15. See General Assembly Resolutions 1004 (E.S.-11), November 4, 1956; 1005 (E.S.-113), November 9, 1956; 1132 (XI), January 10, 1957.
16. UN Document A/3592, June 17, 1957.
17. *Ibid.*
18. See below, Chapter 4.
19. The vote on General Assembly Resolution 1353 (XIV), October 21, 1959, was 45 to 9, with 26 abstentions. The large number of abstentions reflected the feelings of many delegations that it was unwise to pursue this issue, especially because the United States and the Soviet Union were attempting to improve their relations through summit meetings between Khrushchev and Eisenhower.
20. See Eleanor Lansing Dulles, *American Foreign Policy in the Making* (New York: Harper and Row, 1968), p. 181.
21. UN Document S/4314, May 18, 1960.
22. See *SCOR*, Meeting 857, May 23, 1960.
23. See UN Document A/4446, August 20, 1960, "The Menace to World Peace Created by Aggressive Actions of the United States of America Against the Soviet Union," and *GAOR*, First Committee, Meeting 1142, April 5, 1961.
24. Dulles, *American Foreign Policy*, pp. 327–339.
25. UN Document S/6316, May 1, 1965.
26. The debate occupied the attention of the Security Council for *thirty* meetings between May 3 and July 26, 1965. The ability of the Soviet Union to sustain its attack for this period of time, and to force the United States into a defensive posture for so long, demonstrates the relative success that the Soviet Union could now expect to achieve when it decided to engage in embarrassment politics.
27. UN Document A/L.355, October 9, 1961.

28. UN Document A/L.366 and Add. 1–3, October 9, 1961.
29. See *Yearbook of the United Nations,* 1960, pp. 47–48.
30. There is of course some evidence for this. At the Twenty-second Party Congress, Chairman Khrushchev said: "We believe that it is the inalienable right of peoples to put an end to foreign oppression and we shall support their fight. Colonialism is doomed and a stake will be driven into its grave." See the *New York Times,* October 18, 1961.
31. See, for example, UN Document A/AC.109/SR.345, July 14, 1965.
32. UN Document A/AC.109/SR.263, August 5, 1965.
33. See, for example, UN Documents A/AC.109/SR.350, July 29, 1965, and A/AC.109/SR.357, July 29, 1965.
34. UN Document A/AC.109/SR.350, July 29, 1965.
35. *Ibid.*
36. *GAOR,* Fourth Committee, Meeting 264, November 5, 1952.
37. *GAOR,* Plenary, Meeting 929, November 30, 1960.
38. *Ibid.*
39. *GAOR,* Plenary, Meeting 938, December 16, 1960.
40. See *GAOR,* Fourth Committee, Meetings 1458–1465, October 28, 1963–November 1, 1963. The debates in 1963 do not differ significantly from those in later years. If anything, the speeches became progressively more hostile.
41. *GAOR,* Fourth Committee, Meeting 1461, October 30, 1963.
42. *GAOR,* Fourth Committee, Meeting 1457, October 25, 1963.
43. *GAOR,* Fourth Committee, Meeting 1581, December 9, 1965.
44. General Assembly Resolution 2012 (XX), October 12, 1965.
45. *New York Times,* March 22, 1973.
46. UN Document S/10810, October 18, 1972.
47. See Ali A. Mazrui, "The United Nations and Some African Political Attitudes," *International Organization,* Vol. XVIII (Summer 1964), pp. 499–520.
48. For a brilliant analysis of conflict strategies, see E. E. Schattschneider, *The Semi-Sovereign People* (New York: Holt, Rinehart and Winston, 1960), Chapter I.
49. *New York Times,* March 23, 1973.

3. *The Politics of Status*

1. Article 4, para 1.
2. See Leland M. Goodrich, *The United Nations* (New York: Thomas Y. Crowell, 1959), pp. 88–91.
3. The Soviet Union cast fifty-one vetoes to block membership of Western-sponsored applicants. However, thirty-four of these were "repeats" on the same applicants: Italy, for example, six vetoes; and four each for Portugal, Jordan, Ireland, Ceylon, South Korea, South Vietnam, and Japan.
4. General Assembly Resolution 620A–G (VII), December 21, 1952.

5. General Assembly Resolution 114 (11), November 17, 1947.
6. Advisory Opinion of the International Court of Justice, May 28, 1948, *ICJ Reports of Judgements and Advisory Opinions*, 1948, p. 114.
7. The states admitted in 1955 were: Albania, Austria, Bulgaria, Cambodia, Ceylon, Finland, Hungary, Ireland, Italy, Jordan, Laos, Libya, Nepal, Portugal, Rumania, and Spain.
8. John G. Stoessinger, *The United Nations and the Superpowers* (New York: Random House, 1970), pp. 18–19.
9. General Assembly Resolution 510 (VI), December 20, 1951.
10. UN Document A/2122/Add. 1, May 1, 1952.
11. See *GAOR*, Plenary, Meeting 38, September 21, 1947. The Soviet Union argued that by bringing the issue to the United Nations, the United States was violating the Moscow Agreements, which called for consultation among the foreign ministers of the Soviet Union, the United States, and the United Kingdom.
12. General Assembly Resolution 112 (II), November 14, 1947.
13. UN Document A/575 and Adds. 1 and 2, August 1948.
14. General Assembly Resolution 195 (III), December 12, 1948.
15. General Assembly Resolution 376 (V), October 7, 1950.
16. See *GAOR*, Meetings on the Korean Question, any year between 1951 and 1971.
17. *UN Monthly Chronicle*, October, 1972, pp. 37–38.
18. See Stoessinger, *The United Nations and the Superpowers*, p. 9.
19. See "Agreement on the Cessation of Hostilities in Vietnam (July 20, 1954)" and "Final Declaration of the Geneva Conference (July 21, 1954)," in Marvin E. Gettleman, ed., *Vietnam* (Greenwich: Fawcett Crest, 1965), pp. 137–154.
20. See *Yearbook of the United Nations*, 1963, p. 49.
21. General Assembly Resolution 498 (V), February 1, 1951.
22. "Issues Before the 26th General Assembly," *International Conciliation*, September, 1971, p. 15.
23. See, for example, Irving Louis Horowitz, "The United Nations and the Third World: East-West Conflict in Focus," in Robert Gregg and Michael Borkun, eds., *The United Nations System and its Functions* (Princeton: Van Nostrand, 1968), pp. 350–357. See also Inis L. Claude, Jr., *The Changing United Nations* (New York: Random House, 1967), Chapter IV. Professor Claude views the organization's "legitimization" of anticolonialism as an important indication of the United Nations' ability to encourage the collective acceptance of international conduct norms.
24. See *United Nations Conference on International Organization (UNCIO)* Documents X, May 5, 1945, pp. 446–448.
25. *UNCIO* Documents VIII, June 21, 1945, p. 146.
26. *UNCIO* Documents III, May 6, 1945, p. 610.
27. *UNCIO* Documents X, May 15, 1945, pp. 439–444.
28. *UNCIO* Documents X, May 12, 1945, pp. 433–434.
29. *Charter of the United Nations*, Article 73.

30. For a view that the colonial powers acquired legal as well as moral obligations under Chapter XI, see Josef L. Kunz, "Chapter XI of the United Nations Charter in Action," *American Journal of International Law*, 48 (January, 1954) , p. 103.

31. Article 75 bases the coverage of the trusteeship system on the conclusion of "individual agreements." The International Court of Justice has interpretated Article 75 as requiring the prior "consent" of an administering member to bring a territory under United Nations trusteeship. International Court of Justice, *Reports 1950*, p. 139.

32. *GAOR*, Plenary, Meeting 19, November 13, 1946.

33. A special subcommittee was created for this purpose. Although the colonial powers participated in its work, they consistently opposed the creation of *any* machinery to implement the terms of Article 73. See *GAOR*, Plenary, Meeting 64, December 14, 1946.

34. General Assembly Resolution 66 (I) , December 14, 1946. Despite the relatively innocuous nature of the resolution, all the colonial powers cast negative votes except New Zealand, which abstained.

35. Until 1959, the Special Committee on Information, as the ad hoc committee came to be called, was renewed for three-year periods. Although this did not fully satisfy anticolonial demands for permanent machinery, the effect was to keep the issue of supervision alive until majority support for permanent machinery could be achieved. Pressure was also applied through the refusal of France and the United Kingdom to participate in the activities of a permanent committee. See *GAOR*: Plenary, Meeting 268, November 10, 1952. Since all decisions of the equally divided Committee on Information were reviewable to the Fourth Committee, where simple majority voting dictated outcomes, anticolonial members controlled a permanent forum for the articulation of their demands.

36. In a considerably weaker form than anticolonialists preferred, the General Assembly expressed the view in 1947 that the transmission of political information was "in conformity with the spirit of Article 73" and should be "duly noted and encouraged." UN Document A/385, September 18, 1947, p. 213. Despite the continued warnings of the colonial powers, in the words of the Dutch representative, ". . . the only possible result would be that no information of this kind would be available in the future" (*GAOR*, Plenary, Meeting 107, November 3, 1947) , anticolonial members repeatedly called for the transmission of political information. See UN Documents A/C.4/L.349/Rev.1, November 6, 1954; and A/C.4/L.624/Add. 1, December 3, 1959.

37. These included the British territories of Malta and Pitcairn Island; the French territories of Indochina, establishments in Oceana and India, Guadeloupe, New Caledonia, French Guiana, and Martinique; and the American Panama Canal Zone.

38. The views of the colonial powers were simple and direct: "If the administering power could decide to transmit information for a territory," the French delegate said, "it could also decide unilaterally to

cease doing so." The United Kingdom's decision to discontinue trans-
mitting information was, according to the British delegate, ". . . not
subject to any higher review." *GAOR*, Fourth Committee, Meeting
124, November 14, 1949. Anticolonialists were able to force through
a modest resolution which considered it to be "within the responsibility of the General Assembly to express its opinion" on the "principles employed by the administering members in determining the
territories for which they would transmit information under Article
73e of the Charter." UN Document A/1159, November 29, 1949, p. 120.
39. Egypt, for example, stated: "As a general rule, the goal to be attained
[is] independence. The United Nations must be satisfied beyond all
doubt that the will of the people had been expressed freely either by
means of a plebiscite under its auspices or by some other appropriate
democratic procedure." *GAOR*, Fourth Committee, Meeting 274, November 14, 1952. The colonial powers rejected this view, but, more
importantly, opposed the competence of the United Nations to interfere by any measure in their affairs. See *GAOR*, Fourth Committee,
Meetings 322, 326, 327, 330, October 1–9, 1953.
40. Drafts calling for such a study were submitted to the Fourth Committee each year between 1956 and 1959. See UN Documents A/C.4/L.
467, February 12, 1957: A/C.4/L.504, November 1, 1957; and A/C.4/L.
569, December 5, 1958.
41. Yugoslavia, a cosponsor of the 1957 draft, explained: "To admit that
Portugal did not administer non-self-governing-territories amounted
to accepting the argument of the administering members that the fate
of the dependent peoples was exclusively within their competence."
GAOR, Fourth Committee, Meeting 690, November 4, 1957.
42. In a not unrepresentative statement of this counterproductive tendency, the French delegate said: "The Committee [on Information]
whenever it considered a question was confronted with a resolution
which presented an extreme point of view and it therefore had to
seek a compromise. The amendment process in the Fourth Committee
inevitably led to a fundamental dispute between the Administering
Powers and a majority of the Fourth Committee." *GAOR*, Fourth
Committee, Meeting 121, November 10, 1949.
43. The Mexican delegate said of the Committee on Information and in
defense of majoritarianism: "In moments of crisis we saw our majority
melt away and found ourselves discussing fundamental questions on
a footing of equality with the Administering Powers." *GAOR*, Plenary,
Meeting 459, November 27, 1953.
44. UN Document A/L.323 and Adds. 1–6, November 28, 1960.
45. UN Document A/L.366 and Adds. 1–3, November 17, 1961. The membership of this committee was subsequently expanded to twenty-four.
46. Scholars have tended to view this support as indicative of a change
in attitude. See, for example, Edward T. Rowe, "The Emerging Anti-
Colonial Consensus in the United Nations," *The Journal of Conflict
Resolution*, VIII (September, 1964), pp. 209–320.

47. After bitter debate, the General Assembly voted to accept the credentials of President Kasa-Vubu's representatives by a vote of 53 to 24, with 19 abstentions. General Assembly Resolution 1498 (XV), November 22, 1960.

4. The Politics of Legitimization

1. *New York Times*, November 15, 1972.
2. General Assembly Resolution 2851 (XXVI), December 20, 1971. See also *UN Monthly Chronicle*, December, 1971, p. 91.
3. See W. Phillips Davison, *The Berlin Blockade* (Princeton: Princeton University Press, 1958), Chapter I.
4. See "Protocol of the Proceedings of the Berlin Conference," in *Department of State Publication 3556 Germany 1947–49*, pp. 47–57.
5. "Council of Foreign Ministers, London Session, November 25, December 16, 1947: Report by Secretary Marshall, December 19, 1947," in *ibid.*, pp. 63–67.
6. "Proclamation to the German People on the Western Currency Reform by Marshal Sokolovsky, June 19, 1948," in O.M. Von der Gablentz, ed., *Documents on the Status of Berlin 1944–1959*, pp. 53–54.
7. Walter Millis, ed., *The Forrestal Diaries* (New York: Viking Press, 1951), pp. 454–455.
8. See Lucius Clay, *Decision in Germany* (New York: Doubleday, 1950), p. 374.
9. See *"Aide-memoire* delivered to the U.S., U.K., and French representatives by Foreign Minister Molotov," September 18, 1948, and "Identic Notes Addressed to the USSR," September 22, 1948, in *Department of State Publication 3556 Germany 1947–49*, pp. 215–219.
10. *SCOR*, Meeting 361, October 4, 1948.
11. See *Yearbook of the United Nations*, 1948–49, p. 285.
12. *SCOR*, Meetings 363–364, October 6, 1948.
13. UN Document S/1048, October 22, 1948.
14. *New York Times*, October 26, 1948.
15. For an account of the steps leading up to these talks, see Dean Acheson, *Present at the Creation* (New York: W. W. Norton, 1969), pp. 352–357.
16. See, for example, Daniel S. Cheever and H. Field Haviland, Jr., *Organizing for Peace* (Boston: Houghton Mifflin, 1954), p. 450. In commenting on the Berlin agreement, the authors write: "Yet the United Nations continued to prove useful. Mr. Jessup of the United States and Mr. Malik of the Soviet Union . . . met unobtrusively in the corridors at Lake Success to explore the possibility of a settlement that had been hinted earlier in the Soviet press."
17. See Trygve Lie, *In the Cause of Peace* (New York: Macmillan, 1954), p. 216. Lie was convinced that the Western states were uninterested in any compromises.

18. A good brief background of the Suez Canal crisis can be found in Wolfgang Friedmann and Lawrence A. Collins, "The Suez Canal Crisis of 1956," in Lawrence Scheinman and David Wilkinson, eds., *International Law and Political Crisis* (Boston: Little, Brown, 1968), pp. 91–125.

19. UN Document S/3645, September 23, 1956.

20. Friedmann and Collins, "The Suez Canal Crisis of 1956," p. 102.

21. UN Document S/3675, October 13, 1956.

22. Cited in Friedmann and Collins, p. 107.

23. *SCOR*, Meeting 749, October 30, 1956.

24. Robert F. Kennedy, *Thirteen Days* (New York: W. W. Norton, 1969), p. 1.

25. *Ibid.*, pp. 57–89.

26. Quoted in Theodore C. Sorensen, *Kennedy* (New York: Harper and Row, 1965), p. 793.

27. See UN Documents S/5181, S/5183, S/5185, and S/5186, October 22–23, 1962.

28. *SCOR*, Meeting 1022, October 23, 1962.

29. See, for example, Kennedy, *Thirteen Days*, p. 53, and Sorensen, *Kennedy*, p. 783. Both clearly join the United Nations initiative to developing favorable public opinion on whatever course of action might become necessary. Sorensen writes: "We should go to the U.N. first, said this adviser, before the Russians do, and have ready an acceptable resolution our way. With this the President agreed."

30. Kennedy, *Thirteen Days*, p. 52.

31. Sorensen, *Kennedy*, p. 800.

32. See Harry S Truman, *Memoirs, Vol. 2: Years of Trial and Hope* (New York: Doubleday, 1958), p. 381.

33. UN Document S/1500, June 25, 1950.

34. Truman states: "I then called on Acheson to present the recommendations which the State and Defense Departments had prepared [on June 26]. He presented the following recommendations for immediate action." Truman then goes on to outline the military steps to be undertaken, and concludes: "Two things stand out in this discussion. One was the complete almost unspoken acceptance on the part of everyone that whatever had to be done to meet this aggression, had to be done." Truman, *Years of Trial and Hope*, pp. 380–381. See also p. 384.

35. See UN Documents S/1517 and S/1579, 1950.

36. UN Documents S/1527 and S/1554, 1950.

37. See *SCOR*, Meeting 480, August 1, 1950.

38. General Assembly Resolution 376 (V), October 7, 1950.

39. In *Years of Trial and Hope*, p. 395, Truman clearly states that the offer did not meet the "needs of the Far East Command within the over-all requirements of *national* policy *and* the use of Allied troop elements in Korea" (italics ours).

40. *Ibid.*

41. Indeed the President, on June 27, went out of his way to assure the congressional leadership that the operation was under United Nations auspices. *Ibid.*, p. 385.
42. See George McTurnan Kahin and John W. Lewis, *The United States in Vietnam* (New York: Dial Press, 1967) , p. 32.
43. One high-ranking State Department official said: "It would be an understatement to say we do not like the terms of the cease-fire agreement just concluded." Statement of Assistant Secretary Walter S. Robertson, *Department of State Bulletin* (Washington: Department of State, December, 1961) , p. 3.
44. *Pentagon Papers* (New York: Bantam Books, 1971) , Ch. II.
45. See especially McGeorge Bundy to Ambassador Lodge, October 30, 1963. *Ibid.*, pp. 230–231.
46. *Ibid.*, pp. 53 ff.
47. National Security Action Memo 288, March 17, 1964. *Ibid.*, pp. 283–285.
48. *Ibid.*, pp. 286–288.
49. *Ibid.*, pp. 260–261.
50. UN Document S/5849, August 4, 1964.
51. *SCOR*, Meeting 1140, August 5, 1964.
52. On that occasion Secretary of State Dulles said: ". . . If we were to agree that the existence of injuries in the world, which this organization so far has been unable to cure, means that the principle of renunciation of force is no longer respected and that there exists the right wherever a nation feels itself subject to injustice to resort to force to try to correct that injustice, then . . . we would have, I fear, torn this Charter into shreds and the world would again be a world of anarchy." *Department of State Bulletin* (Washington, November 12, 1956) , p. 752.
53. *SCOR*, Meetings 1140–1141, August 5, 1964.
54. UN Document S/5907, August 19, 1964.
55. *Pentagon Papers*, p. 270.
56. UN Document S/6174 and Corr. 1, February 7, 1965.
57. *Pentagon Papers*, pp. 428–429.
58. *New York Times*, February 2, 1966. Hanoi said: "Consideration of the United States war acts in Vietnam falls within the competence of the 1954 Geneva Conference on Indochina and not of the United Nations Security Council." Hanoi has never wavered on this question. In January, 1968, the foreign minister said: "The US imperialists are scheming to bring the Vietnam question before the Security Council. . . . It is necessary to point out that the United Nations has no right to discuss the . . . question. Whatever resolution . . . is adopted . . . is null and void." Foreign Minister Nguyen Duy Triak, on Hanoi radio, *New York Times*, January 3, 1968.
59. See UN Document A/6400, September 1, 1966.
60. UN Document S/7105, January 31, 1966.
61. *SCOR*, Meetings 1271–1273, February 1–2, 1966.
62. *Ibid.*

63. *Ibid.*
64. *SCOR*, Meeting 1272, February 1, 1966.
65. UN Document S/7168, February 26, 1966.
66. *Yearbook of the United Nations* 1966, pp. 151–152.
67. *Ibid.*, pp. 152–153.
68. See Inis L. Claude, Jr. *Swords Into Plowshares*, 4th ed. (New York: Random House, 1971), p. 271.
69. Commenting on this incident. Ali A. Mazrui writes: " 'Colonialism is permanent aggression.' This became an important theme for Afro-Asian argumentation mainly following India's annexation of Goa." *International Organization*, Vol. XVIII.
70. William D. Coplin writes: "With a multitude of battlefields, a loser in one arena might not be so desperate if he knows that there will be numerous other arenas and many other chances to redress the loss. . . . International law and organization have merely contributed to the development of an international bargaining process whereby conflict can be expressed in many forms which do not involve the use of violence." *The Functions of International Law* (Chicago: Rand McNally, 1966), p. 100.

5. *The Politics of Socialization*

1. See E. E. Schattschneider, *The Semi-Sovereign People* (New York: Holt, Rinehart and Winston, 1956), Ch. I.
2. In effect, by not considering these issues the organization acknowledges the legal argument that it is banned from intervening in matters that are essentially within the domestic jurisdiction of a member state. See *Charter of the United Nations*, Article 2, Paragraph 7.
3. See *SCOR*, Meeting 357, September 16, 1948.
4. *SCOR*, Meeting 359, September 20, 1948.
5. In a cable to the Secretary-General on November 1, 1956, Imre Nagy asked that the defense of Hungarian neutrality be placed on the agenda of the General Assembly. UN Document A/3251.
6. *New York Times*, November 12, 1972.
7. For example, Stephen S. Goodspeed says flatly: "The eventual withdrawal of Soviet troops in May, 1946, was influenced by the Council's repeated urging of the disputants to continue to negotiate and to inform the Council of any progress made." *The Nature and Function of International Organization*, 2nd ed. (New York: Oxford University Press, 1967), p. 184.
8. UN Document A/2924, and Add. 1, July 26, 1955.
9. See *GAOR*, Plenary, Meeting 530, September 30, 1955.
10. General Assembly Resolution 909 (X), November 25, 1955.
11. *GAOR*, Plenary, Meeting 578, November 15, 1956.
12. *Ibid.*
13. General Assembly Resolution 1012 (XI), February 15, 1957.

14. UN Document S/4195 and Add. 1, July 10, 1959.
15. General Assembly Resolution 1573 (XV), December 19, 1960. The crucial paragraph calling for a United Nations-administered referendum was, however, stricken from the resolution by a vote of 40 to 40, with 16 abstentions, thereby failing to obtain the required two-thirds majority.
16. An excellent brief account of French policy during this period is found in Bernard E. Brown, "The Decision to End the Algerian War," in James B. Christoph, ed., *Cases in Comparative Politics* (Boston: Little, Brown, 1965), pp. 154–179.
17. See *Yearbook of the United Nations 1946*, p. 332.
18. "Domestic Policies and UN Activities: The Cases of Rhodesia and the Republic of South Africa," *International Organization*, Winter, 1967, p. 56.
19. *SCOR*, Supp. No. 1, Annex 4, January 21, 1946.
20. See *SCOR*, Meeting 14, February 10, 1946.
21. Alastair M. Taylor, *Indonesian Independence and the United Nations* (Ithaca: Cornell University Press, 1960), Chapter I.
22. See *Department of State Bulletin*, Vol. 18, No. 454 (March 14, 1948).
23. UN Document S/426, July 31, 1947.
24. UN Documents S/447 and S/449, July 30, 1947.
25. UN Document S/459, July 31, 1947.
26. *SCOR*, Meeting 172, August 1, 1947.
27. *SCOR*, Meeting 194, August 25, 1947.
28. UN Document S/477, August 7, 1947.
29. For the substance of these negotiations, see *Congressional Record*, Senate, Vol. 95 (April 5, 1949), "Speech of Senator Graham to the Senate on the Indonesian Question."
30. See UN Document S/1129, December 19, 1948.
31. UN Document S/1128, December 19, 1948.
32. *SCOR*, Meeting 388, December 22, 1948.
33. *Department of State Bulletin No. 499*, Vol. 20 (January 5, 1949), p. 84.
34. *SCOR*, Meeting 398, January 11, 1949.
35. UN Document S/1234, January 28, 1949.
36. *Congressional Record*, Senate, Vol. 95 (April 6, 1949), p. 4004.

6. A Dangerous Place

1. For a comprehensive theoretical work dealing with functionalism, see David Mitrany, *A Working Peace System* (London: Royal Institute of International Affairs, 1943). See also Richard N. Gardner, "The United Nations Conference on Trade and Development," *International Organization*, Vol. XXII, No. 1 (Winter, 1968), pp. 99–130, and Richard W. Van Wagenen, "The Concept of Community and the Future of the United Nations" in Norman J. Padelford and Leland M. Goodrich, eds., *The United Nations in the Balance* (New York: Frederick A. Praeger, 1965), pp. 448–463.

2. See, for example, Ruth B. Russell, "Changing Patterns of Constitutional Development," *International Organization*, Vol. XIX, No. 3 (Summer 1965), pp. 410–425, and Gabriella Rosner Lande, "The Effect of the Resolutions of the United Nations General Assembly," *World Politics*, Vol. XIX, No. 1 (October 1966), pp. 83–105. See also Evan Luard, *Conflict and Peace* (Boston: Little, Brown, 1968), pp. 260–261.

3. See Bruce M. Russet, "Toward a Model of Competitive International Politics," *Journal of Politics*, Vol. XXV, No. 2, pp. 226–247. For a comparison of the growth of national legislatures with the United Nations, see Herbert J. Spiro, *World Politics: The Global System* (Homewood, Ill.: Dorsey Press, 1966), pp. 128–139.

4. See, for example, Geoffrey L. Goodwin, "The Commonwealth and the United Nations," in Norman J. Padelford and Leland M. Goodrich, eds., *The United Nations in the Balance* (New York: Frederick A. Praeger, 1965), pp. 320–331.

5. *UN Charter*, Article 2, Paragraph 3.

6. *Ibid.*, Article 2, Paragraph 4.

7. *Ibid.*, Article 33, Paragraph 1.

8. See William D. Coplin, *The Functions of International Law* (Chicago: Rand McNally, 1966), p. 91.

9. See General Assembly Resolution 3034 (XXVII), December 18, 1972. The resolution stressed the need to find "just and peaceful solutions to the underlying causes which give rise to such acts of violence." Further, it "condemned the continuation of repressive and terrorist acts by colonial, racist and alien regimes. . . ." The vote on this resolution, which in effect found Israel guilty of provoking the murders in Munich, was 76–35–17.

10. See Chadwick F. Alger, "Non-Resolution Consequences of the United Nations and Their Effect on International Conflict," *Journal of Conflict Resolution*, Vol. V (1961), pp. 128–145.

11. See Keith S. Petersen, "The Uses of the United Nations," *Southwestern Social Science Quarterly*, Vol. 44, No. 1 (June 1963), p. 59. According to the author: "How much of a tension releasing element there is in any formal U.N. presentation can only be guessed at. . . . Either the pacifying or the vaunting of egos, more commonly national or cultural than personal, is clearly one of the functions that the U.N. performs. It is an important function. It is performed almost continuously."

12. See, for example, Sydney D. Bailey, *The General Assembly of the United Nations* (New York: Frederick A. Praeger, 1964), pp. 6–7.

13. See Chadwick F. Alger, "Personal Contact in Intergovernmental Organizations," in Robert W. Gregg and Michael Barkun, eds., *The United Nations System and its Functions* (Princeton: Van Nostrand, 1968), pp. 104–127.

14. See, for example, *GAOR*, Special Political Committee, Meetings 148–162, November 10–20, 1959. Linking the refugee problem with Arab

political objectives in Palestine, as on this occasion, has been a significant feature of debate on the issue at each session of the Assembly
since 1948.

15. *SCOR*, Meeting 1360, June 13, 1967. See speech by Saudi Arabian
representative, Jamil M. Baroody.

16. A notable example was the insistence of the Albanian delegate to
force a vote during the "non-session" of the General Assembly in
1964–65. By so doing Albania threatened the political compromise
between the United States and the Soviet Union to avoid a showdown
on the issue of depriving the Russians of their vote in the General
Assembly for nonpayment of dues. See *Yearbook of the United Nations*
1964, pp. 41–44.

17. *SCOR*, Meeting 675, June 20, 1954.

18. Thus Herbert J. Spiro insists that at the United Nations, "the regular
observance of certain procedures, methods, ways of doing things, no
matter how mechanical, merely formal, and reluctant it may be,
affects the behavior of those who practice this observance. It may
even affect their motivation." *World Politics: The Global System*,
p. 129.

19. Israeli concern about possible Soviet intervention and uncertain support from Washington is discussed in Walter Laqueur, *The Struggle
for the Middle East* (New York: Macmillan, 1969), pp. 54–55.

20. Laqueur notes that following the ejection of the British from Palestine, the Soviet Union had no incentive to continue its support of
Israel. He observes further that short of the most extreme Arab
demands "the Soviet Union began to give full support in the United
Nations to all other Arab complaints." *Ibid.*, p. 45.

21. In discussing the 1965 cease-fire, for example, Lynn H. Miller attributes its acceptance to the fact that "for Pakistan it became a war
that could not be won and for India a war which she had no desire
to fight." "The Kashmir Dispute," in Scheinman and Wilkinson, eds.,
International Law and Political Crisis, p. 79.

22. See K. J. Holsti, *International Politics* (Englewood Cliffs, N.J.: Pren-
tice-Hall, 1967), p. 444. Holsti writes: "Since tensions have no single
source, they are more difficult to resolve than those conflicts whose
origins lie in expansive demands and in the incompatibility of recog-
nizable objectives."

23. For Soviet objections to the Baruch Plan, which culminated in the
use of the veto on June 22, 1947 (UN Document S/836), see *SCOR*,
Meetings 318, 321, and 325, June 11, 16, and 22, 1947. On "open skies"
see General Assembly Resolution 914 (X), adopted December 16, 1955,
by a vote of 56 to 7.

24. *New York Times*, January 25, 1973.

25. For an excellent brief account of this dispute, see Lynn H. Miller,
"The Kashmir Dispute," in Scheinman and Wilkinson, eds., *International Law and Political Crisis*, pp. 41–89.

26. UN Document S/726, April 21, 1948.

27. Miller, "The Kashmir Dispute," p. 67.
28. At this time, the Indian delegate stated: "The accession of the state of Jammu and Kashmir was full and complete because there was no such thing as provisional accession in the Indian constitution." *Yearbook of the United Nations* 1962, p. 129.
29. *SCOR*, Meeting 1238, September 6, 1965.
30. Miller, "The Kashmir Dispute," p. 79.
31. A typical resolution that resulted from complaints by both Israel and Syria of cease-fire violations was UN Document S/5111, April 9, 1962. The resolution "deplores the hostile exchanges," but goes on to "reaffirm" a January 19, 1956, condemnation of Israel "whether or not undertaken by way of retaliation." The resolution then determined that the Israeli attack on Syria "constitutes a flagrant violation" of the earlier resolution.
32. General Assembly Resolution 194 (III), December 11, 1948.
33. See, for example, General Assembly Resolution 2253 (ES-V), July 4, 1967.
34. General Assembly Resolution 2628 (XXV), November 4, 1970. See also General Assembly Resolution 2149 (XXVII), December 8, 1972. The United States opposed the pro-Arab resolution on the ground that it failed to link the withdrawal from occupied territories to "the terms of a just and lasting peace." *UN Monthly Chronicle*, Vol. X, No. 1 (January, 1973), p. 21.
35. *New York Times*, August 13, 1973.
36. Occasionally even United Nations advocates become aware of the relationship between nonaction at the United Nations and chances for peaceful settlement. Thus in an editorial on December 24, 1972, the *New York Times* wrote: "It is a sad commentary on the current state of international cooperation for peace that the Assembly was probably most helpful when it did nothing, as in the case of Korea where tentative moves toward a North-South détente are best served by silence at Turtle Bay."
37. For a précis of these arguments see, for example, *Yearbook of the United Nations* 1967, pp. 137–138.
38. *Yearbook of the United Nations* 1950, pp. 292–293.
39. *New York Times*, February 9, 1973.

Index